P9-AOZ-549

Pr... for

THE BRIDE WORE WHITE

"Quick's seventh Burning Cove romance (after *When She Dreams*) will please series fans eager to return to the glamorous golden age of Hollywood setting. . . . Quick remains a master of sparkling dialogue that builds believable chemistry between her leads. This is good fun."

—*Publishers Weekly*

"Ready-made for adaptation as a play, television series, or movie . . . Mystery meets romance meets the paranormal in this glossy golden age of Hollywood thriller."

—*Kirkus Reviews*

"Quick gracefully returns to the glamour-tinged, wit-infused world of her 1930s Burning Cove Books with another spot-on story that flawlessly fuses danger, deception, and desire into the literary equivalent of catnip for both romance and mystery readers."

—*Booklist* (starred review)

"An action-packed mystery, suspenseful from page one, with intensity and plot twists that don't let up. The follow-up to *When She Dreams* is a compelling romantic mystery with psychic connections and sparkling dialogue."

—*Library Journal* (starred review)

Praise for

WHEN SHE DREAMS

"With its perfectly executed plot, snappy dialogue, and generous dash of dry wit, this is proof positive of why Quick's novels continue to be the platinum standard for stylish American historical romance kissed with a hint of sophisticated suspense and a dash of the supernatural."

—*Booklist* (starred review)

"The metanarrative commentary about storytelling and genre plus the prewar West Coast glamour and noirlike incidents make for an updated gothic with . . . appeal."
—*Kirkus Reviews*

"A fun, perfectly crafted escape read. The glitz and glamour is there on the pages along with the down-and-dirty and its greed and violence. . . . When you pick up *When She Dreams*, set aside some time to enjoy, because putting it down until the last page is very hard to do."
—*Fresh Fiction*

"It was nice to revisit Burning Cove and some of the characters we have seen before. I love the unique 1930s California setting, and I am entertained by the mysteries."
—*Smexy Books*

"An exciting, intriguing, intense, and suspenseful story that has a number of surprises and twists. . . . *When She Dreams* was fast paced, enthralling, with a romantic couple whose chemistry was sizzling. Amanda Quick once again gives us a complex mystery that has a bit of everything in this glamorous historical world of 1930s."
—*The Reading Cafe*

"Fans of historical mysteries, the 1930s, and paranormal woo-woo will enjoy *When She Dreams* and the Burning Cove series."
—*Caffeinated Reviewer*

THE
BRIDE WORE
WHITE

AMANDA
QUICK

BERKLEY ROMANCE
New York

BERKLEY ROMANCE
Published by Berkley
An imprint of Penguin Random House LLC
penguinrandomhouse.com

Copyright © 2023 by Jayne Ann Krentz
Penguin Random House supports copyright. Copyright fuels creativity, encourages
diverse voices, promotes free speech, and creates a vibrant culture. Thank you for buying
an authorized edition of this book and for complying with copyright laws by not
reproducing, scanning, or distributing any part of it in any form without permission.
You are supporting writers and allowing Penguin Random House to continue to
publish books for every reader.

BERKLEY and the BERKLEY & B colophon are registered trademarks of
Penguin Random House LLC.

ISBN: 9780593337882

Berkley hardcover edition / May 2023
Berkley Romance mass-market edition / March 2024

Printed in the United States of America
1   3   5   7   9   10   8   6   4   2

Book design by Laura K. Corless

This is a work of fiction. Names, characters, places, and incidents either are the product
of the author's imagination or are used fictitiously, and any resemblance to actual persons,
living or dead, business establishments, events, or locales is entirely coincidental.

If you purchased this book without a cover, you should be aware that this book is stolen
property. It was reported as "unsold and destroyed" to the publisher, and neither the author
nor the publisher has received any payment for this "stripped book."

For Frank, as always, with love

THE
BRIDE WORE
WHITE

Chapter 1

The moment she removed one long black glove and touched the rim of the crystal bowl, Madame Ariadne knew the client on the other side of the table intended to murder her.

Damn. As if she didn't have enough problems at the moment. She'd had it with the profession. If she survived the night, Madame Ariadne, Psychic Dream Consultant, was going to disappear forever.

Her real name was Prudence Ryland, but those who paid to have her interpret their dreams knew her only as Madame Ariadne. She had never really felt that the dream reading business was her true calling. Yes, there was very good money in it, and yes, she had a talent for it, but she had never liked the work. Tonight it might get her killed.

"This is the first time I have consulted a psychic

about the meaning of my dreams," Thomas Tapson said. In the shadows of the darkened room, his eyes glinted with the reflected light of the old-fashioned lamp in the center of the round table. "I look forward to the experience."

He had walked into the reading room with an air of amused curiosity. He had stopped in the center of the shadowed, heavily draped surroundings and removed his expensive fedora with a gracious gesture. The perfect gentleman. His hand-tailored suit, elegantly knotted tie, and gold signet ring were the hallmarks of wealth and high social status.

On the surface, his voice carried the unmistakable accent of an upper-class boarding school education. It was the voice of a man who had been raised in the rarefied world of San Francisco society. But if you knew how to listen, you could detect the sick lust he was working hard to conceal.

She knew how to listen—it was a requisite skill in the psychic trade. The question was whether or not she knew how to survive the night.

"I will certainly do my best to interpret your dreams, Mr. Tapson," she said, managing to keep her own voice cool and professional with just the right touch of mystery and drama.

The ability to put on a good performance was another skill essential to success in her profession. She had been raised in the dream reading business. She was an accomplished actress.

"I apologize again for my late arrival this evening," Tapson continued. "I was unavoidably detained at a meeting with some business associates."

"I understand," she said.

Tapson had been her last appointment of the day. When he had failed to arrive on time, she had assumed he was a no-show. She had been about to put the Closed sign in the window when he had appeared out of the foggy twilight of the damp San Francisco night.

Obviously it had been a mistake to open the door to him, but when she tried to tell him he would have to book another appointment, he immediately offered to double her already sky-high fees—if she would agree to consult for him tonight.

She had allowed herself to be persuaded because she could not resist the prospect of the extra cash. She intended to close down the business soon, and her future looked uncertain. She needed a comfortable financial cushion to see her through until she could reestablish herself in a new career in Southern California.

This was what came of allowing oneself to be tempted by money, she thought. One accidentally opened the door to a murderer. Lesson learned, but perhaps too late.

"If you would please place your fingertips on the rim of the crystal bowl," she continued, "I will begin the reading."

She thought she had braced herself for the nerve-jarring jolt she knew was coming—even the most fleeting contact with the stuff of another person's dreams was deeply disturbing—but there was no way she could have protected herself from the horror of Thomas Tapson's dream storm. She knew then that she would not be his first kill. The euphoric thrills he had derived from the terror and pain of his previous victims were infused into the hellish energy that slammed through the crystal. Her chest tightened. She suddenly could not breathe.

"I hope you can help me," Tapson said. "I've had a very strange recurring nightmare for some time now. At first I tried to forget it, but now I'm starting to wonder if it might have some significance."

She studied him from behind the veil of her wide-brimmed black felt hat. Unlike many in the psychic profession who conducted readings and séances swathed in exotic robes and colorful turbans, she preferred modern, fashionable attire, and she stuck with one color—black. She thought it reinforced an aura of serious professionalism. She was not a fraud. There was no need to dress like Hollywood's version of one.

Marketing required some drama. She had an intuitive talent for reading dreams, but she had learned the business side of things from her grandmother, who had always impressed upon her the importance of establishing a style that set one apart from the crowd. Selling psychic dream readings was no different from selling perfume or jewelry. Packaging was everything.

In addition to the veiled hat, she wore a sharply tailored black jacket, a slim black skirt, and black gloves. Her jewelry was limited to a small colorless crystal pendant, a family heirloom that had been given to her by her grandmother.

She had capitalized on the glamorous fashion for veiled hats because she thought the delicate netting covering her face added just the right touch of mystique and mystery without conjuring images of carnival fortune tellers.

"Our intuition often speaks to us in our dreams, Mr. Tapson," she said. "It is always a wise idea to pay attention."

"I don't mind telling you I've developed insomnia because of this particular dream," Tapson said. "It has become quite annoying."

She forced herself to breathe with control while she fought to overcome her instinct to shield herself from the nerve-shattering intimacy of Tapson's dreams. Using the crystal made it much easier to focus, but it also intensified her vulnerability to the psychic lightning that flashed in the heart of his dream storm. The only other means of achieving such clarity was with physical contact, but the thought of actually touching the monster on the other side of the table was more than enough to ignite an anxiety attack.

Tapson watched her across the rim of the crystal bowl with the glittering eyes of a large insect about to leap upon its prey. He tightened his grip on the rim of the bowl, his fingers like claws. The lamplight sparked on his signet ring, inexplicably drawing her attention. She glanced at it and saw that the front was engraved with a key.

"How does this work?" Tapson asked.

"Crystal is an excellent conductor for psychic energy," she explained. In spite of her incipient panic, she managed to slip effortlessly into the glib explanation. Clients always wanted to know the secrets of a reading. She told them the truth because there was no reason not to. It wasn't as if they could do what she did, not without her kind of talent. "I cannot visualize your dreams, of course, but when you describe them, the crystal will transmit impressions of what your intuition is trying to tell you. My task is to interpret those impressions for you."

"That sounds very scientific," Tapson said. He smiled, displaying teeth yellowed by cigarette smoke. Here and there gold fillings gleamed in his mouth. "I was expecting a Ouija board."

"That is a very old-fashioned technique."

She met his eyes and held them while she painstakingly began to thread her way into the hurricane of his dream energy. Her goal was the center of the storm, the dark pit where his primal impulses and desires seethed. The process took time. She needed to buy some of that precious commodity.

"I take it you are not a believer in the paranormal," she said, anxious to keep the conversation going.

"Let's just say I have my doubts, like a lot of other people. I am, however, desperate to discover the meaning of this particular dream. I didn't know where else to turn."

"Who referred you to me?" she asked.

She was closer now, slipping through the roiling waves of dark energy.

"An acquaintance." Tapson frowned, impatient. "I'm paying a great deal to hear your interpretation of my dream, Madame Ariadne. Get on with it."

"Of course. Very well, I am ready to conduct the reading, Mr. Tapson."

It was all she could do to maintain her grip on the

crystal bowl. With most clients, she cheated, not quite touching her fingertips to the rim. After all, in the majority of cases there was no need to make contact and subject herself to the nightmarish energy of another person's dreams because, in general, the stories told in dreams were not that hard to analyze. They tended to fall neatly into one of several broad categories. She usually got all the information she needed during the conversation that took place before the actual reading. It was just a matter of paying attention.

She had memorized a list of useful interpretations designed to satisfy most clients.

Your dreamscape indicates that you are under a great deal of stress. I recommend that you drink a cup of chamomile tea before bedtime to calm your nerves.

It is obvious that you are facing a difficult decision. You should take a step back emotionally, drink a cup of chamomile tea, and then make a list of reasons for and against this project.

She also had a couple of specialty interpretations on hand for specific categories of clients. *Your intuition is telling you that the nice gentleman you are expecting for tea this afternoon is not your new best friend. Whatever you do, don't take his investment advice and do not entrust him with your money* was reserved for lonely, wealthy widows and single women who had come into an inheritance.

She kept *You say you wake up in a nightmare that involves being buried alive under a mountain of white satin? These dreams strike every night on the days that you go for a fitting for your wedding gown? The meaning is obvious. You should call off the wedding. You are marrying the wrong man. Trust me on this* available for women on the brink of marriage who were clearly having doubts.

She knew that when it came to wedding nightmares, most clients would not take her advice because it was not what they wanted to hear. She could not blame them. How many times had she awakened with similar nightmares before her own disastrous marriage? And yet she had gone through with the runaway wedding in Reno.

Her intuition had been warning her for months that it was time to get out of the dream reading business. But here she was, sitting across the table from a maniac who planned to kill her—all because she had ignored what her psychic senses had been trying to tell her. She had decided to keep the doors open just a little while longer. A fresh start in Southern California was going to be a risky venture. She had wanted to put more money aside.

She tightened her fingers on the rim of the crystal bowl and succeeded in slipping through the last of the storm that swirled around the dark pit of energy that fueled Tapson's dreams.

It was all she could do not to scream. She had known that getting so close to the well of primal energy and raw emotions at the center of the hurricane was going to be an appalling, terrifyingly intimate experience that would no doubt give her nightmares far into the foreseeable future. Nevertheless, she was unprepared for the sheer horror that awaited her in the darkness.

Her grandmother had explained to her that her version of the family talent was unusual. She did not merely catch fleeting sensations generated by a client's dreamscape, as most dream readers did. She could ride the currents of that energy to the source. She had been told time and again that there was considerable risk involved. Invading another person's dreams and attempting to manipulate them could destroy a reader. There was always the possibility, Grandma had said, that the client would prove to be more powerful than the reader.

It was not as if she had ever wanted to do what she was going to attempt tonight, she thought. She hated the sensations she was experiencing. She was literally in a waking nightmare—someone else's nightmare, which made it so much more awful. When she got out of this—if she got out alive and with her sanity—she would probably have panic attacks for the rest of her life. But she dared not retreat. Not yet.

"Tell me your dream, Mr. Tapson," she said.

"It always begins the same way," he said, his voice deepening into a husky whisper. "I see a pure, virginal bride draped in white satin and lace. She waits for me near the bridal bed. She pretends to be perfect. Innocent. Flawless. But I know the truth. She is a succubus. She seduces men in their sleep, draining their life energy. The only way to control her is to kill her before she can destroy another man. When I am finished with her tonight, her wedding gown and the bed will be drenched in her blood."

No doubt about it, Prudence thought. It was past time to find a new career.

On the other side of the table, Tapson watched her with eyes hot with a ghastly desire. The currents of dream energy pulsing through the crystal confirmed that she was looking at a man in the grip of a blood-lust. Her jangled nerves shrieked at her to run but her common sense warned her that would not solve the problem. She could not outrun Tapson. Even if she managed to escape him tonight, he would follow her. She knew obsession when she saw it.

"Well?" he prompted, his voice thickening with anticipation. "What is my dream trying to tell me, Madame Ariadne?"

"Your dream script indicates that you are under a great deal of stress, Mr. Tapson," she said, striving to maintain her professional aplomb. "I suggest you get more exercise and drink a cup of chamomile tea before bedtime."

Tapson's eyes glittered. "There are other activities I prefer to engage in at bedtime."

"Yes, I know," she said. Her fury surfaced, temporarily overcoming her fear. "You like to murder innocent women, don't you? How many have you killed? I'm sure I'm not meant to be your first."

Shock and confusion flashed in Tapson's eyes. Whatever he had been expecting, an outright accusation wasn't it. But in the next instant, a demonic rage flared in the atmosphere around him.

"Do you claim to be innocent, Madame Ariadne?"

"I am the one who asks the questions," she said. "Why did you decide to target me? We have never met. We have no connection. What made you decide to kill me?"

Tapson's mouth twisted in a dreadful parody of

a seductive smile. "You are a fraud, aren't you? Admit it."

"No, Mr. Tapson. I am not a fraud."

He tried to release his grip on the crystal and get to his feet, but he discovered that his fingers were frozen to the bowl, locked in place by the electrical charge of the energy she was channeling through the crystal.

He used his other hand to reach inside his jacket and pull out a knife.

She fought down the new surge of panic. He was physically more powerful than she was. Her only hope was to stay in control.

"What are you doing to me?" he shrieked. *"Succubus."*

"You picked the wrong psychic," she whispered. "Or maybe you picked the right one. It all depends on your point of view."

She tightened her grip on the rim of the bowl and concentrated on the icy currents of Tapson's dream energy. Deliberately she began to distort and reverse the waves. She sent the wildly oscillating pulses slamming back around the crystal.

Tapson's mouth opened on a soundless shriek. Unable to release the bowl, he tried to lunge at her across the table, knife in hand, intending to slice her throat. But he could not move.

She was trapped. If she released her own grip on the crystal, she would lose control of the situation. She sent another jolt of disrupting energy through the crystal. She was working on instinct now. She had never before used her talent to try to destroy the energy at the heart of someone's dreams.

Tapson stiffened violently as if he had touched a live electrical wire.

In a sense, that was exactly what had happened.

Tapson stared at her in disbelief and mounting horror. He began to tremble. The tremors became spasms. The knife fell to the carpet, landing with a soft plop.

"No," he said. "You can't do this to me."

His eyes rolled back in his head. His right hand went limp. He no longer had a death grip on the rim of the bowl—he was incapable of gripping anything. He collapsed on the floor and lay still.

She took a shaky breath and yanked her hand off the crystal. The pain of the psychic burn wasn't from a physical injury—her fingertips had not actually been singed—but her nerves were severely rattled. She could not afford to succumb to an anxiety attack, not now. She needed to stay focused on survival, because it was obvious her entire world had just been turned upside down.

"Damn you, Tapson," she whispered to the unconscious man. "I hope you are trapped in a nightmare. I hope you are locked in it for the rest of your life."

She had to think. She had to concentrate on her next move.

She took a step and then stopped and put a hand on the table to keep from losing her balance. When she had her nerves under control, she made her way around the table. Crouching beside Tapson, she groped for and found a faint, erratic pulse. He was alive, but she was sure he would never be the same.

There was no way to calculate how much damage she had done to his nerves and his senses. The technique of channeling energy through crystal with enough force to destabilize the source of a person's dreams was highly unpredictable. It was hardly the sort of skill one could easily practice and refine, at least not in an ethical way.

The talent for doing what she had just done was rare, even in a family with a long history of psychics who could read dreams. But the few accounts left by her ancestors who had possessed the ability had been clear on one point—disrupting an individual's dream energy was guaranteed to cause considerable damage.

First things first. Her own survival was at stake. She had to get rid of Tapson. She could not let him continue to lie there on the floor of her reading room. What if he woke up and was still capable of killing her? What if he never woke up at all?

She briefly considered trying to hide the unconscious man. Even if she could manage the process—doubtful, because Tapson was large and powerfully built—there was no practical way to haul him any significant distance in the busy city.

There was really only one solution to her problem. She would call an ambulance and explain that Tapson had suffered a stroke during a reading. If or when he woke up, there was a good chance he would not remember exactly what had happened. Even if he did remember what she had done to him, he would have a hard time convincing the police she had tried to murder him with psychic energy.

For her part, she had no way to prove that he had tried to murder her, let alone that he had killed others.

Regardless of what happened to Tapson, her reputation would be destroyed if the press got hold of the story. The rumors alone would ruin her. Clients would certainly not be eager to book appointments with a psychic known to have had a client collapse during a reading. That sort of thing did not make for successful marketing.

She did not believe in omens and portents, but this situation was about as close as one could get to a sign from the universe informing her that it was time to move on.

She squared her shoulders and walked out of the reading room into the small reception area. She picked up the phone.

"Hospital, please," she said to the operator. "It's an emergency. I wish to request an ambulance."

After making the call, she put the receiver back into the cradle and went to the door of the reading room to take another look at Tapson. He had not moved, but he was still breathing. The light glittered on the blade of the fallen knife. She wondered briefly if she ought to get rid of it but decided not to worry about it. There was no evidence that a crime had been committed.

She heard the siren wailing in the distance and turned to go back across the reception area to open the door. But she paused again when she saw the lamplight gleam on Tapson's gold signet ring. She did not know why it was important, but her intuition was whispering to her. *Pay attention.*

When the ambulance arrived, she explained to the two men who loaded the patient onto a stretcher that the knife belonged to the client. They shrugged and took it with them.

"The streets can be dangerous at night," one of them said.

She closed the door, locked it, and went upstairs to pack. It was definitely time to find a new future.

Chapter 2

The following morning Prudence descended the stairs dressed for travel in an unmemorable brown tweed suit and a small plain hat. It felt like the right costume for slipping out of San Francisco unnoticed. She did not move in society, but she had several clients who did. There was also a very efficient rumor network among her colleagues and competitors. Sooner or later the news that a gentleman client had collapsed in her reading room would circulate. She wanted to disappear before the telephone started ringing.

She crossed the front room of the town house, a suitcase gripped in one gloved hand. She had packed only the essentials. She was no longer Madame Ariadne, but she was not yet sure who she was going to become. Regardless, she doubted she would need her psychic dream reading costumes for her future self. She did not want to go back into that line of work.

When she arrived in Los Angeles she would contact the housekeeper and ask her to pack up the rest of her personal possessions and hold them until she had a new permanent address.

Her handbag was stuffed with the cash she had stored in the small concealed safe in the bedroom. The habit of keeping a sizable sum of money conveniently available had been passed down to her from her grandmother, who had lost her savings at the start of the Depression several years earlier. Yes, everyone said President Roosevelt had made the banking system safe, but her grandmother had never entirely trusted banks again.

At the front door she took a moment to say farewell to the comfortable little town house that had been her home since she and her mother had moved in with her grandmother. That had been after her father was killed in the Great War. Her mother had died of the flu the following year.

She and her grandmother had been on their own. They had done well in the psychic business. But a year ago her grandmother had died and Prudence had found herself utterly alone in the world. For a while a strange sense of despair and desperation had come over her. It was during that terrible, crushing time that she had made the biggest mistake of her life. She had rushed into marriage. *You learned from that experience,* she reminded herself. *You won't make that mistake again.*

She paused at the front door to take one last look

around. She wasn't sure what she ought to be feeling in that moment. A sense of melancholy, perhaps, or sadness, maybe.

But for some reason what she experienced was akin to a feeling of relief. She was escaping San Francisco and the life she had lived there. She was going to re-invent herself. By the time she reached L.A. she would be a new woman.

She went out into the damp early-morning fog that had seeped in off the Bay, locked the door, and hailed a cab to take her to the train station.

She did not see a newspaper until that evening when she carried her suitcase off the train in Los Angeles. She dug some coins out of her handbag and purchased a couple of local papers and two Hollywood gossip magazines. It was time to get to know her new home. There were a number of small towns, neighborhood enclaves, and communities scattered around the city proper. She needed to decide where she wanted to live while she looked for a job. It would be lovely to rent an apartment by the beach.

She scanned the newspapers with a sense of antici-pation. The front-page headlines consisted of the usual fare—tensions were continuing to rise in Eu-rope, trouble was brewing in the Far East, the FBI was investigating more gangland killings, and a divorce lawyer had been accused of falsifying a judge's signa-ture on some annulment papers. She paused to read the details of the fraudulent annulment but relaxed when she concluded it did not affect her.

It was the lead story on the society page of one of the papers that stunned her.

HEIR TO TAPSON MINING FORTUNE
COLLAPSES IN NIGHTMARE PSYCHIC'S READING
ROOM. DIES IN HOSPITAL.

"He's dead?" Prudence whispered, horrified. Belatedly the label the press had branded her with registered. "*Nightmare Psychic?*"

The cabdriver caught her eye in the rearview mirror. "You okay, miss?"

"Yes, yes, I'm fine. I was just rather shocked by a news story."

"I know what you mean. I get shocked every time I pick up a newspaper. That's why I usually stick with the racing form. By the way, I got a tip from a jockey about the next race at Santa Anita that I don't mind passing along. Rising Star in the seventh on Thursday."

"Thank you," she said, because she couldn't think of anything else to say.

She plunged into the article with a sense of dread.

Last night Thomas J. Tapson III, grandson of the founder of Tapson Mining Company, collapsed during the course of a psychic dream reading. An ambulance was called and Mr. Tapson was rushed to the hospital, where he later died.

The tragedy occurred on the premises of a fashionable psychic known to the city's upper crust as Madame Ariadne. Rumors of what may have caused

Mr. Tapson's death are currently swirling among the city's psychics and their many clients. Some have taken to calling the dream reader the "Nightmare Psychic."

Mr. Tapson has not circulated in San Francisco society in recent years, having been on an extended tour abroad, where he engaged in such pursuits as big game hunting and mountain climbing. His family was apparently unaware that he had returned.

Your correspondent went to Madame Ariadne's address with the intention of interviewing her, but she was not at home. A neighbor reported seeing her get into a cab with a suitcase early this morning.

Madame Ariadne claims to be a psychic who can reveal the meaning of dreams. There is bound to be a great deal of speculation about her unusual techniques in the wake of Mr. Tapson's death. Some are asking if it is possible to murder a man with the paranormal powers of the mind. Others suggest that, in addition to dream readings, Madame Ariadne offered more intimate services . . .

Prudence folded the paper and watched the street scene on the other side of the cab window.

Had she actually killed a man with her psychic talent? If so, what did that make her? Was she really the Nightmare Psychic?

"Rising Star in the seventh at Santa Anita, you said?" she asked after a moment.

"Yep."

"Has that particular jockey given you a lot of tips?"

"A few."

She turned away from the street scene and surveyed the ripped upholstery in the well-worn cab.
"Have you made a lot of money off the jockey's tips?"

"A few bucks here and there. But I've never been in
a position to put enough down to make a serious
profit until now. This time is different. I'm going in big
with my bet on Rising Star. Got a feeling that horse is
a winner. How about you?"

She rolled down the window to savor the warm
breeze of the city night. Her spirits lifted with anticipation of the bright new future she would create for
herself in Southern California.

"I'm going in big with my bet, too," she said.

"Gotta think positive, right?"

"Absolutely," she said. "Got to think positive."

Had she killed a man with her talent?

Chapter 3

Jack Wingate's dream began the way it always did . . .

. . . The mesmerizing flames burned in the mirror, summoning him. The answer to his question was waiting for him on the other side of the looking glass. All he had to do was walk through the fire into the unknown.

There was someone or something hiding deep inside the flames. From time to time he caught glimpses of the figure. He was certain that if he could just get a closer look he would be able to recognize who or what was attempting to lure him into the firestorm.

He fought to resist the pull of the flames, but the more he struggled, the harder it was to stay on his side of the mirror. He could not take the risk of exploring the mystery on the

other side, because if he went through the flames, he might
not be able to return to the real world. He might be lost
forever in a nightmare of insanity . . .

He came awake the way he always did after the
dream struck: in a cold sweat, his heart beating as if
he had just run a marathon. He took a moment to let
the disorientation pass. When he was certain he was
firmly grounded in the waking state—in reality—he
shoved the quilt aside and got to his feet.

For a time he stood there in the lavishly decorated
bedroom suite, absorbing the echoing silence of the
big house. Strictly speaking, the dramatic, ultramod-
ern, two-story residence perched on the cliffs outside
Burning Cove was not filled with silence. He could
hear the low, muffled rumble of the crashing waves
on the beach down in the cove. But the mansion,
known locally as House of Shadows, felt silent and
still in a way he could not describe. He had lived alone
all of his adult life, but he had never been so aware of
being alone as he was in this house.

You got a deal on the place, he thought. *Stop whining.*

Maybe he should get a dog.

After a moment he went into the adjoining bathroom and toggled the light switch on the wall. The
fixtures came on, illuminating the gleaming aqua-
blue and black tile work. He crossed to the pedestal
sink and made himself take a good look in the
mirror.

The man who gazed back at him had once had an
ordinary face, an unremarkable face. It was a face that
would never have landed him a Hollywood contract,

but that had been fine with him. Unlike the movie star who had built the house, he had never wanted to be a film legend. He had goals that could be achieved with a face that did not attract second looks.

The Bonner case had changed everything. Most of the left side of his face was now a chaotic road map of scars. There were more scars on his left shoulder and part of the left side of his chest. Those could be hidden with clothing. But the man in the mirror had a face that was guaranteed to attract attention on the street. A well-angled fedora could only conceal so much.

He hadn't had the guts to try inviting a woman out on a date since he had recovered from his injuries. It wasn't just that he lacked the fortitude to deal with rejection or, worse yet, pity. It was that he seemed to be missing the desire needed to motivate the risk. This was a depressing realization.

He wanted to focus on his new, cloistered life. He longed to sink into solitude and devote himself to his work. But he no longer slept well, because his nights were interrupted by the damned nightmare.

The burning mirror dream was bad, but what really worried him was the faint music of the invisible chimes. He heard the distant notes at odd moments during the day, and he had learned the hard way that he could not ignore them or pretend he was imagining things. Sometimes the chimes signaled a warning. At other times they told him to *pay attention*. They sounded when he was closing in on the truth; when he was observing something very important. And they forced him to confront the terrifying possibility that he might be delusional.

One thing was clear. He would not be able to move forward with his life until he identified the figure hidden in the flames.

Chapter 4

A few months later . . .

Prudence woke up at dawn with a knife in her hand and the fragments of a nightmare clouding her vision.

It took her a frantic, disorienting moment to realize that the wispy fog she was trying to peer through was actually a voluminous lace veil. There was something wrong with the netting. It was stained a reddish-brown color, as if it had been splashed with tea.

No, not tea. Blood.

The shock of horror paralyzed her for a couple of heartbeats. Her breath caught in her chest. Her throat was so tight she could not even give voice to a scream.

In the next instant she sat up with the violent force induced by raw panic. That was when she discovered that she was not alone on the bed. There was a man dressed in a tuxedo stretched out beside her. The front of his elegantly tailored white shirt was saturated with the reddish-brown evidence of multiple stab wounds.

The rising tide of terror threatened to drown her when she recognized the dead man—Gilbert Dover, the heir to the Dover fortune.

She was trapped in a nightmare. That was the only rational explanation for what was happening. She had to wake up. She managed to roll to the side of the bed, away from the dead man, and fell off the edge. She landed on her hands and knees with a jarring thud. The painful jolt forced her to face reality. She was not ensnared in a terrible dream. This was real.

When she tried to get to her feet, she got tangled up in the heavy satin skirts of a long, billowing gown—a once-white wedding gown that, like the veil, was stained with blood.

With a fierce effort of will she managed to scramble upright. She could feel fabric under her feet. When she looked down she saw that she was not wearing shoes. She stood on a rug.

She yanked off the wedding veil and flung it aside. Hoisting the folds of the gown, she nearly collapsed in relief when she realized she was still wearing the garter belt, stockings, panties, and slip she'd had on beneath the black business suit she had worn to work. There was no blood on any of her underthings. No signs of violence.

Memories came back in a rush. *She is deep in the stacks of the library of the Adelina Beach College Department of Parapsychology. She is tracking down* An Investigation of Dreams *for Professor Tinsley. She turns to go down an aisle lined with towering bookshelves. She senses movement behind her. An arm snakes around her throat, dragging her back against a man's chest. A wet cloth covers her nose and mouth. She recognizes the sweet, medicinal smell of chloroform, tries to struggle, reaches up for the crystal pendant, and then . . . nothing.*

It had all happened so fast. She had not had the time she needed to focus her psychic energy and fight off her attacker.

She looked around the room, trying to orient herself. The gray predawn light revealed a luxuriously appointed suite. Heavy curtains were tied back with gold tassels. Through the windows she could make out lavish gardens.

It occurred to her that she was viewing the scene from a perspective that indicated the suite was several floors above the ground.

Whisking up a fistful of the satin skirts, she hurried across the room and stopped at one side of a window. Four, maybe five floors below were a sweep of lawn and a grand porte cochere. Several impressive limousines were parked in the long, curving drive. Liveried chauffeurs lounged against the fenders of the big cars, smoking and chatting. Bellhops came and went, escorting weary socialites who were returning from nightclubs and, no doubt in some cases, the wrong beds.

The scene answered one question. She was in a hotel that catered to the wealthy upper classes—people like Gilbert Dover.

She was about to turn away from the window when she noticed the small scrum of news photographers gathered near the lobby entrance. She knew they were there to catch the arrival of a Hollywood celebrity or a rising politician emerging from a limo with a woman who was not his wife on his arm. The press thrived on such scandals.

The grisly murder scene in which she was standing combined all the elements required to ensure that the photographers and reporters would get front-page pictures and screaming headlines that would hit every paper on the West Coast.

It did not take the keen intuition of a former-psychic-dream-reader-turned-librarian to conclude that she had to escape the hotel without being seen.

She loosened the gold tassels that secured the curtains. Feeling her way across the darkened room, she found the bathroom and toggled the light switch. The glow of the ceiling fixture illuminated the tiled space and spilled through the doorway. She tried not to look at the bed as she searched the suite for her business suit or a robe—anything she could wear in place of the ghastly wedding gown.

She found the crumpled black skirt, the snug-fitting tailored black jacket, and the prim white blouse in the towel hamper. Her sensible mid-heel lace-up black oxfords were on the floor.

She was relieved to discover that it was not difficult to remove the wedding gown. It had been made for a taller woman, one with more impressive cleavage. Whoever had dressed her had been in a hurry. Only a few of the long row of delicate satin buttons on the back had been fastened.

When she yanked at the fabric on the back of the

gown, the little buttons popped off. The horrid dress fell away and crumpled on the floor. She looked down at the inside of the bodice. A few loose threads indicated that the label had been cut out.

She stepped out of the gown and tugged on the tight skirt of her business suit. Her fingers shivered as she fumbled with the zipper. She had to take a deep breath and concentrate to get the blouse buttoned. She pulled on the jacket but did not attempt to fasten it. Tying the laces of the oxfords required concentration.

She caught sight of herself in the mirror when she turned to leave the bathroom. Her hair, which had been pulled back into a severe bun the last time she had seen her reflection, now hung around her shoulders. Her eyes were stark with fear. She told herself to stay calm. She was making progress. She was out of the damned wedding gown and properly dressed once again, more or less.

No, she was not properly dressed. Something was wrong.

She stared at her image for a couple of beats longer before she realized what was missing—the gold-framed spectacles she had purchased to complete the look she had created to land her new job as a research librarian.

She did not need to wear glasses—her eyesight was fine—but the spectacles were an important accessory. Like the bun and the plain watch on her wrist, they enhanced what she considered her Professional Woman image. Her best friend, Maggie Lodge, called the ensemble her Stern Governess costume, but that was beside the point. For the most part, the look achieved the goal of convincing the faculty and visiting academics who came into the library that she was serious about her work and was most definitely not interested in having a sexual fling in the Rare Books & Manuscripts vault.

The glasses had no doubt been lost when she had been chloroformed. Luckily she had a spare pair at home. Right now she had to concentrate on escaping the murder scene and vanishing before room service or a maid or—horror of horrors—a policeman opened the door of the suite.

She was halfway across the main room, heading for the door, when it occurred to her that she had no idea where she was. She might be miles from her little apartment in Adelina Beach.

There was no sign of her handbag. That was not a surprise. She had not had it with her when the kidnapper grabbed her and put a chloroformed cloth over her face. She might need cab fare. Reluctantly she made herself turn around and take one more look at the gory scene on the bed. Dover probably had some cash in the pocket of his trousers, but she could not bring herself to search the dead man. She would hitchhike if necessary.

Her gaze snagged on the bloodstained knife. *Fingerprints.* Hers were all over the murder weapon. Gritting her teeth, she made herself go back to the bed. She used the end of a sheet to wipe the handle.

It occurred to her that her prints were elsewhere in the suite. She went back into the bathroom, kicked the bloody wedding gown out of the way, and grabbed a towel. She made a quick tour through the room, wiping down any surface she could remember having touched.

When she was done, she used the towel to open the door. Bracing herself for disaster, she peeked into the hall. Relief swept through her when she saw that the corridor was empty.

She could not risk the elevator or the main stairwell. The chance of being seen was too great. She hurried to the far end of the corridor and opened the door of the fire escape. Four flights of metal steps descended into the shadows of an empty alley.

She went out onto the landing and started down. The structure rattled, squeaked, and clattered with every step. To her ears the noise was as loud as a police siren. She held her breath, certain that someone would open a window and look out to see if there was a cat burglar trying to escape with a hotel guest's jewelry.

She made it to the ground without anyone shouting at her, took a deep breath, and ran for the far end of the alley. When she turned the corner, she glanced toward the entrance of the hotel and saw the stately gold lettering emblazoned on the sign: *Pentland Plaza*.

It was not until she was safe in the front seat of a truck driven by a farmer on his way to an early-morning market that she allowed herself to examine the full extent of the disaster that had befallen her.

She had thought she had left the past behind when she fled San Francisco and moved to Southern

California. It was obvious now that she could no longer live in that comforting fantasy.

One way or another she had to deal with the nightmare in which she found herself.

The nightmare had a name—Clara Dover.

Chapter 5

"You've given me no option, Miss Ryland. I am forced to terminate your employment." Burgess Attwater folded his hands on top of the big desk. "You will collect your personal effects and depart the library within fifteen minutes. Is that clear?"

"Quite clear," Prudence said. "And you needn't look as if you are merely carrying out your responsibility as the director of the library. We both know you have been looking for an excuse to fire me from the moment I arrived."

Attwater watched her with a steely glare. "If that is true, you certainly gave me an excellent reason to let you go, didn't you? Your sudden disappearance yesterday was a clear dereliction of duty, exactly the sort of flighty, unpredictable, irresponsible behavior I was afraid of when I was pressured to hire you as a research librarian. If Professor Tinsley had not insisted on giving you a chance, I would not be in this unpleasant position."

"Oh, shut up," Prudence said. "You're thrilled that you have a reason to get rid of me. You don't think women have any place in academic libraries."

"And you have just proven me correct," Attwater said. "You must admit your behavior yesterday afternoon was intolerable. You vanished into the stacks with a man at a quarter to five in the afternoon and you didn't reappear until this morning. You can't possibly expect me to keep you on in a professional capacity after such disgraceful behavior. You will pack up your desk immediately."

"I assumed you would fire me this morning, so I'm already packed, but I would like to know the name of the man you say accompanied me into the stacks."

"You don't even know his name? Really, Miss Ryland, that is beyond disgraceful. You are a prime example of what comes of allowing females to enter the upper echelons of academia."

"And you are a fine example of a jackass." Prudence took a step forward and flattened her palms on the desk. "I don't intend to waste my time begging for another chance. I just want to know the name of the creep who followed me into the stacks yesterday afternoon."

"I have no idea whom you seduced, Miss Ryland, and even if I did, I would not give you his name. Perhaps next time you will obtain an introduction before you fornicate with a gentleman in the stacks."

"Whoever he was, he was no gentleman and there

was no fornication, but I don't expect you to believe me. All I want is a name."

"Well, you're not getting one. I've had enough of this nonsense. You will leave the library immediately or I shall have you escorted off the premises."

It had been too much to expect Attwater to give her the name of the man who had followed her into the stacks. She suspected he was telling her the truth when he said he didn't know. He had been in a meeting at the time.

"Never mind," she said. "You are useless, Attwater. Don't worry, I will see myself off the premises." She strode to the door and opened it. Pausing on the threshold, she glanced back over her shoulder. "By the way, when Professor Tinsley asks about the research I was doing for him yesterday, you may tell him that I found that treatise he was looking for."

Attwater scowled. "What treatise?"

"*An Investigation of Dreams.* Anonymous. Eighteenth century. It contains a reference to a seventeenth-century alchemist named Sylvester Jones." Prudence summoned up a bright, shiny smile. "I'm sure the professor will be thrilled. Evidently he considers it critical to his work."

For the first time, Attwater's expression registered some unease. "Where is the treatise?"

"Somewhere in the stacks." Prudence swept out a hand to indicate the extensive rows of shelving on the other side of the glass-paned office window. "Or maybe it was in the Rare Books and Manuscripts vault. I don't recall precisely. I was very busy at the time. But don't worry, I jotted down the Dewey number in my notebook. It won't be difficult to find it again."

Attwater got to his feet, brows snapping together. "Where is your notebook?"

"You'll be thrilled to know that Professor Tinsley intends to credit the library in his paper—assuming he gets the treatise, of course. When it's published, the library and its director will be famous in the most exclusive academic circles that take paranormal research seriously. I'm sure Duke University's Parapsychology Laboratory will be madly jealous."

"Now see here, Miss Ryland—"

She went briskly through the doorway. "Goodbye, Mr. Attwater. Give my best to Professor Tinsley."

"One moment, Miss Ryland. Where is that treatise?"

"I told you," she said over her shoulder, "I can't recall precisely, but the exact location is in my notes. Took me days to track it down. I'm afraid my Latin is a bit rusty. But being the professional that you are, I'm sure you'll find it very quickly."

"Where is that notebook?"

"In my handbag." She patted the leather bag slung over her shoulder.

Attwater stared, aghast, at the handbag. "That notebook is library property."

"No, it's not. I purchased the notebook myself and I use it to keep track of personal information."

Attwater's mouth fell open. Something approaching panic flashed in his eyes. His face was suffused with an unflattering shade of red. Her Latin might be rusty, but his was nonexistent. They both knew he was never going to find the treatise that Tinsley was after. That meant there would be no credit for the director of the library of the Adelina Beach College Department of Parapsychology in Tinsley's paper.

She closed the door very firmly and went down the hall to her desk.

Otto Tinsley was currently the most powerful professor in the department. It was important to keep him happy. The only reason she had obtained the position of research librarian in the first place was because Tinsley had been impressed with her and had insisted she be hired. He was not going to be pleased when he found out that she had been fired, regardless of the cause. If he did not get the treatise he was desperate to reference in his paper, he would be even more irate. Academic politics being what they were, a professor of Tinsley's stature always outranked a librarian, including a librarian who happened to be the director of the library.

Reginald Herring, the library clerk, was at his desk. He pretended not to notice when she emerged from Attwater's office. When she passed him, she gave him a beatific smile.

"Goodbye, Mr. Herring," she said. "It was so very helpful of you to inform Director Attwater that I disappeared into the stacks with a man yesterday."

Herring, thin and bitter because she had been given the title of research librarian and therefore outranked him, looked up. Behind the lenses of his spectacles his eyes glittered with vengeful satisfaction.

"It's not my fault you chose to engage in a dalliance in the stacks, Miss Ryland," he said.

"It was a whirlwind affair," she said. "I didn't even

catch the gentleman's name. But you're the observant type, especially where I'm concerned, and we both know that only the most distinguished members of the faculty are allowed to browse the stacks. I'm sure you noticed which professor followed me yesterday."

Herring blinked a couple of times. "I can assure you your paramour wasn't a member of our faculty."

"Oh, I see. You allowed a *stranger* to wander into the stacks."

Herring started a little at the accusation. "He mentioned that he was a visiting professor from a small college in San Francisco."

Prudence held her breath. "I see. I assume he gave you his name?"

"Smithton. He said he was here to see you." Herring sneered. "He mentioned something about your unique talents."

She ignored the sarcasm. "Did you see him leave?"

"No. I left promptly at five." Herring gave her a superior smile. "I assumed you would escort your visitor out of the library and lock up when the two of you were finished with whatever you were doing back there."

"What did he look like?"

"Really, Miss Ryland, I have better things to do than catalog your male acquaintances. If you can't remember what they look like, you can't expect me to recall them or take notes. I will say he was quite fashionably dressed. I certainly could not afford his tailor on my clerical salary."

Prudence gave Herring's cheap, ill-fitting suit and plain tie a once-over and then smiled a pitying smile. "That's too bad. You could use a good tailor."

She went out into the hall and closed the door with considerable force before Herring could come up with another snide comment. She marched past the glass-paned door of the cataloging department, aware that Mr. Bryerly, the cataloger, was watching to see who had just slammed the door.

She went outside onto the front steps and paused to let the warm light of the California morning envelop her. It was just after nine. Attwater had been waiting for her when she had arrived promptly at eight thirty. It had taken him a full half hour to fire her because he had been unable to resist the opportunity to lecture her on his firmly held belief that women did not belong in the academic world.

She went down the steps and walked across the campus. Adelina Beach College was a new institution that aimed to attract students from the small towns and beachfront communities near Los Angeles. Eager to make its mark in the academic world, it had boldly invested in the Department of Parapsychology. The goal was to establish a reputation for cutting-edge research that would allow the college to compete with the prestigious work of Rhine and McDougall at Duke and Harry Price at the London National Laboratory of Psychical Research.

The day she had landed the position of research librarian she had been thrilled. Her long-term dream was to open a bookshop focused on paranormal literature, but she wanted to have a little more cash put aside before she took the risk of going into business on her own. Working in the library at Adelina Beach College had seemed like the ideal position. She would gain experience in the field and establish a professional reputation that would enhance the appeal of the bookshop. At the same time she would earn a salary that would allow her to put a little more money aside for her dream.

True, she could earn more if she went back to her old line of work, but the very thought of having to do dream readings again was depressing. It would mean taking on clients who might give her nightmares and anxiety attacks. Yes, the business had paid the rent and put food on the table for her grandmother and herself during the hard times. It had covered the doctors' fees and medicine that the elderly woman had needed during those last few horrible months.

Yes, there was a lot to be said for the profits to be made in dream reading, and if it became absolutely necessary, she would do what she had to do. But going back to her old life was a last resort. There were risks. The mess in which she found herself was directly attributable to her career as a psychic.

She walked home to her aging beachfront apartment house. She had resisted the temptation to buy a car, preferring to save the money. She stopped at a corner market to pick up some tea, a loaf of bread, and a carton of eggs.

She was sitting at the small dining room table eating an egg salad sandwich, drinking a cup of tea, and trying to come up with a plan when she saw the *Adelina Beach Courier* delivery truck cruise down the street in front of the apartment house. It stopped at the newsstand at the end of the block.

Electricity snapped across the back of her neck,

rattling her senses. It was too early for the afternoon edition of the local paper. That meant a special edition was being delivered.

She leaped to her feet, grabbed her handbag, and hurried out the door. She went down the two flights of stairs to the street and walked quickly to the newsstand.

She could read the headline from several yards away:

DOVER INDUSTRIES HEIR MURDERED BY KILLER BRIDE

She chucked three cents into the machine, grabbed a copy of the paper, and rushed back to her apartment to read the full story.

The body of Gilbert Dover, eldest son of Mr. and Mrs. Copeland Dover of San Francisco, was found savagely murdered in the bridal suite of a Los Angeles hotel this morning. Police report that Mr. Dover, attired in a tuxedo, had been stabbed multiple times. A discarded bridal gown drenched in what appeared to be the victim's blood was discovered on the floor of the bathroom. The knife used to kill Mr. Dover was left on the bed.

There was no sign of the bride, who somehow escaped unseen. Indications are she may have exited the hotel by way of the fire escape.

The hotel manager stated that the bridal suite had been booked in the name of a different guest, who never checked in. None of the staff recalls seeing Mr. Dover or the missing bride. The detective in charge of the case suspects that the couple used the service stairs to sneak into the hotel and let themselves into the bridal suite.

"We think the fake bride lured Mr. Dover, who is said to possess unusual tastes in such matters, into what he believed to be a romantic liaison," Detective Andrews said. "The woman then proceeded to stab him to death. It is obvious we are now searching for a ruthless murderess who may well be insane. If you have any knowledge of this madwoman, please contact the police immediately."

Sources say that Mr. Dover cut a well-known figure on the San Francisco social scene and was said to be an eccentric when it came to his notions of entertainment . . .

Prudence lowered the paper and sat very still for a long time. She had known this was coming. She had thought she was prepared for the inevitable. But the shock of seeing it in print left her on the razor-thin edge of panic. The police were looking for her—they just didn't know it yet.

There was no way to estimate how much time she had, and asking her friend Maggie and Maggie's very new husband, Sam Sage, for help was out of the question. The couple was on a leisurely honeymoon road trip. They had not left an itinerary, so there was no way to contact them at a hotel or an auto court. Besides, when you got right down to it, there wasn't anything Maggie or Sam could do. She needed assistance from someone who was capable of dealing with the weird and powerful Dover family.

It was time to call an expert. She reached for the phone.

"Long distance, please," she said when the Adelina Beach operator responded.

"One moment, please. I'll connect you," the woman said.

There was another short wait until another woman came on the line.

"Long distance," she said.

"I wish to place a call to Mr. Luther Pell in Burning Cove, California," Prudence said. "I have the number."

Chapter 6

Jack Wingate heard the music of the invisible chimes and knew that Prudence Ryland was going to be a problem—not because she was almost certainly a fraud and quite possibly a murderess but because she was showing every indication of being unpredictable.

He was very, very good at fitting people into neatly defined categories that, in most cases, made predicting their behavior a relatively straightforward business. But as he watched Prudence deal with Luther Pell, it became clear that the only predictable thing about the woman was that she was—yes—unpredictable.

According to Luther, she had made the appointment yesterday afternoon from her home in Adelina Beach. She had arrived on the noon train from L.A. today and taken a cab straight to Pell's office. She had not bothered to check into a hotel. Her suitcase was on the floor beside her chair.

The three of them were gathered in Pell's office. The expensively appointed room was located on the floor above the Paradise, the hottest nightclub in town. Luther was seated behind his large polished wooden desk. Sleek, well-dressed in a hand-tailored jacket and a silk tie, his dark hair gleaming with a judicious amount of oil, his eyes unreadable, he looked like what he was: a dangerous man who had mob connections.

Very few people were aware that Pell had other connections as well, including the private phone number of the director of a clandestine government intelligence agency.

Jack had taken up a position near the French doors that opened onto a wrought iron–trimmed balcony overlooking citrus-scented gardens and the sapphire-bright Pacific beyond. The position allowed him to observe Prudence without being obvious about it. It also had the advantage of making it more difficult for her to see him clearly. He knew that when she looked at him, he was cast in shadow by the glare of the sun behind him.

She should have been almost unaware of him—he was good at fading into the woodwork—but he could tell by the not-so-subtle glances she occasionally sent in his direction that she was trying just as hard to do a read on him as he was trying to do on her. She was maintaining a polite, businesslike facade, but he got the feeling she was not thrilled with what she saw. It was as if she had already decided they were going to be adversaries.

For absolutely no rational reason he could think of, he found that . . . intriguing. Interesting. It also deepened the mystery of Prudence Ryland.

He reminded himself that she was a client. Luther was going to pay him good money to keep her from being arrested for murder.

The real question was whether or not she was an innocent caught up in a Machiavellian conspiracy designed to make her appear guilty of murder. From what he knew of the case, it was obvious there had to be more to her story.

The important element in the equation was that Luther was not concerned with the possibility that Prudence Ryland had murdered Gilbert Dover. That, of course, made her even more interesting. When it came to assessing clients, Luther's intuition was nothing short of amazing.

At the moment she appeared to be precisely what she claimed to be—an innocent librarian, a woman alone in the world, who had been set up for a murder rap by an unhinged killer.

She perched on one of the padded leather chairs, a delicate porcelain teacup in her gloved hand. She appeared very prim and proper in a crisply tailored rust-brown jacket; a slim, modest skirt that covered her knees; and a pair of sensible lace-up oxfords. Her midnight-dark hair was tightly pinned beneath a tiny felt hat in the same rust-colored shade as her suit. Her gloves and purse were in the same color. Her jewelry consisted of an almost unnoticeable crystal pendant and a plain businesslike watch.

It was the spectacles that gave away her game. Something about the way she wore them—as if they were a bit of a nuisance—told him there was no prescription ground into the lenses. The glasses were intended to enhance the unassuming image she wanted to project.

To some extent they did succeed in veiling the intense energy in her watchful amber eyes, but that just made him more curious. Prudence Ryland was a woman in hiding, but what was she hiding from?

"I will be honest with you, Mr. Pell," she said. There was a faint clink as she set the cup down on the saucer. "We both know I can't afford the fees that I'm sure you charge for your investigative work. But as I told you on the phone, I hope to be able to repay you in kind. I really am a very good researcher. I think I could be of service to you in the future."

"I agree," Luther said. "I am aware of the research you provided to Maggie Lodge and Sam Sage a few weeks ago when they became involved in the murder case out at the old Carson Flint estate."

"Paranormal literature is my specialty," Prudence said. "Particularly dream research. The study of dreams is a foundation for much of the work that is done in the field. But as I'm sure you're aware, research skills can be useful in any area of investigation."

Luther's eyes glinted with cool satisfaction. "I discovered long ago that information is an extremely valuable commodity, Miss Ryland. I look forward to having your phone number in my directory of experts. We have an agreement. You are now a client of Failure Analysis. Please explain your situation to Mr. Wingate and me."

"I'm not sure I understand Mr. Wingate's role in this matter," she said. "Is he your secretary?"

"Don't worry," Jack said. "I'm very good at taking notes, and I'm a skilled typist."

Prudence shot him a steely glare. Luther stepped in quickly.

"Sorry," he said. "I should have made it clear when I introduced you. Mr. Wingate is the consultant I've selected to handle your case."

"Consultant?" Prudence said. "Is that the same thing as an investigator?"

"The two professions overlap in many important respects," Luther assured her.

"I see."

"But they are not exactly the same," Jack said. "My responsibility is to analyze the information that is acquired in the course of an investigation."

"I'm afraid I don't understand the difference," she said, her voice very cold now. Before he could respond, she turned back to Luther. "It seems to me that at this stage of the investigation I need a real investigator."

"In my opinion, you need Jack," Luther said. "I hope you will trust me, Miss Ryland. This is what I do best. I match agents and cases."

Jack watched her closely, but he could not get a clear read on her. It wasn't hard to figure out that she

was not excited by the news that he would be handling her case. But he was not sure why she was uncertain about his role in the investigation. With any
other woman he would have assumed that the scars
had put her off. But aside from a brief, assessing
glance at the ruined side of his face, she had appeared
unfazed. It hadn't been a polite act designed to pretend she hadn't noticed the marks—he knew what
that kind of acting looked like. After noting the scars,
she had dismissed them as unimportant.

True, she had more worrisome things on her
mind—like the fact that she was in danger of getting
arrested for murder. He could see why that might
push his scars far down her list of priorities.

So if it wasn't the scars that made her wary of him,
what was it?

"All right," she said. "You are the one with expertise in this sort of thing, Mr. Pell. I accept your
recommendation."

"Thank you," Luther said. "Now, tell us what
happened."

"The day before yesterday, shortly before five
o'clock in the afternoon, I went into the stacks to locate
an old treatise for one of the professors in the Department of Parapsychology," Prudence said. Her tone
was brisk and professional now, a researcher delivering a report. "The library was very quiet at the time.
The clerk was at his desk but there were no patrons.
However, a stranger entered and followed me into the
stacks. He grabbed me from behind and rendered me
unconscious with chloroform. That is the last thing I

remember until I woke up next to Gilbert Dover, who was . . . dead."

Jack watched her. "You must have talked to the clerk. What did he tell you about the stranger who followed you into the stacks?"

For the first time since they had been introduced, Prudence gave him her full attention. Behind the lenses of her spectacles, her eyes flashed with awareness. He smiled a little, satisfied that she was still trying to figure him out. *Good luck, lady. I've had a lot of experience staying in the shadows, too.*

The ability to intuitively read people was a talent that had its uses in his work, but when it came to his personal life, it was a curse. Sure, it was helpful for law enforcement to know whether a killer intended to go on murdering people or if a particular murder was a one-time event. And yes, his talent could be employed to track down the bad guys. But being able to predict that a friend's marriage would fail or that there was a high probability a lover would betray you forced a man to view other people in a cold, realistic light. His motto was *Don't expect too much and you won't be disappointed.*

"The clerk's name is Reginald Herring," Prudence said. "He did not go out of his way to be helpful."

Jack reached inside his jacket and took out a notebook and a pencil. "Think he might have been involved?"

"No," Prudence said. She watched as he made notes. "Herring disliked me intensely because I got the job that he was convinced should have been his.

He was very happy to see me fired, but I can't imagine he is mixed up in the murder of Gilbert Dover."

Jack looked up. "What else did he tell you?"

"He said the man identified himself as a visiting professor named Smithton. That was no doubt a lie, but Herring did tell me that Smithton mentioned being affiliated with a college in San Francisco. I think that is important."

Jack heard the chimes but he did not need them to see the obvious. "Because the Dovers live there," he said.

Prudence nodded encouragingly, evidently pleased that he had been able to make the connection. Jack wondered if he should be offended. Luther gave a soft, amused snort.

"I'm sure it was a slip of the tongue or else Smithton did not think that bit of information would reveal anything useful," Prudence continued. "He was probably just trying to provide some background to make his story look solid."

"Did you ask the clerk for a description?" Luther said.

"Yes." Prudence looked grim. "Again, Mr. Herring was not helpful. He assumed the worst, of course."

Jack frowned. "What the hell is worse than getting kidnapped and set up for murder?"

"Not much," Prudence admitted. "But what I meant was that Reginald Herring chose to believe that I invited Mr. Smithton to join me in the stacks."

For the first time in a very long while, Jack realized he had just gone blank. "Why would you do that?"

Prudence gave him a pitying look that had nothing to do with his scars and everything to do with her opinion of his intelligence.

"Take a wild guess, Mr. Wingate," she said.

Jack caught the glint of amusement in Luther's eyes. It was all he could do not to groan with embarrassment. He had been so focused on the kidnapping and murder that he had missed the obvious.

"Got it," he said. "Herring thought you and Smithton had planned a, uh, a *tryst* in the stacks."

Prudence flushed—not from embarrassment, Jack realized, but from outrage.

"Mr. Herring made no secret of the fact that he did not approve of my being hired as research librarian," she said. "Director Attwater didn't want to put me in the position in the first place. I discovered later that he was pressured into employing me. He'd spent the past few weeks looking for an excuse to fire me, and thanks to Mr. Smithton, he got one."

"Right," Jack said. "Let's get back to the case. You woke up in the bridal suite of the Pentland Plaza."

Prudence tightened one gloved hand into a small fist. "Wearing a wedding gown and veil. I still had on all of my underthings, thank goodness, but whenever I think of that horrible man putting me into that awful dress, I want to kill him."

Luther's brows rose a fraction of an inch.

She winced and tapped one gloved finger on the arm of the chair. "I probably should not have said that."

"Under the circumstances, your reaction is understandable," Luther said.

"The thing is, even if I had the opportunity, I would prefer to do it with a weapon other than a knife," Prudence said, very earnest now.

Curiosity glinted briefly in Luther's eyes. "Why not a knife?"

"Too messy," Jack said before Prudence could respond.

She looked at him, startled. Then her eyes tightened a little, telling him he was right.

"Exactly," she said. "Much too messy. All that blood. It was just awful."

"There's another reason you would not have used a knife," Jack continued, thinking it through. "You'd have to take the risk of getting dangerously close to your target. You are not a large woman. According to your story, you were easily overpowered by the man who followed you into the stacks."

Irritation flashed in Prudence's electric eyes. "I was not easily overpowered, Mr. Wingate. I was taken by surprise and attacked with chloroform. There's a difference."

He ignored that. "And then there's the fact that a knife does not always make for a quick kill. It takes skill and expertise to guarantee efficiency. As a librarian you would have known about those factors because you would have done the research."

Prudence gave him a wary look. "Skill and expertise?"

"You might get lucky with the first strike and hit an artery," he said. "The odds are not good, though, unless you know a great deal about the human body. But mostly it's the mess that would persuade you to use another means. From a purely practical point of view, there would be the possibility of leaving too many clues. Bloodstained clothing is difficult to get rid of. No, you might pick up a knife as a last resort, but it would not be your first choice if you had time to plan."

Prudence was distracted by the observation. "That scene in the hotel bridal suite indicates a great deal of advance planning, doesn't it?"

"Yes, it does," Jack said. He paused as another thought occurred. "The newspapers said the gown was drenched in blood."

Prudence frowned. "No, not drenched. There were several stains on it, and on the veil, too, but it wasn't actually soaked in blood, if you see what I mean."

"What about the bed?" Jack asked. "Was there a great deal of blood on it?"

"No, there wasn't. There was a lot of blood on Gilbert's clothes but not on the bedspread."

"The bed had not been turned down?" Jack said.

"No." Prudence gave him an expectant look. "Well? What does that tell you?"

"Not a lot," Jack admitted. "Just that Dover was killed somewhere else. His body was smuggled into the hotel, probably in a laundry cart or a large traveling trunk. You must have been transported the same way."

Prudence shuddered. "What a ghastly thought. But I see what you mean."

"Whoever set the scene in the suite probably dressed in hotel livery or workman's clothes," he added.

"I suppose it would have been tricky to stab a man to death in a classy hotel like the Pentland Plaza without drawing attention," Prudence said.

"Or without making a considerable mess in the process," Jack said. "In a stabbing there is always a lot of blood, and it tends to stain everything in the vicinity."

She gave him an approving look. "That is a very good observation, Mr. Wingate."

"Thank you," he said, aware that he was speaking through set teeth. "This is not my first murder investigation, Miss Ryland."

"Please continue with this line of questioning," she urged, apparently unaware of his attempt at sarcasm or Pell's barely concealed amusement.

Best to forge ahead, Jack decided. It was either that or get into a verbal sparring match with the client. "Tell me about the wedding gown."

"What do you want to know?"

"Did it fit?"

Prudence blinked, evidently surprised by the question. "No. It was a little too large in . . . certain places." She gestured vaguely toward her bosom. "And it had been made for a woman who was somewhat taller than me."

That would not take much, Jack thought. Prudence was a petite woman.

"Was the gown expensive?" he asked.

"For obvious reasons I did not spend a lot of time examining the dress, but yes, it was beautiful. At least it would have been if someone hadn't splashed blood on it. There was a great deal of heavy satin in the skirts and a lot of delicate pearl work on the bodice. It certainly didn't come from the sale rack at a department store. It was handmade."

"I don't suppose you thought to check for a label," he said.

Prudence gave him an irritated look. "As a matter of fact, I did."

"Good thinking," he said. "And?"

"It had been cut out," she said. Her eyes glinted with annoyance.

"Too bad."

"It was not my fault, Mr. Wingate."

"No, I suppose not." He studied his notes. "So we have an expensive gown made to fit another woman."

"Obviously," she said, her tone sharpening. "It's not as if it would have been made for me, is it?"

Jack looked at her. Okay, he was still new to the private consulting business. Until the Bonner case, he had always worked with law enforcement and government agencies. Dealing with bureaucracies was a hazard of the business, but for the most part, he had been able to navigate those waters. It was rapidly becoming clear, however, that dealing with private clients like Prudence Ryland was going to be a much bigger problem. Then again, there couldn't be many like her. It was statistically impossible. She was definitely unique.

"I need more information in order to refine my hypothesis," he said. He tapped the pencil against the notebook. "The first step is to find out why you were included in the script, Miss Ryland. You must have some idea. It's obvious you were not selected at random to play the part of the Killer Bride."

She winced but she did not ask him why he had come to that conclusion. Probably because she knew it was obvious.

"I don't know why Gilbert Dover was murdered," she said. "But, unfortunately, I have a somewhat complicated connection to the Dover family."

"Somehow that does not come as a surprise," he said.

She shot him a quelling glare. "Gilbert's father died several years ago, leaving Dover Industries in the hands of his wife, Clara Dover. Clara is a very formidable woman, both in society and in the business world. When it comes to business, she is known to be brilliant and ruthless. It's no secret in San Francisco that she is the one who transformed Dover Industries from a small regional manufacturing company into the powerful corporation it is today."

"That's true," Luther said. "I made a couple of phone calls after you and I set up this appointment, Miss Ryland. There's no question but that Clara Dover is an impressive businesswoman. She pushed most of her competitors into bankruptcy along the way to building her empire."

"Several months ago, she became obsessed with her plan to persuade me to marry Gilbert," Prudence continued.

Jack heard the faint clash of distant chimes and got the ghostly frisson on the back of his neck that told him he was finally getting some truly important information.

"Go on," he said, aware that his voice had hardened. The words came out sounding like an order.

Prudence slanted him another wary glance. "Before I became a librarian, I worked as a psychic in San Francisco."

"Did you now?" he said, almost under his breath.

"You must be wondering why Clara Dover would settle on me as an appropriate bride for the heir to the Dover fortune," Prudence said. "It's true I enjoyed some success as a psychic. Most of my clients came from upper-class circles. But I never personally moved in those circles. I don't have an inheritance. I can't claim to be related to any of the important families in the city. To understand Clara's obsession with convincing me to marry Gilbert, you need to know that she is certain she possesses a powerful psychic talent. She thinks Gilbert inherited her ability."

Jack frowned. "Hard to believe that an individual smart enough and strong-minded enough to build a business empire would put any credence in the paranormal, let alone convince herself that she actually possesses some psychic talent."

"Try employing your imagination, Mr. Wingate," Prudence said, her voice dangerously sweet.

"Excuse me," Luther said, once again interrupting before Jack could respond. "Please continue, Miss Ryland."

"I'm afraid Clara Dover was fixated on a ridiculous plan to repair what she believed to be a flaw on the male side of the Dover family bloodline," Prudence said. "She concluded marriage to me would somehow fix the problem."

"What was the flaw?" Jack asked.

Luther answered the question. "My San Francisco sources told me that the Dover men were known for their volatile tempers, as well as certain eccentricities."

Jack looked at him. "Eccentricities?"

"I was told that Gilbert Dover was not welcome in the city's brothels," Luther said. "He was rumored to have injured several women."

"Clara Dover thought marriage would change her son's vicious temperament?" Jack shook his head. "That seems unrealistic, to say the least."

"I doubt very much that she believed I could change Gilbert," Prudence said. "Her concern was for his offspring, her grandchildren."

"The problem in the Dover bloodline goes back at least three generations," Luther said. "In the course of my calls to San Francisco, I learned that years ago there were rumors that Clara's husband, Copeland Dover, was responsible for the deaths of at least two prostitutes, but no charges were ever brought. He was said to have had a violent temper. No one mourned his passing when he keeled over from a heart attack, although his widow gave him a lavish funeral."

"Clara Dover, like most people in society, goes to great lengths to maintain appearances," Prudence said.

"Copeland Dover's father, Gilbert's grandfather, apparently disappeared from San Francisco society altogether," Luther added.

"The rumor is that the family had him locked up

in a private asylum," Prudence said. "That's where he died."

"Clara and her husband, Copeland, produced two sons," Luther said. "Gilbert is the oldest. The younger brother, Rollins, is, by all accounts, stable. He got married a few months ago. His mother gave him a title and an office at Dover Industries, but everyone knew he was not in line to take control of the company. That was supposed to be Gilbert's job. Evidently there was never any question but that he was the favorite."

"Everyone in San Francisco knew that," Prudence said. "As I was saying, Clara was well aware of the problems in the bloodline, although she would never in a million years acknowledge them."

"Of course not," Luther said. "Rumors like that can destroy a family and, in this case, a business empire."

"*Her* empire," Prudence said. "She built Dover Industries. But all the money and power in the world can't fix a bloodline. Unfortunately, she thought I could take care of the problem as far as the next generation was concerned. Thankfully, I was warned of her intentions by the psychic circuit."

Jack paused his pencil over his notebook. "Psychic circuit?"

Prudence waved a hand. "You know how it is. Members of every profession tend to share news that affects others in that particular line of work. It's no different in the community of psychics."

"A gossip network for psychics," Jack said, thinking about the possibilities. "Interesting."

Prudence gave him a chilly smile. "It was because of the information available on the psychic circuit that my grandmother made it a point to avoid booking appointments with Clara Dover whenever possible. After Grandma passed, I tried to follow the same practice. But once in a while there was no diplomatic way out of a reading."

Jack nodded. "Refusing outright to do a séance for Clara would have been extremely risky for your business."

Prudence gave him a repressive glare. "I don't hold séances. Neither did my grandmother. In my opinion, mediums who claim to be able to speak to the dead are frauds."

"On that point we are in complete agreement, Miss Ryland," he said.

She raised her brows. "You think all psychics are frauds, don't you, Mr. Wingate?"

"My opinion is not important," he said. "I'm here to consult on your case. I can do that without having to believe in the paranormal."

"As you said, your views on metaphysics are of absolutely no importance. You are correct about something else as well, Mr. Wingate. Clara Dover had the power to destroy a small business like mine, and she would have done it in a heartbeat. That is why I had to handle her in a diplomatic fashion."

Luther sat forward at his desk. "Did Clara expect you to overlook her son's dangerous temper for the sake of marrying a Dover?"

"Yes, of course," Prudence said. "In her view, he was irresistible because he was a Dover, her son and heir. While she was trying to sell me on the idea of marrying him, she made a point of insisting that he was a man of keen intelligence and strong psychic ability. She said those traits occasionally made him impatient and temperamental, but she informed me that would not be a problem for the right woman."

"You," Jack said.

"Me. Clara's theory was that marriage to a woman who also possessed some strong psychic talent would act as a calming influence because such a woman would understand Gilbert's high-strung temperament. But, more importantly, as far as she was concerned, it would ensure that her grandchildren would be not only psychically gifted but stable."

"She really believed you had some genuine psychic ability?" Jack asked.

Prudence gave him another of what he was coming to think of as her go-to-hell smiles.

"Oddly enough, Clara did believe that," she said. "I understand why a man such as yourself, a man of apparently limited imagination, might find it impossible to grasp the concept of the paranormal. But not everyone takes such a narrow view of the world. Clara Dover, whatever her faults might be, does not lack intelligence or imagination. She believes in the paranormal, and yes, she was convinced I possessed some psychic talent."

Jack looked at Luther. "Have I just been insulted?"

"I think so," Luther said.

"Just wanted to confirm my own conclusion," Jack said. He turned back to Prudence. "I'll try not to take it personally."

"If I were you, I would definitely take it personally."

"If you insist." Jack flipped a page in his notebook. "To return to the main topic—Clara Dover didn't need a daughter-in-law who could bring money or social status into the family. She wanted one she believed could help her strengthen and stabilize her son's so-called paranormal talent so that her grandchildren would inherit so-called psychic abilities but not the bad blood in the Dover line."

"Yep, that pretty much says it all," Prudence said. "You're right; you do take very good notes."

"Just wait until you have the opportunity to observe my typing skills," he said.

Luther cleared his throat. "Clara Dover sounds as if she is more than a little unhinged. Maybe Gilbert's instability came from her side of the family as well as his father's."

"No," Prudence said, "I don't think so. Clara was obsessed and very determined to get what she wanted, but she never seemed unstable, at least not when I knew her as a client. However, there's no knowing how Gilbert's death might have affected her."

"Because he was the object of her obsession?" Jack asked.

"It would be more accurate to say Gilbert was the means by which she intended to secure the empire she had created," Prudence said.

He thought about that. "I see what you mean. His death crushed her dreams of founding a dynasty of psychically gifted Dovers."

"She will be enraged because she'll see herself as stuck with her other son, Rollins," Prudence said. "Perhaps one day she'll realize she was more fortunate than she thinks."

"Maybe," Jack said. "But from the sound of it, I doubt it. How hard did she push you to marry Gilbert?"

"Very hard." Prudence gave a visible shudder. "She brought him, unannounced, to a reading appointment she had booked for herself and introduced him to me. Gilbert was very charming, but it was obvious he was simply humoring his mother. I could tell he had no personal interest in me, however, so I hoped that would be the end of the matter. But a day later he asked me out to the theater. I'm sure his mother ordered him to do it."

"You declined, I assume?" Luther said.

"Yes, of course. I explained I didn't have the proper attire for the theater. That was a mistake, because the day after that a very expensive evening gown was delivered to my door, along with another invitation. I sent both back. Matters went on like that for a while, but eventually the invitations stopped. I knew Gilbert had been going through the motions to please his mother. Apparently he'd had enough of the charade. I was very relieved until the day Clara Dover walked into my reading room in a towering rage."

"She threatened you?" Jack asked.

"She said that she had made me the offer of a lifetime, and if I was too stupid to take advantage of it, she would destroy me," Prudence said. "I tried to calm her down, but she was beyond reason. I knew she could ruin me, but I was already planning to shut down my business and move to L.A. That last scene with her convinced me to speed up my plans."

There was a short, brittle silence. Jack made no attempt to break it. Neither did Luther. They both watched Prudence.

With great care she set the cup and saucer on the small table next to the chair. "Shortly after the very unpleasant visit from Clara, I shut the doors of my business and moved to Los Angeles. Well, Adelina Beach, to be precise."

Jack listened to the chimes and knew he was not hearing the complete truth.

"How long has it been since you made the move?" he asked.

"Several months," she said.

He smiled. He didn't need the sound of the chimes now. He just did the math.

"Do you think you might have arrived in L.A. around the first of November?" he asked.

Prudence went very still. Behind the lenses of her spectacles, her eyes got bone-chillingly cold. "Possibly. I can't recall the exact date. Is it important, Mr. Wingate?"

"No, I've got enough information." He tucked the notebook and pencil into the pocket of his jacket. "I just wanted to confirm a theory I have been working on since Luther suggested I take your case."

Prudence clenched the arm of her chair with a gloved hand. "What is that theory?"

"You are Madame Ariadne. You have a knack for attracting publicity, don't you? First you hit the headlines as the Nightmare Psychic who vanished after her last client collapsed during the course of a reading. Now you are on the front page as the Killer Bride. Do you plan to order another set of business cards?"

Chapter 7

Prudence stopped breathing for a small slice of time that felt like an eternity.

When she recovered from the shock, she reminded herself that she had known her past would come back to haunt her if she sought help from Luther Pell. Still, she had assumed she would be attempting to explain the situation to Pell, who was something of a known quantity. Jack Wingate, on the other hand, was a complete mystery. The fact that he had been the first one to connect the dots was unsettling.

She had to admit it was also not surprising. She had known the moment she walked into the room and saw him standing in the shadows near the window that he was going to be a problem.

"You have an excellent memory for scandal, Mr. Wingate," she said, working hard to maintain a cool, professional demeanor. She knew how to handle difficult clients. She'd had ample experience first as a psychic and then as a librarian. Okay, Jack was not, technically speaking, a client, but it amounted to the same thing. "I trust you know better than to believe everything you read in the press."

He smiled a faint, cold smile. "Perhaps you would care to set the record straight?"

"For starters, Thomas Tapson did not drop dead in my reading room. He suffered a seizure. I immediately called an ambulance. I learned much later, after I arrived in L.A., that he had died. The authorities ruled the death as natural causes. The scandal sheets sensationalized the story and hinted at murder by psychic means. I must admit, I'm surprised you pay attention to that sort of cheap journalism."

"The case caught my eye because of the psychic element," he said.

"Why? I was under the impression that you considered all psychics to be frauds."

"I like to keep an open mind."

"Really? I've seen no evidence of that."

Luther cleared his throat again. "Jack is currently working on a book about a method of crime scene analysis that he has developed. He is probably including a chapter on investigations involving psychics or the paranormal. Right, Jack?"

"Or something," Jack said.

"Perhaps we should direct this conversation back to the problem at hand," Luther said.

"Good idea," Jack said. He did not take his attention off Prudence. "It has not escaped my very *open mind* that this is the second time you have been involved in the mysterious death of a man who moved in upper-class social circles in San Francisco."

"It's a coincidence," Prudence shot back.

"Do psychics believe in coincidence?"

"I did not murder anyone in San Francisco, and I thought we had established that I did not kill Gilbert Dover," Prudence said, fighting to keep her temper under control.

"No," Jack said. "What we established was that you would not have murdered Dover with a knife. It doesn't mean you did not convince someone else to assist you."

"What?" So much for maintaining a professional facade. She had never been so angry in her life. "Are you accusing me of murder?"

"I'm not accusing you," Jack said. "I'm just making an observation." He glanced at Luther. "You were right. Miss Ryland is a very interesting case."

"I am not a *case*, Mr. Wingate," Prudence said. It was too much. She had been under enormous stress since waking up in the Pentland Plaza honeymoon suite with a dead man beside her. And now this. "I am an innocent woman who is seeking professional investigative assistance."

"What, exactly, do you want me to do?" Jack asked.

"Fortunately for you, I have decided I don't want *you* to do anything," she said. "I am here to obtain the services of Mr. Pell's firm. I'm sure he has other consultants available."

Luther grunted. "It's true I contract with a number of investigative experts, Miss Ryland. My job is to select the individual I believe is best suited to deal with a particular case. In my professional opinion, Jack is the right person for your situation. I realize he can be difficult, but believe it or not, he knows what he's doing."

She eyed Jack, not bothering to conceal her skepticism, and then turned back to Luther. "What in the world makes you think Mr. Wingate is the right consultant to handle this disaster?"

"Mostly because he appears to be interested. Isn't that right, Jack?"

Jack inclined his head once in short, brusque agreement. "It's an intriguing case."

She could hardly believe what she was hearing. "That's the reason you are assigning him to this investigation, Mr. Pell? Because he appears *interested*? I'm sorry if Mr. Wingate has a problem with boredom, but I'm not here to keep him busy or to distract him. He can go to the movies if he needs entertainment."

"Jack doesn't take an interest in every case," Luther said. "When he does, it usually means he's the right person for the job. Also, he happens to be convenient. He recently moved here to Burning Cove."

She shot another look at Jack. He appeared interested, all right. Maybe a little too interested.

Initially she had detected what she had concluded was detached curiosity in his hard-to-read eyes. She had asked Pell if Jack was his secretary, but that had been pure sarcasm. The truth was that when they were introduced, she had wondered if Jack was one of Pell's mobster associates. Maggie had told her that Luther was rumored to have connections to the criminal underworld.

Dark haired and cold eyed, with a face that looked as if it had been chiseled from granite, and the attitude to match, Wingate certainly could have been a visiting crime lord. But she had been forced to reevaluate her conclusion when she realized he was watching her the way a dedicated lepidopterist might examine an unusual butterfly. She got the feeling he was trying to decide if she was a rare enough specimen to be added to his collection.

Her intuition had stirred. *Who or what are you collecting, Jack Wingate?*

She realized it was her reaction to him that disconcerted her the most. She was both wary and intrigued, and that was confounding, because he was definitely not her type. In fact, he did not fit into any of the usual categories.

She got the impression that at some point he had made the decision to take a step back from life and watch others from a safe distance. She would not be surprised to learn that the scars had been the reason for his retreat into the shadows.

Something about his hard eyes told her that he saw more than he wanted to see. He was not so much lonely as alone, but he deliberately generated that isolation.

She reminded herself that she was not attracted to the dour, withdrawn type. After the fiasco with Julian, she had made a conscious decision to date only cheerful, optimistic, good-natured men who liked to dance until dawn. Men who laughed easily. Men who were not ready to get serious about romantic relationships. Men who did not press for the kind of physical intimacy she now knew she could not risk. Men who were not inclined to be possessive. When it came to romance, she was determined to become a professional flirt. She planned to pursue that objective just as soon as she got the rest of her life back on track.

No question about it—Jack did not meet any of her requirements. Optimism and a cheerful nature were clearly alien concepts to him. He would never be a charming flirt. He was not a man who would ever laugh easily. If he did allow himself to get involved in a romantic relationship, he would be very, very serious about it.

Nope, not her type. But that was a good thing because she needed a professional investigator, not a date.

She gave him a chilly smile. "When was the last time you got involved in a case because you happened to be interested and you found the situation convenient, Mr. Wingate?"

"It's been a while," Jack said. "I can check my appointment calendar if it's a matter of concern to you."

She watched him for a long moment, but she knew she was wasting time. It was not as if she had a meaningful choice.

She turned back to Luther. "I'm sure Mr. Wingate and I will get along splendidly. What could possibly go wrong?"

"Good question," Jack said. "I can work out the probability of disaster if you give me a little time."

She pretended to ignore him and kept her attention on Luther.

"Well, then, that's settled," Luther said. He looked

relieved. "Let's get back to the details of this case. How did you and Clara Dover become acquainted, Miss Ryland?"

Might as well get it over with, Prudence thought.

"I grew up in my grandmother's house in San Francisco," she said. "She made her living as a psychic, and she raised me in the profession. Her stage name was Madame Oriana. She specialized in reading and interpreting dreams. She managed to build a reputation with the city's social set. Clara Dover was an occasional client. You could say I inherited her after Grandma died."

Jack looked intrigued. "She asked you to interpret her dreams?"

"Yes," Prudence said.

"What sort of dreams did she want you to analyze?" Jack said.

"Not surprisingly, she was mostly interested in discovering what her intuition was attempting to tell her regarding her business."

"Did she ever make any decisions based on your readings?"

"I never had to actually read her dreams to try to figure out what her intuition was saying. I thought I made it clear: Clara is a very forceful woman. She doesn't actually listen to anyone else, and she certainly doesn't take advice from others. On the occasions when I met with her, she sat on the other side of the table and told me what she was sure her dreams were trying to tell her. I, in turn, advised her to pay attention to her intuition."

Jack nodded once as if she had again confirmed

some conclusion he had already arrived at. "Got it. In other words, you told her what she wanted to hear."

"As I'm sure you've discovered in your own career, it's usually wise to tell clients what they want to hear."

"Did you make exceptions to that rule?" Jack asked.

"Yes. But telling clients what they don't want to hear rarely goes well. I'm sure you've learned that lesson, too."

He had the grace to wince. "I won't argue that point."

"There's a reason I got out of the psychic dream reading business, Mr. Wingate. I am much better suited to working with books. I was an excellent librarian."

"Right up until you got fired," Jack observed.

She managed what she hoped was a serene smile. "I can certainly understand why you have trouble dealing with clients."

"They are a nuisance," he agreed. "Moving along—in your professional opinion, does Clara Dover have any genuine psychic talent?"

"Yes, I think so."

"You *think* so?"

"It's extremely difficult to prove that an individual has a paranormal talent. The line between intuition and psychic ability is very blurred, to say the least."

To her surprise, Jack appeared to give that some serious consideration.

"You may have a point," he allowed.

She contemplated the ceiling. "Thank you. I have had some experience in the field."

"About Clara Dover's talent," Jack said, evidently unaware of her irritation.

"She clearly has a gift for business, but whether or not it's a true psychic talent, I can't say. For what it's worth, my grandmother was convinced that Clara perceives human auras, although she may not realize it."

"That's interesting," Luther said. "Theoretically, if you could read auras, you might be able to tell a great deal about individuals. Their strengths. Weaknesses. That sort of thing. That would certainly be useful in investigative work. Applied to the business world, that information might allow you to make useful assessments of your competitors and clients."

"I agree," Prudence said. "It might explain Clara's success."

"If you don't mind," Jack said, "I've got a few more questions."

She gave him a polite smile. "Of course you do. What do you want to know, Mr. Wingate?"

He watched her with his grim eyes. "What kind of talent did Clara think her son possessed?"

"Gilbert? She was convinced he had inherited her aptitude for business. The fact that he displayed little or no interest in Dover Industries did not seem to alarm her. She was sure that once he was married to a nice stable psychic he would settle down and assume his responsibilities."

"Any reason to think that might have been true?" Jack asked.

"Nope."

"You met Gilbert, you knew his mother, and you had information about the family from the psychic circuit," Jack said. "What was your opinion of him?"

"Gilbert Dover believed himself to be quite charming, and his mother certainly agreed." She shivered. "I found him repulsive."

"Why?" Jack asked, more interested than ever.

"You mean aside from the fact that he had a reputation as an arrogant bully who was known to take advantage of women he considered his social inferiors?"

"Aside from those things," Jack said.

"Let's just say I knew from the start that I could never marry Gilbert Dover." *Or anyone else,* she added silently. But her problems with sex and marriage had nothing to do with the case. She was certainly not going to discuss them with these two men.

"Tell me about your last client," Jack said. "Thomas Tapson. The man who died in your reading room."

"I thought I made it clear that Tapson did not die in my reading room," she said. "He suffered a seizure and died several hours later in the hospital."

"My apologies. I forgot the details."

No, you did not forget a damned thing, she thought. He had been trying to trip her up.

"I would have thought a memory for details would be important to an investigator," she said sweetly.

"Consultant," he corrected.

"Consultant."

"What did you learn about Tapson from his dreams?"

"Nothing that has anything to do with my case. The man wanted to kill me. He called me a succubus. I'm quite certain he had murdered other women. I am very glad he collapsed when he did. That is all I can tell you."

"How, exactly, did he collapse?" Jack asked, looking disturbingly thoughtful.

"How does someone usually collapse? He lost consciousness and dropped to the floor. Try not to get distracted, Mr. Wingate."

"You never know how odd bits and pieces of information might be important," Jack said.

Luther must have decided it was time to intervene again. "We are veering off topic. Do you have enough information to formulate a plan for dealing with Miss Ryland's case, Jack?"

"What?" Jack made an obvious effort and refocused. "Oh, right. Miss Ryland's situation is convoluted, but at its core, it's not complicated."

Prudence stared at him. "Excuse me? You don't think my case is complicated?"

"It's not complex in terms of the basic motive, but it's going to take a while to unravel because there are a number of players involved," he said.

Luther folded his hands on top of the desk. "Talk to me about motives."

"This isn't about greed or power," Jack said, "at least not primarily. This situation feels personal. I'm approximately ninety-six percent sure we're looking at a revenge motive."

"Revenge?" Prudence said, horrified. "Against me? Whatever for?"

"You were not the target. There's a high probability that you're just a pawn."

"Somehow that does not reassure me."

"It's not meant to reassure you," he said. "At this moment and for the foreseeable future, you are in serious danger."

"From whom?"

"Clara Dover is at the top of the list, at least at this moment. She will be obsessing over you."

"But she has no reason to suspect that I am the woman the press is calling the Killer Bride."

"Whoever murdered Gilbert Dover went out of the way to make sure you took the fall," Jack said. He sounded as if he was working hard to exercise patience. "The scheme did not play out as planned, but we should assume that the killer will make sure Clara believes you were the woman in that bloody wedding gown. Right now she will be fixated on making you pay for the death of her son and heir. The next person on the list of those who probably want you dead is the real killer."

Prudence clenched her fingers on the arm of the chair again. "The man who followed me into the library stacks and kidnapped me."

"You're going to need a bodyguard, Miss Ryland," Jack said.

"I think Jack is right, Miss Ryland," Luther said quietly.

Prudence caught her breath. "It might be smart to employ a bodyguard for a while. Where does one find someone with those skills? How much would it cost? I'm afraid I'm on an extremely limited budget at the moment."

Luther and Jack exchanged unreadable looks. Jack turned back to her.

"Professional bodyguards are expensive," he said. "In this case, one might also get in the way."

She went blank. "Get in the way of what?"

"My plan," Jack said. "We need to draw the killer out into the open."

"Again, I agree," Luther said.

Prudence got the uneasy feeling that she was losing control of the situation. She was the client. She needed to make it clear she was in charge. "One moment, gentlemen. If I'm not supposed to hire a bodyguard, what do you propose I do? I'd like to hear the details of Mr. Wingate's so-called plan, if you don't mind."

"Don't worry," Jack said. "I've got the basic outline of one that has a high probability of success. Once I've worked out the details, I can provide you with a more accurate estimate."

"Is that right?" She gave him a smile that she knew probably looked as if it could cut crystal. "And just what is this brilliant plan?"

"Isn't it obvious?" Satisfaction heated Jack's eyes. "You will revive your role as Madame Ariadne and move into my house as my personal psychic dream reader. I understand hiring such people is all the rage at the moment."

Chapter 8

"Don't panic, Miss Ryland," Luther Pell said.

"Too late, Mr. Pell." Prudence was very careful not to look at Jack. "I'm afraid I'm far beyond panic. I may become hysterical at any moment. You can't possibly be serious about assigning Mr. Wingate to my case."

Luther had the grace to appear mildly apologetic. "Dealing with Wingate requires patience. The problem is that he tends to jump several steps ahead and land on a conclusion—or, in this case, a plan—without taking the time to outline his logic."

"I see," she said. She looked at Jack. "I can't wait to hear this logic, Mr. Wingate."

Her sarcasm evidently eluded him—or maybe he was just accustomed to having that effect on people, she thought. Whatever the reason, he nodded once, clasped his hands behind his back, and began to pace the room in front of the open French doors.

"The goal is to draw out the killer and set a trap," he said. "You are the bait, of course."

"Bait?" she repeated.

"I'm afraid you are all I have to work with. A little acting will be called for, but you obviously have some talent in that department."

"Because I once had a career as a psychic?" she asked, controlling her temper with sheer willpower. "And because in your opinion all psychics are frauds and, therefore, excellent actors?"

He stopped in front of the balcony doors, his face once again unreadable against the glare of the sun behind him. "No. Because you have considerable experience in the role and because our quarry knows who you are and what you look like. I'm afraid no other woman will do."

"You're saying you're stuck with me," she said.

"Exactly." He sounded approving and greatly relieved that she had managed to grasp the logic of the situation. "We could attempt to put on our little drama in San Francisco or Adelina Beach, but it makes much more sense to draw the killer or killers here, where we have the high ground."

She was flabbergasted. "Killer or *killers*? Do you really think there might be more than one murderer involved?"

"At this point I don't have enough information to come to a conclusion, at least not one with a high probability of being correct. Killers have been known to copy the tactics and techniques of other killers."

She tried to ignore the frisson that flickered across her nerves. "That is a disturbing thought."

"But a very real possibility," he said. "In addition to the killer or killers, our play will very likely draw Clara Dover. Once she knows where you are, she will come looking for you."

"Are you certain?"

"Very," Jack said. "Trust me, if she was as obsessed with her plan to use you to save the Dover bloodline as you say, the belief that you murdered her chosen heir will push her over the edge. Because of you, she has lost her vision of founding a dynasty."

"Jack has a point," Luther said quietly. "In spite of appearances to the contrary, he usually knows what he is doing."

"Usually?" Prudence kept her voice perfectly polite.

Jack gave her a cool smile. "Statistically speaking, I have an excellent success rate when it comes to predicting results and outcomes in an investigation." He started to raise his left hand in an unthinking gesture. "But when I screw up, it's usually in a memorable way."

As if he had realized he was about to touch the ruined side of his face, he immediately lowered his hand.

"I understand," she said. "I had a very high rate of success when I was in the dream reading business, but occasionally readings ended badly."

"The Tapson reading, for example?" Jack suggested.

Once again Luther stepped in before the discussion could deteriorate further. "Jack has a talent for putting the pieces of a puzzle together. When he's finished, each piece will connect with the others around it. We'll have a complete picture. But at the moment there are a lot of unknowns. You need an investigator, but you also need around-the-clock protection. Jack can provide that if you will allow him to do so. Frankly, moving into House of Shadows and resuming your role as Madame Ariadne will solve a lot of logistical problems."

"House of Shadows?" she said.

"My place a few miles outside of town," Jack explained. "No, I'm not in the habit of naming houses. The original owner was a movie star. He named the place after his last film."

"I remember that movie," Prudence said. "It was a scary horror film about a haunted mansion. It starred Brent Forrest, the actor who died in a fall."

"The family had to sell the house. I got a deal."

"I see." She unclenched the chair arm and turned back to Luther. "Are you saying that in addition to his *consulting* skills, Mr. Wingate is also a professional bodyguard?"

Luther contemplated Jack with an unreadable expression. "I wouldn't call him a professional bodyguard, but he does have a way of anticipating trouble. In my experience, that skill is a lot more useful than the ability to pull a trigger."

"Am I to understand that you think Mr. Wingate's plan is a good one?"

"I think it's the best one we've got," Luther said.

"Very well," she said.

"I'm sure you'll be comfortable in Jack's house," Luther said, clearly relieved. "It's got a great view of the water, and there's plenty of room, so you'll have privacy."

"There is one problem," she said. "As Madame Ariadne I had a certain style when it came to fashion. I sold off that wardrobe when I moved to Adelina Beach and became a librarian. I'll need some new clothes if I am to resume that role. I can afford a few things, but as I mentioned earlier, I'm on a strict budget at the moment."

Luther glanced at the wall clock. "There's plenty of time for Jack to take you shopping this afternoon. Buy what you need. Jack can put it on his expense account. Be sure to pick up an evening gown."

She stared at him. "What?"

"We need to make certain the press discovers that the notorious Madame Ariadne is in town," Luther said. "The fastest way to do that is for you and Jack to put in an appearance at the Paradise Club this evening. I'll make sure the photographers are on hand."

Prudence got an eerie out-of-body feeling. "This all seems a little . . . excessive."

"That's pretty much how we do things here in Burning Cove," Luther said. He turned to Jack. "If you need any investigative legwork, phone calls to track down information, that sort of thing, feel free to ask Raina for some assistance. Things have been a little slow lately. She could use the business."

"I'll keep that in mind," Jack said.

"Who is Raina?" Prudence asked.

"Raina Kirk," Luther said. "She owns Kirk Investigations, a private detective agency here in Burning Cove."

"Oh, you mean she's a real investigator?" Prudence asked. "Not a consultant?"

Luther fixed her with a stern glare, and then he gave Jack the same look.

"Do me a favor," he said. "Try not to kill each other. Failure Analysis has an excellent success rate of its own. I'd like to keep it that way."

Chapter 9

Raina Kirk sat down in the chair Luther had just pulled out for her. "How did things go between Jack and the new client today?"

"I swear it was like trying to referee a boxing match," Luther said. He took the seat on the other side of the small round table. "Within five minutes of meeting in my office they were throwing punches. I can't even tell you which one started the fight. It's all a bit of a blur."

The waitress arrived to take their orders. Raina gave hers and waited as Luther did the same. It was midafternoon. They were in a shady little sidewalk café in the heart of the town's fashionable shopping district. The offices of Kirk Investigations were a block away in a charming plaza. The wide sidewalks were crowded with visitors from around the country and around the globe. If you were vigilant, you might spot a glamorous star like Cary Grant, a tycoon like Howard Hughes, a notorious mobster, or a bored European aristocrat trying to overcome a severe case of ennui with a vacation in the fantasyland of California.

Burning Cove was a world away from New York and the past Raina had buried there. Like so many others looking to reinvent themselves, she had driven Route 66 west to find a new life, and she had gotten very, very lucky.

Here in the land of golden sunshine, where people were busy inventing the future, she had not only discovered a new future for herself, she had found Luther and the one thing she had never dared to dream would come her way—a soul mate.

The waitress poured coffee and left.

"The important thing is that Prudence Ryland agreed to move into House of Shadows with Jack," Raina said. "Sounds like you accomplished your mission."

"She wasn't thrilled about it, I can tell you that," Luther said. "But she's willing to go along with the plan because she doesn't have much choice, and she knows it. Somehow she managed to get herself tangled up in the murder of the heir to the Dover fortune."

The waitress returned with a tiered tray of tiny sandwiches and pastries. When she disappeared again, Raina sipped some of her coffee and lowered the cup.

"Tell me the important part," she said. "How did Miss Ryland react to Jack's scars?"

Amusement flickered briefly in Luther's usually enigmatic eyes. "The same way you did when I introduced you to him. She noticed them. Who wouldn't? And then she just accepted them as part of Jack."

"She wasn't repulsed?"

"No."

"Any signs of pity? Jack would hate that."

"No. I'm sure she was curious, but that was about it." Luther reached for a sandwich. "It will be interesting to see if he tells her how he came by the scars."

"How did Jack handle her reaction—or lack thereof?"

Luther smiled one of his rare smiles. "I got the impression he didn't know what the hell to do with Prudence Ryland."

"That will be good for him."

"Think so?" Luther said around a bite of sandwich.

"Yes, I do."

"Maybe this case will encourage him to climb out of the hole he's been in since the Cordell Bonner mess."

"You said he seemed genuinely interested in the investigation?"

"No question about it," Luther said. "It's the first time he's taken more than a passing interest in a case since the Bonner affair."

"Any idea why this one caught his attention?"

"At the start I'm pretty sure it was because the case itself is unusual, but also because the client was working in the Adelina Beach College Department of Parapsychology when she was kidnapped."

"Aha. We know Jack has developed something of

an obsession with collecting the literature of the paranormal recently."

"It gets better," Luther said. "Turns out Miss Ryland not only has some expertise in that field but she used to make her living as a dream reading psychic—the one who made headlines several months ago when one of her clients collapsed in her reading room in San Francisco. The papers called her the Nightmare Psychic."

"And now she's the Killer Bride. No wonder Jack could not resist her case."

"I'm pretty sure he took it because he wants to know if Prudence Ryland is the real deal."

"A real psychic?"

"Yes."

"Oh, dear, that might not go well. Even if Miss Ryland does have some psychic talent for reading dreams, how on earth would she go about proving it? Anyone can claim to be able to interpret dreams. Who is to say the interpretation is right or wrong? And why would she even bother to try to prove anything to Jack? It sounds like he's already managed to annoy her."

Luther picked up his coffee. "Jack Wingate is a desperate man, Raina."

"I know. Something tells me things are going to get awkward out there at House of Shadows."

"I'll be satisfied if they manage not to strangle each other before the killer shows up."

Chapter 10

The medium went by the name of Lorelei. She had been in the business of summoning spirits from the Other Side since she was a young girl. Over the years she had developed what could only be called a sixth sense when it came to reading clients. It took a lot to make her nervous, but the new client was having that effect on her.

In hindsight, she should have declined to book the appointment. There had been rumors on the psychic circuit about Clara Dover. She was known to be a difficult client even during the best of times. Her state of mind now that her eldest son had been murdered in a bizarre manner was said to be unstable.

But on the surface Clara Dover was the perfect client—wealthy, socially prominent, and a true believer in the paranormal.

She was also a forceful presence. A small woman, she nevertheless managed to dominate the claustrophobic séance chamber. Her gray hair was pinned up under a fashionable high-crowned black hat trimmed with a black lace veil that was currently crumpled on the brim. She wore an expensive black suit suitable for mourning. But Clara Dover did not appear to be grieving. A fierce, barely controlled rage was the dominant emotion spiking in the atmosphere around her.

Should never have taken the booking, Lorelei thought.

"Please place your hands on the table," she instructed.

Clara slapped her black-gloved hands on the surface of the table. "Get on with the business. I don't have all day."

An invisible cloak of dread shrouded the darkened room. Lorelei could not shake the sensation of impending disaster. She told herself that her sudden attack of nerves was ridiculous. This wasn't her first séance. She was a skilled professional who had been connecting people with the dead for a couple of decades.

She had made good money when the séance business had boomed at the end of the Great War and through the devastating flu epidemic that had followed. Grieving relatives had been desperate to communicate with those who had been taken too soon. Business had soared again after the crash as people sought financial advice and gambling tips from deceased relatives. Currently the demand for expert mediums was reliably steady, but the headlines in the press made it clear that another worldwide war was looming. That would no doubt mean another uptick in profits.

Her mother had been right, Lorelei thought. There would always be a market for practitioners who claimed to be able to speak with the dead. There was really only one rule to success in the medium business—tell the clients what they wanted to hear. The rest was theater.

Showtime.

"I call the spirit of Gilbert Dover," Lorelei intoned. "Can you hear me, Mr. Dover? Your mother is here. She wants to know that you are safe and content on the Other Side. She wishes to say goodbye."

"No," Clara Dover snapped. "That is not why I want to communicate with Gilbert."

This was not going well, Lorelei thought. But she had no choice except to keep moving forward.

A cold draft drifted through the séance room. The lamp on the table dimmed briefly and then flared again. There was a faint, muffled tapping.

Clara Dover tensed with anticipation. "Is he here? Gilbert? Is that you?"

"Welcome, visitor from the Other Side," Lorelei said in her stage voice. "Please identify yourself. Are you the spirit of Gilbert Dover?"

Another whisper of cold air wafted through the small space. There was more tapping.

"Gilbert?" Clara said. "Is that you? Show yourself."

There was no maternal anguish in the demand. Clara's voice was harsh and impatient. Lorelei tried to think of a way to end the séance as quickly as possible.

Another cold draft. More taps.

"The answer is yes," Lorelei said, sticking with the dramatic tone. "The spirit of your son is with us, but I must warn you that he cannot remain for long. The connection to the Other Side is very weak tonight. Something to do with the fog, no doubt."

Clara ignored her. "You are a fool, Gilbert. Just look at yourself. Not only are you dead, you have embarrassed Dover Industries. That dreadful picture of the bridal suite and the wedding gown were on the front page of every paper in the country. The police say they believe you were playing some sort of ridiculous sex game with the woman who murdered you. What were you thinking?"

A sharp silence descended. There was no draft. No tapping. Lorelei rushed to fill the awkward moment.

"Communication with the Other Side is quite difficult, Mrs. Dover," she said. "I'm afraid the answers can seem a bit vague to us."

Clara tightened one gloved hand into a fist. "The police say they don't know the identity of the woman who murdered you, but I found a note on my pillow last night. It said that Prudence Ryland, that woman who called herself Madame Ariadne, murdered you. Is that true?"

There was another silence.

"I'm afraid the atmosphere is quite disturbed this evening," Lorelei said.

Clara ignored her. "When I told Rollins about the note, he said there was no proof. He tried to tell me that we should leave the matter to the police, but everyone knows they are hopeless. I came here so that you could confirm the information in the note. Did that ungrateful creature murder you? Yes or no?"

Icy perspiration trickled down Lorelei's sides. She raised her voice.

"The spirit is slipping back through the veil," she said. "It cannot remain here any longer."

There was a quick series of taps.

"That sounded like a yes to me," Clara said. "Listen to me, Gilbert. The problem is that Madame Ariadne disappeared from San Francisco months ago. *Where is she?*"

There was a blast of cold air, a few more raps, and then a gong sounded, echoing in the shadows.

"The spirit has departed," Lorelei said, raising her voice to make sure she could be clearly heard in the spirit world, which was located on the other side of the wooden paneling.

"Well?" Clara said. "What was the answer? All that tapping must have been Gilbert's response. I'm not leaving until you tell me what he said."

"The answer was unclear," Lorelei said. "I'm afraid that is all I can tell you. The séance is concluded. I am exhausted. I must rest."

"Never mind. I will find her. That creature murdered my son. She will pay for the humiliation she has brought down upon me and my company."

Lorelei cleared her throat. "I know this is none of my business, but perhaps you should not jump to conclusions on the basis of a rather vague response from the Other Side. Shouldn't you leave this matter to the police as your other son suggested?"

"Rollins has no idea what he's talking about." Clara did not bother to hide her disgust. "Not his fault, I suppose. He does not have the gift. Really, I don't know why it skipped over him."

"The gift?"

"I have a psychic talent. Gilbert inherited it. Unfortunately, Rollins did not."

"I don't understand," Lorelei said. "If you can contact those on the Other Side, why did you book an appointment with me?"

"I'm not a medium, you silly woman. My talent is for business."

"Oh, right. Of course."

"Gilbert got my ability, but he resisted assuming his responsibilities at Dover Industries. He was a healthy, vigorous man. I understood that he needed to sow a few wild oats before he settled down, but obviously I should not have been so indulgent."

According to the rumors, Gilbert Dover had done more than sow a few wild oats, Lorelei thought. He had a nasty reputation for forcing his attentions on young women who were not in a position to defend themselves—maids, waitresses, and other working girls who were unlucky enough to attract his attention. His father had possessed a similar reputation.

"How, uh, interesting," Lorelei said.

"I made it very clear to Gilbert that he had an obligation to marry a woman of talent and ensure that the gift was passed down to the next generation. But he insisted on having his fun. Said he wasn't ready to settle down. Now look at what's happened. He's dead and I'm stuck hoping for the best with Rollins."

"I understand the younger Mr. Dover is married," Lorelei ventured, trying to find a neutral way out of the conversation. "I saw the photos in the papers."

"To a fortune hunter," Clara said, not bothering to hide her disgust. "Men. They can't see beyond a pretty face. At least her manners are presentable. I suppose he could have done worse."

"Perhaps your talent will show up in their children," Lorelei said, desperate to end the discussion. "In my experience, paranormal abilities often skip generations, but that doesn't mean they have disappeared from the bloodline."

"I'm wasting my time here," Clara muttered. "This is none of your business."

She turned toward the door.

"I'll get that for you," Lorelei said. She jumped up and hurried around the table. In her haste she nearly blundered into one of the concealed wires that controlled the ectoplasm generator. She made it to the door without further incident and got it open. "The thing is, I don't think it's a good idea to assume you have the right answer to your questions about the identity of the woman who murdered Mr. Dover."

"I am assuming nothing," Clara grated. "I have the note and now I have confirmation from Gilbert. I know who murdered my son."

"Contact with the Other Side is an extremely delicate business. The spirits often misinterpret our questions, and we, in turn, may not always comprehend their answers."

"A misunderstanding is not a problem in this case." Clara swept through the door of the séance chamber and went out into the small reception area. "Gilbert knows perfectly well who murdered him. Unfortunately, he failed to tell me where Madame Ariadne is, but I'm certain that a private investigator will be able to find her."

Lorelei could not think of a suitable response to that, so she hurried past the desk where her daughter was usually seated and opened the front door.

Clara frowned at the empty chair behind the desk. "Where is your assistant?"

"She's probably running an errand," Lorelei said. "I'm sure she'll be right back."

Clara clicked her tongue in a disapproving manner. "It is so hard to get good help. I was forced to hire a new chauffeur this week. That is the third one in six months."

She sailed through the front door and outside to where the big Pierce-Arrow limousine waited. The liveried chauffeur was lounging against the fender, smoking. When he saw Clara, he dropped the cigarette, ground it out beneath a boot, and opened the door of the passenger compartment.

Lorelei waited until the heavy vehicle motored away down the street before she closed the door, turned, and sagged back against it in relief.

"She's gone," she announced.

Sheila opened the concealed door and stepped out of the narrow passageway behind the wall of the séance chamber.

"I'm so sorry, Ma," she said. "I wasn't sure what to do. I couldn't figure out what answer you wanted me to give her so I turned on the fan again and did a few raps and then the gong."

"It's not your fault." Lorelei straightened away from the door. "It wouldn't have mattered how we handled the session. Clara Dover is convinced Prudence Ryland, the psychic who used to work as Madame Ariadne, murdered her eldest son. That may be true, but if so, all I can say is she did the world a favor."

"Was Gilbert Dover so awful?"

"Rumors about his appalling behavior have been circulating for years. No one will miss him."

"Except Clara Dover. What do you think she'll do?"

"I don't know," Lorelei said. "I just wish I could warn Madame Ariadne, but no one knows where she went after she left San Francisco. Listen to me, Sheila. If the police come around asking about this séance, we must be very clear that we did not hear a clear answer from the Other Side. Do you understand?"

"Yes," Sheila said. "I just hope Mrs. Dover doesn't book another appointment. That woman is very odd."

Lorelei shuddered. "There has always been gossip about the strain of eccentricity in the Dover family bloodline, but the problem was said to be on the male side. After meeting Clara, however, I wouldn't be surprised to discover that Gilbert Dover got his nasty temperament from both his parents. If Mrs. Dover telephones for another appointment, tell her that I don't have any openings in my schedule. If that doesn't work, tell her I've left town."

"All right." Sheila hesitated. "I wonder where Madame Ariadne went?"

"I don't know," Lorelei said. "But wherever she is, I wish her good luck. She'll need it. I don't think Clara Dover will stop until Madame Ariadne is dead."

Chapter 11

House of Shadows should have been a truly impressive example of modern architecture—a stunning combination of glass and wood and stone—but for some inexplicable reason it felt like a mausoleum.

Prudence told herself she was allowing her grim mood to influence her reaction to what was, in reality, a very handsome residence. She had to be practical about the situation. She had contacted Luther Pell for assistance. He had provided it in the form of Jack Wingate, who evidently possessed the investigative—make that analytical—abilities her situation required. That was all that mattered. Jack might lack rudimentary social skills, but that was not important. She needed his professional expertise. She could ignore everything else, including her odd reaction to his beautiful home.

Besides, it wasn't as if she had much choice. It was just too bad she would have to spend an unknown number of days in a house that was soaked in shadows.

Determined to be mature, she walked across a living room that looked as if it had been decorated by a designer who specialized in lavish Hollywood movie sets, opened the glass doors, and stepped out onto a terrace.

"Mr. Pell was right," she said. "You've got a spectacular view."

"I know," Jack said. "The real estate agent talked it up a lot. Said I couldn't go wrong with waterfront property."

She glanced over her shoulder. He was standing in the shadows of the living room, watching her as if he was genuinely curious to observe her reaction to his home. She got the feeling that he, too, was trying to restart their rocky relationship. Evidently he had realized they were going to have to find a way to coexist until the investigation was concluded. It would be pointless to snipe at each other. They were both adults.

The drive from the Paradise Club to House of Shadows had been made mostly in silence. Under other circumstances she would have enjoyed the short trip. Jack drove a maroon Packard convertible, and he drove it very well. She could only hope that he was equally good at conducting murder investigations.

"I'm sure the real estate agent was right," she said. "About the value of waterfront property, I mean." She paused, trying to think of something else positive to say. "You certainly have lots of privacy."

"It's one of the reasons I bought the place," Jack said.

She could have sworn that he actually sounded defensive, as if he felt he had to explain something he wasn't sure he understood himself. Curious, she turned around to face him.

"I take it privacy is important to you," she said.

"I'm not a complete recluse."

"Are you sure? When was the last time you took advantage of the amenities of Burning Cove?"

"I visit the library once a week to read newspapers from around the state and to do research. I shop at the grocery store. The gas station. I've been known to visit the hardware store."

She smiled. "But you prefer to be alone most of the time."

"I find it makes life simpler."

"Probably more boring, though," she said.

He hesitated, as if he had not considered that particular side effect. "My work keeps me busy."

"Given your desire for privacy, I'm surprised you came up with a plan that involves inviting a complete stranger into your home."

"You're not a stranger," he said, sounding vaguely surprised. "You're a client."

"Right. Glad we got that settled. Don't worry, I shall do my best to stay out of your way while you do your consulting. If you will show me to my room, I'll unpack."

"Upstairs." Clearly relieved at the change of topic,

Jack hoisted her suitcase and led the way to an impressive staircase. "There's a private guest suite on the second floor. Three of them, in fact. None of them has ever been used. The actor who built House of Shadows planned on entertaining a lot of houseguests, but he only lived here a couple of weeks."

She gripped the wood railing and followed Jack up the stairs. "Because he died."

"Right."

A frisson of knowing sparked across her nerves. She tightened her grip on the railing. "In a fall."

"Right."

She glanced back at the dramatic sweep of the staircase. "Where, exactly, did he fall?"

"Stairs."

"Please don't tell me Brent Forrest died on this staircase."

"Okay, I won't tell you."

"Damn."

"It gets worse," Jack said. "Brent Forrest didn't fall down this staircase by accident. He was pushed."

"He was murdered?" She stopped on the stairs. "No wonder you got a deal on the house."

"We didn't know about the murder." Jack reached the landing and turned to look at her. "No one did. The cause of death was declared an accident."

Her attention snagged on the one word that glowed like a neon sign in the night. "We?"

"I was engaged at the time," Jack said. "My fiancée loved the house."

"Oh." She let that go because she got the impression the subject was closed. It did not require any great detective skills to conclude that the fiancée was no longer in the picture. "So how did you come to learn that Forrest's death was a murder?"

"I got curious about the story of the accident after I moved in."

She thought about her own reaction to the staircase. "Because you sensed the bad energy on these stairs?"

"No," he said evenly. "Because I got *curious* about Forrest's death."

"Uh-huh." Something had triggered his curiosity, she decided. She was pretty sure he had picked up the bad energy on the staircase, but it was obvious he would never admit it.

He pretended he hadn't heard the doubt in her voice. "I started looking into reports of Forrest's accident. It wasn't hard to put the pieces together, but there is no evidence left that would stand up in a court of law."

"So a famous movie star gets pushed down the stairs and the killer gets away with it?"

"Yep."

She started climbing again, keeping her grip on the railing.

"Any idea who shoved Brent Forrest down this staircase?" she asked when she reached the landing.

"Ninety-eight percent probability that Forrest was murdered by his lover, Laura Gray."

"The *actress*?"

"Yes." Jack started down the hall. "I think you'll like the red suite best."

"Wait." She hurried after him. "I want to know the whole story."

"I told you, I can't prove anything. And it's old news anyway. Forrest died a couple of years ago."

"Still—"

"Also, I think Laura Gray was fighting for her life. There are reasons to believe Brent Forrest was a brutal man, although the studio fixers did a good job of covering up his history of abuse and violence. After his death, Gray went into seclusion for nearly two months. I'm pretty sure she was badly beaten during her last encounter with Forrest. She needed time to heal."

"So it was self-defense," Prudence said quietly.

"As far as I'm concerned, yes."

"Okay, I can see why you didn't push to open an investigation, but I have to tell you, I don't think you are ever going to be comfortable in this house."

"Because I know what happened here? That doesn't bother me. Why should it?"

"Fine. Forget I said anything. Hey, it's your house."

"Yes," he said. "It is."

Time to change the subject, she realized. Its history of violence and death aside, the house was all wrong for Jack. It was too big and too empty. The bad energy was probably affecting his dreams—he just didn't realize it. One thing was clear: He would not appreciate her observations and thoughts on the subject.

He opened a door and stood back. "The red suite."

She walked across the threshold of the suite—and stopped, torn between amazement and amusement.

"It looks like a movie set," she said, more than a little awed.

Jack grunted. "I know."

The suite was decorated in shades of red accented with gold. A four-poster bed draped with diaphanous hangings and covered in a fluffy satin quilt served as the centerpiece. The mattress was so high off the floor that a small step stool had been placed on one side. A long padded bench sat at the foot of the bed.

The remainder of the furnishings consisted of a mirrored dressing table accented with a velvet stool, a cushioned chaise longue, and a large chest of drawers.

Glass-paned doors opened onto a shaded balcony. A door inside the suite stood ajar, revealing a large bathroom decorated in red tiles.

"You're welcome to take a look at the other two suites," he said. "But I'll warn you, one is done in dark blue and the other is very purple."

"This will do nicely," she said. "I'll unpack and freshen up. Then we can make plans."

"No, we're going to go shopping, remember?"

She winced. "For my Madame Ariadne wardrobe."

"Luther was right. The first step in this case is to put in an appearance at the Paradise Club. I want to get that over with so that we can make sure your photo makes it into the papers as soon as possible, preferably tomorrow."

She went still. "I see."

"The sooner the killer comes looking for you, the sooner I can close this case."

She swallowed hard and gave him a polished smile. "Wouldn't want you to get bored sitting around waiting for someone to try to murder me."

He surprised her with a flummoxed expression. Evidently unable to decide on a response, he stepped back into the hall. "When you're ready, I'll be in the library."

She brightened. "There's a library?"

"This place was designed for entertaining on a big scale. There are several unnecessary rooms. I turned one into a combination office and library."

Chapter 12

It was early evening and they were in Jack's library, the one room of the big house that felt welcoming. Maybe that was because it was the one room that felt lived in, Prudence thought, the one room that did not feel empty and sunk in shadows. It was obviously the only room in the mansion where Jack seemed comfortable.

"We have plenty of time before we leave for the Paradise," Jack said. "Is there anything else you can tell me about the Dover family?"

"Not much," Prudence said. "But keep in mind that although Clara Dover was an occasional client of my grandmother's and I saw her for a few readings, most of what I know about the rest of the family is gossip from the psychic circuit."

Jack got a thoughtful expression. It was not a

difficult look for him to achieve. It seemed to be one of a very limited repertoire of visible moods that he allowed himself to display. So far she had identified only two others—there was his cold, remote, detached observer look, and his cold, remote, detached skeptic expression. Now and again he spiced things up with a sprinkle of disdainful amusement or disapproval, but that was as far as he was willing to go, at least when it came to visible evidence of emotion.

From time to time she thought she glimpsed hints of deeper, darker stuff lying in wait just under the surface, but she was pretty sure it would be a really dumb idea to try to stir those waters.

The late-afternoon shopping expedition had gone surprisingly well, probably because she hadn't made any effort to enjoy the experience. Under other circumstances it would have been delightful to browse Burning Cove's fashionable boutiques. But there was no pleasure to be had in re-creating a minimalist version of her Madame Ariadne wardrobe, so she had gone about the business with precision and efficiency.

Nevertheless, she had to admit that she was thrilled with the black crystal-studded evening gown and the dramatic accessories that went with it. She would probably never get another chance to wear the dress after tonight, but it was hard not to be excited by the prospect of walking into the Paradise Club dressed for the occasion.

Yes, she had discovered the evening ensemble on sale; still, she was going to be doing research for Luther Pell for a very long time in order to pay off the cost of hiring Failure Analysis, Inc.

"Did either of Clara's sons consult psychics in San Francisco?" Jack asked.

"Not that I know of. As far as I'm aware, they were not interested in the paranormal. Clara sometimes mentioned Rollins and Gilbert in the course of her readings, but she never indicated they were in the habit of consulting psychics. Well, mostly she talked about Gilbert. Poor Rollins was always an after-thought."

"And now he's next in line for the throne." Jack glanced at his notes. "What about Mrs. Ella Dover?"

"Rollins's wife? I can't tell you much about her, ei-ther. I never met her or her husband. Ella and Rollins got engaged shortly before I left San Francisco. As Lu-ther said, they were married a few months ago. Clara complained that Ella was marrying Rollins for his money. To be fair, that is probably true, but I'm sure the same could have been said about anyone who married into the Dover family. It would take some-thing like a vast fortune to convince any woman to overlook the fact that she was going to have to put up with a mother-in-law like Clara."

Jack went back to his notes. Feeling restless, she got out of the chair and began to peruse the contents of the library.

The walls were lined with shelves crammed with books and journals representing a wide range of top-ics, including psychology, anthropology, and, intrigu-ingly, folklore. File boxes of *Scientific American* occupied a large portion of one shelf. There was an-other shelf devoted to historical accounts of notorious murders. One section featured pamphlets illustrating the tricks magicians and psychics used to fool their audiences.

But it was the bookcase containing treatises, books, journals, and records of investigations into the paranormal that intrigued her the most. Jack had made his opinion of the subject clear. Labeling him a skeptic would be putting it mildly. So why collect materials relating to dreams and metaphysics?

She turned to study her new consultant. He was seated behind his large desk, making notes with one of a dozen precisely sharpened pencils that projected from a Bakelite pencil holder.

A stack of typed pages anchored by a heavy crystal paperweight was on one corner of the desk. A typewriter was positioned on a side table. It was obvious that a manuscript was in progress. She remembered Luther Pell saying Jack was writing a book about analyzing crime scenes.

He looked up suddenly, as if he had just realized she was studying him from the other side of the room.

"Did Clara always book private readings and consultations?" he asked.

"Yes, but that's not unusual. Most dream readings are private."

Jack nodded. "All right, let's continue. How would you describe Clara Dover?"

"A small tornado in a business suit and gloves. To know her is to want to stay out of her path. She is intelligent, strong-willed, wealthy, and powerful. It's no secret in San Francisco that she is the brains behind Dover Industries. As I told you, she is a firm believer in the paranormal, and she is obsessed with the notion that she possesses some psychic ability. She is convinced that she owes her business success to the insights she gains from her dreams."

Jack glanced at his notes. "Copeland Dover died years ago, leaving her a widow with two young sons. She never remarried."

"No. Why would she? Dover Industries is her passion. She's devoted to the business."

"Did she ever mention her dead husband in the course of her readings?"

"At one reading she let slip that she blamed Gilbert's failure to settle down and pay attention to the business on his having inherited his father's taste for eccentricity."

"Did she define *eccentricity*?"

"No, but everyone on the psychic circuit knew that was a polite term for his volatile temper."

"Do you know anything about Copeland Dover?"

"No. He died when I was just a little girl. But I do know there was general agreement that Copeland Dover's passing was not a great loss to the world."

"The eccentricity problem."

"Yep."

Jack leaned back in his chair. "What else can you tell me about Clara Dover?"

"She has no patience with people who fail to perform to her satisfaction. I believe that group includes almost everyone on the planet. I'm sure that's why she kept rotating through various psychics." Prudence paused, thinking. "It will come as no surprise to hear that she is rumored to be a very demanding employer. With the exception of her housekeeper, who, I was told, has been with her forever, there is a high turn-over on her staff."

"Did that information come from the psychic circuit?"

Prudence smiled. "Nope. That gossip came from Mrs. Hanks, the housekeeper who looked after Grandma and me. People in that line of work have their own gossip circuits. When Mrs. Hanks found out I was booking sessions with Clara, she advised me to get my fees up front. Clara Dover has a well-earned reputation for refusing to pay for services she deems unsatisfactory."

"I keep coming back to Rollins Dover. Any rumors of eccentricities or a violent temper?"

"Rollins?" She shook her head, thinking. "Not that I know of. I don't recall any particular psychic circuit gossip about him, not like there was about Gilbert."

"You mentioned that there was a high turnover on Clara Dover's staff with the exception of a devoted housekeeper. Ever meet her?"

"Maud Hollister, yes. She accompanied Clara to some of the readings, but she always waited in the reception room. I got the impression that Clara relies on her the way one would rely on a confidential sec-retary. I think most people felt sorry for her. She al-ways seemed sad and bitter."

"Is there a Mr. Hollister?"

Prudence hesitated and then shook her head. "I don't think so. I don't remember a wedding ring. But as I said, I really don't know anything about her ex-cept that everyone said she was the one loyal member of Clara's household staff."

"Huh."

"Come up with something interesting?"

"I find it fascinating that a woman who built an empire is in the habit of consulting psychics."

Prudence went with her charm-the-client smile. *Fake* psychics."

Chapter 13

"The ironic thing about this situation is that I have been hoping to spend a night here at the Paradise ever since my friend Maggie told me about it," Prudence said. She surveyed the dramatically shadowed interior of the nightclub. "I just assumed the experience would be under somewhat different circumstances. I suppose this is a classic example of *be careful what you wish for.*"

Jack studied her from the opposite side of the intimate booth and concluded that he had been right that afternoon when he met her in Luther's office. Prudence Ryland was a problem, not because her case was complicated—he relished complex investigations—but because he was no closer to finding an appropriate category for her.

The metamorphosis from the cool, aloof, professional woman he had met that afternoon to the mysterious lady in black tonight was a case in point. She was wearing a column of flowing black silk studded with crystals that she had picked up during the shopping venture. He had been prepared to spend hours waiting in the Packard that afternoon while she browsed, but she had sped through Burning Cove's boutiques with the ruthlessness of an FBI raid on a gangster's hideout.

Belatedly it dawned on him that she had taken no pleasure in the task, and for some reason that was . . . disappointing. Damned if he knew why.

She might not have enjoyed the shopping, but the costume change had definitely worked. In Luther's office she had been a modest, unassuming professional spinster in a tailored suit. Tonight she was a dramatic, mysterious vision in black. The crystals on her gown caught the candlelight. The long black gloves made every move of her hand a captivating little dance. The spectacles were gone. Her fascinating eyes glowed behind a black net veil.

It was all an act, he reminded himself. Except for the eyes. The compelling mysteries they concealed were very, very real.

There was something else that felt real, too—her reaction to his scars. He had caught no hint of quickly veiled revulsion or pity, both of which he had learned to recognize instantly. She had noticed the damage on the left side of his face—it would have been impossible not to—and then moved on.

She appeared to have immediately forgotten the horror mask he would wear for the rest of his life, and that made it possible for him to forget it, too, at least when he was with her—just as he did when he was with Luther and Raina.

He found himself wanting to savor what felt like a couple of stolen hours in the company of a fascinating woman in a darkened nightclub. He had, after all, spent the past five months and three days—not that he was counting—without any female companionship. He had been alone with his books, his manuscript, and his nightmares for a very long time.

Perhaps the most intriguing aspect of the situation was that he had been just as riveted by Prudence Ryland that afternoon, when she had been playing a very different role, as he was tonight. The combination of her acting ability and his reawakened interest in sex was a dangerous mix, the kind of volatile situation that could make a man reckless.

He raised his martini in a small salute to the transformation that had come over her. "If it makes you feel any better, you look like you hang out in nightclubs like the Paradise on a regular basis," he said.

Her crimson lips curved in a cryptic smile. "Should I take that as a compliment?"

He grimaced. Shit. He really was out of practice when it came to talking to women. "Sorry, that didn't come out well. I'll try again. I'm impressed with your acting skills. This afternoon you looked like a serious academic. This evening you appear to be at home in the hottest nightclub in Burning Cove. I admit I find the ability to make the switch . . . interesting."

She picked up her sidecar and looked at him over

the rim of the glass. "You're wondering which is the real me, aren't you?"

"I don't think either version provides a complete picture of the real you, but each gives me a glimpse. I do have a question, though."

"Just one?"

"Why the glamorous look for Madame Ariadne? It's not the classic costume of a professional psychic. I expected turbans and scarves."

"I learned the trade from my grandmother. She had a talent for marketing. She felt it was important to establish a distinctive image in order to stand out in the field. There's a great deal of competition in the psychic business."

"Makes sense. Why all the black?" A thought struck him. "Are you a widow?"

"That's two more questions. I thought you had only one."

"Can't help myself. Asking questions is what I do."

Her mysterious smile came and went again. "No. I'm not a widow. The black outfit and veil allowed me to add an element of mystery to my performance."

"Are you saying it was an act?"

"People who pay a psychic to read their dreams expect a performance. I did well in the business because I delivered one. The black gowns and veils also sent the message that I was not an ingenue. It told clients that I was a sophisticated woman with some experience of the world and, therefore, was qualified to read the dreams of other sophisticated people. The costume ensured that clients viewed me as a professional rather than as a cheap carnival act. And last but definitely not least, wearing black put some distance between me and my clients. It indicated that I was not interested in establishing a personal relationship."

"A personal relationship," he repeated, examining the words with great care. "In other words, you did not want customers to get the impression that you might be available for a romantic liaison."

"Clients."

"What?"

"My grandmother taught me to always refer to customers as *clients*."

"Your grandmother sounds like a very wise businesswoman."

"She was. My turn, Mr. Wingate. How did you settle on your professional image?"

That stopped him for a beat. He gave the question some thought and then shook his head. "I don't have a professional image, unless you count a suit and tie as a uniform."

She looked amused. "Oh, you have an image, Mr. Wingate. It is very polished and very impressive and very effective."

He was not sure he liked the direction in which the conversation was going. He felt as if he was sitting in the front car of a roller coaster poised at the high point of the track, gazing down at the steep drop. He probably should not have bought the ticket in the first place, but it was too late now.

"How would you describe my professional image?" he asked.

"Enigmatic, aloof, cerebral, and detached. You are

obviously trying to project a Sherlock Holmes persona, but I regret to inform you that you are not entirely successful."

"No?"

"Sherlock Holmes is a man with no secrets of his own, so he obsesses over other people's secrets," she said. "You, however, possess some real secrets. They are what motivate you to do the work you do."

"Does that sort of psychic talk work well with clients?"

"Are you saying I'm wrong?"

"Everyone has secrets," Jack said. "Everyone wants answers. It doesn't take any psychic talent to come up with that analysis."

She smiled a very knowing smile. "But not every consultant would convince a stranger to move into his home so that he could study her at close quarters in order to get answers."

That was an annoying observation, because it contained a whisper of truth.

"I'm just trying to do my job," he said. He knew he was speaking a little more firmly—more assertively—than was absolutely necessary. All right, he sounded as if he was trying to defend himself. "Luther Pell is employing me to protect you and to find out who tried to set you up for murder."

"Never mind. I've got a few questions of my own. Why do you find me and my case so interesting?"

He watched her for a long moment, trying to decide how much to tell her.

"Do you remember the reason Pell asked me to consider taking your case?" he asked.

"He said you were skilled at this sort of work, that you were convenient because you live here in Burning Cove, and, most important of all, you had taken an interest in my problem." Prudence paused. "I got the impression that I was supposed to be quite thrilled by that last bit."

"All true," he said, ignoring the sarcasm. "But there is one more reason. As Luther told you, I'm developing a technique of criminal analysis that I'm hoping will be applicable to a wide variety of cases. Your situation is unique and, therefore, interesting. Luther is curious to see if my methods can be applied to your case. So am I."

"In other words, I am a research project for you." She looked as if she could not decide if she was relieved to have her suspicion confirmed or if she was irritated. "That explains a great deal."

He watched her intently. "Does it worry you that I am motivated by scientific curiosity?"

"Nope." She took a tiny sip of her cocktail. "I wanted an answer and I got one." She paused ever so briefly before adding, "Or maybe I should say I got a partial answer. Tell me about your theory of criminal analysis."

"I'm sure you would find it extremely boring."

"Try me."

It was a dare, a challenge, and he realized he was going to respond to it.

"All right," he said. "Feel free to stop me when you realize you are about to fall asleep."

"I will."

He deliberately launched into the lecture using his

most pedantic voice. "Law enforcement personnel, especially the FBI, and others who study the criminal mind have been searching for methods of studying crime scenes and using the observations to create descriptions of the perpetrators."

"You mean a picture? A drawing? How would that be possible unless there was an eyewitness?"

"Not a photographic likeness, although ideally it should be possible to deduce several specific aspects of a person, such as age and gender." Jack sat forward and folded his arms on the table. He had set out to prove he could be a monumentally boring conversationalist, but he could feel the passion for his subject rising to the surface. "I'm talking about an analysis that produces a list of personality and behavioral characteristics that makes it possible to compile a number of reasonably accurate assumptions about the subject."

"Such as?"

"A good crime tree could provide—"

"A tree?"

"Right, like a family tree. In fact, ideally, a crime tree would include some information about the subject's family and associates. It would indicate the motives and emotions driving the criminal. It would tell us if he went about the crime in a disciplined fashion or if he acted on impulse. Whether he was insane or simply a cold-blooded sociopath. It should provide some sense of the subject's educational background, his age, the sort of career he is in, and even a sense of where he lives."

"In other words, your goal is to narrow the field of

suspects so that the investigators can focus their attention on the most likely bad guys."

"Exactly," he said. "The idea is to stop criminals, especially killers, before they can strike again."

"Ah, so you are attempting to devise a method of predicting the behavior of the criminal." Prudence paused for emphasis. "No offense, but it sounds a lot like a psychic reading."

"No, damn it," he said, his voice tightening. "You are not going to sucker me into an argument about the differences between metaphysics and real science. You wanted an explanation of my method. I'm giving you one."

"Okay."

"My technique is designed to provide an evidence-based approach to solving violent crimes. After all, we do know a great deal about criminal behavior."

"Really? Such as?"

"It's astounding how many times the criminal is standing just offstage, watching the progress of the investigation from the shadows."

Prudence got a thoughtful look. "I've heard that old theory about criminals returning to the scenes of their crimes."

"It's true."

"That seems rather risky from the criminal's point of view. Why would someone do that?"

"Any number of reasons. To make sure he didn't leave any evidence behind that could lead the police to him. To observe the progress of the investigation so that he'll have some warning if it looks like he might be in danger of arrest. Or to try to point the investigators and the press in a different direction."

"I see what you mean," Prudence said. "Staying close to the investigation would be dangerous, but there is some logic to doing so."

"Exactly." He was uncomfortably aware of how he had allowed his own sense of urgency and enthusiasm for his work to seep into his voice. He tried to read her expression through the black netting of her veil. As far as he could tell, she was not bored yet. He did not detect any hint of amusement or outright derision, either. She was paying close attention. He was not sure how to read that. Not knowing what else to do, he kept going.

"There are other reasons why criminals sometimes try to inject themselves into the investigation," he said.

Prudence studied him with a knowing look. Her eyes glowed with understanding. "Because they can't resist the compulsion to get intimately involved? They need to observe the reaction of the spectators? Perhaps toy with the police? Taunt them?"

He watched her for a long moment. "That is very . . . insightful."

Her lips curved in a humorless smile. "Thank you. One does learn a few things about human nature in the psychic dream reading business."

"I suppose that is true. Hadn't thought of it that way."

Prudence didn't say a word. She continued to study him from the other side of the veil, her eyes more mysterious than ever. He took a deep breath.

"As it happens, you're right," he said, determined to move forward. "For some, the crime is their art, the way they experience a sense of their own power. They need an audience to affirm that power. They want to savor the reaction of the onlookers, so they are driven to stay close to the investigation."

"You think that is the mind-set of the person who murdered Gilbert Dover, don't you? The killer wants to stay close in order to observe the reaction of his so-called audience?"

"Everything about the scene in that bridal suite suggests a picture of cold, well-planned revenge. Yes, I think the killer was excited to see the effects of his art on his audience. But you partially vandalized the finished piece."

Prudence caught her breath. "Do you believe the killer will want revenge on me because I ruined his masterpiece?"

"No. The revenge was aimed at someone else. But the killer will want you dead because you know too much."

"But I don't know anything."

"The killer will be sweating now because you escaped. He has no way of knowing how much you observed. So yes, he would prefer that you be dead. The one who will want revenge on you is Clara Dover."

"Right. Thanks for that clarification. Let's hope you are as good at the consulting business as Luther Pell seems to think."

He picked up his martini. "Yeah, let's hope."

Prudence watched him swallow some of his drink.

"Given my uncertain future, I think I'd better make the most of my one night in the hottest nightclub in Burning Cove," she said. "Let's dance."

He half choked on the martini, coughed, sputtered, and hastily lowered the glass. "I don't dance." *Not anymore.*

"Don't worry, I don't mind taking the lead. It's a slow number. We'll keep it simple."

"Damn it, Miss Ryland."

"If you're going to swear at me, I think you should call me Prudence, don't you? After all, we are house-mates for the foreseeable future." She slipped out of the booth and extended a gloved hand. "You've just explained that at least two people want me dead. The least you can do is let me have one dance. I may never get another chance to spend an evening in a club like this one."

"Miss Ryland—"

"Prudence."

"We're here because we're in the middle of an investigation."

"You owe me this dance. If you won't take the floor with me, I'll find someone who will. Maybe one of these nice waiters—"

"That sounds a lot like blackmail."

"Yes, it does, doesn't it?"

"Fine. You win. This time."

He got up, seized her hand, and hauled her down the aisle and onto the crowded dance floor. She went into his arms with the triumphant air of a battlefield general who had just won a decisive victory.

"The war isn't over, lady," he growled.

"Oh, look," she said, her eyes suspiciously bright behind the veil. "You do know how to dance."

"And how to lead."

"Yes, I can see that."

He flattened his palm against the small of her back and pulled her closer. She smelled good and she felt good. It really had been a long time since he'd had a woman in his arms.

They walked out of the nightclub into a disorienting, senses-dazzling hail of camera flashbulbs. As Luther had promised, the press was waiting. Shutters clicked. The reporters and photographers crowded around, shouting questions and instructions.

"Look this way, Madame Ariadne. That's it."

"Over here, Madame Ariadne. How about raising the veil and giving me a smile?"

Jack felt Prudence tighten her grip on his arm, but aside from that small move, she gave no indication that she was anxious or unnerved. He steered her toward the waiting Packard. Fortunately he had put the top up on the convertible before leaving the house that evening.

The valet saw them approaching and opened the passenger side door. Jack sensed Prudence trying to quicken their pace. He applied some subtle braking action.

"We don't want to look like we're trying to run," he said quietly.

"I know."

Reluctantly she slowed her steps to match his. The

scrum of photographers followed, flashbulbs exploding. The questions kept coming.

"*Is your new client here gonna survive his private psychic readings, Madame Ariadne? Or is he gonna end up like your last client in San Francisco?*"

Jack gave Prudence a sidelong look. Outwardly she was not displaying any emotion aside from cool, sophisticated reserve, but she was clenching his arm as if hanging on for dear life.

"Not much farther," he said quietly.

"*Can you really kill a man with your psychic energy, Madame Ariadne? They say that's what happened to your last client in San Francisco.*"

A shock wave shivered through Prudence. Jack felt it all the way to his bones. He eased her into the front seat and closed the door. He went swiftly around the long hood of the Packard, got behind the wheel, and put the big car in gear.

Another round of flashbulbs lit up the night as he drove away from the Paradise.

Chapter 14

A fraught silence gripped the front seat of the Packard. Jack made no attempt to break it. After a few minutes, Prudence recovered her cool aplomb.

"Do you really think your plan will work?" she asked.

"Ninety-six percent probability that it will," he said, turning onto Cliff Road.

"How soon will we know?"

"The news that Madame Ariadne is living in Burning Cove and working as a private dream reader will hit the local paper in the morning. The photos will go out on the wire, and the San Francisco papers will have the story in the afternoon editions. I think we will be hearing from Clara Dover soon after that."

"There will be some drama," Prudence warned. "Clara Dover is not the subtle type."

"She's not the one I'm most concerned about."

"Says the man who has never met her." Prudence folded her arms and watched the road unspool in front of the Packard. "She is quite capable of hiring a professional hit man. I can only hope she will discover that good help is as hard to find in that line of work as she seems to think it is in every other category of service."

"I realize Clara will cause us some problems, but we know a lot about her. That gives us an advantage. It's the person who murdered Gilbert Dover and set you up as the Killer Bride we need to worry about. We don't have nearly enough information about him."

"I guess you're right."

"You *guess* I'm right?"

"Never mind." Prudence glanced at him briefly and then turned her attention back to the road. "On the plus side, you're a good dancer."

"Thanks. It's been a while."

"It's been a while for me, too."

"How long?" he asked, because he could not stop himself.

"The last time I danced was the day I got married in Reno," Prudence said. "Julian and I went out to a nightclub that evening. Nothing fancy like the Paradise, of course, but there was a band and—"

"*What?*" The chimes clashed so loudly he could scarcely think. "Luther never said anything about you being married. There was nothing in the papers about Madame Ariadne being married, either."

"The marriage didn't last long." Prudence unfolded her arms and widened her hands, a magician calling attention to a clever trick. "About three weeks. And then, one day, it just disappeared. It was as if it never happened."

"Three weeks?" he said. He tightened his grip on the steering wheel. This was important, and he had not seen it coming. That was . . . disturbing.

"The truth is that it ended on my wedding night, but it took three weeks for the annulment to come through," Prudence said. "Before you ask, it wasn't Julian's fault. I'm the reason for the annulment. Enough about me. Let's talk about you. Why haven't you danced in a very long time?"

"You're changing the subject."

"You're damn right, I am. Tell me why you haven't danced in a long time."

He hesitated, wanting answers. But he knew she would shut down if he pushed too hard.

"I was engaged," he said. "And then this happened." He took one hand off the wheel long enough to gesture toward the scars. "And then the engagement ended. Haven't danced since. Not until tonight. Satisfied?"

"Something tells me there's a lot more to the story," Prudence said.

"Something tells me there's a lot more to the story of your annulled marriage."

"Everyone has a right to their secrets."

"True," he said. "But I should remind you that my career is based on learning other people's secrets."

"I grew up in the psychic dream reading business. I'm very good at learning other people's secrets, too. I'm also very good at keeping them."

"I've noticed."

He downshifted for a curve. Somewhere in another dimension the chimes were still clanging. He would give a great deal to know more about her annulment, but that was not her most important secret. It was another question that required an answer. *Can you really kill a man with your psychic energy, Madame Ariadne?*

Chapter 15

She had spent the evening dancing in a hot night-club with the most fascinating, the most infuriating, the most intriguing man she had ever met. Now, tonight, she was sleeping in his bed.

Okay, now she was overdramatizing the situation, Prudence thought. Yes, technically speaking, the bed belonged to Jack Wingate, but he was nowhere near it. He was in another bedroom located at the far end of the other wing of the big house. She was very much alone in the big bed, and that's how things had to be. If her annulled marriage had taught her one thing, it was that she could never again risk going to bed with a lover.

Not that Jack had shown any indication that he was interested in becoming her lover. He had made his opinion of her clear. In his eyes, she was nothing more than a fraud who happened to be his client.

But she had enjoyed that dance tonight, and she was pretty sure he had not exactly hated it when she more or less coerced him into taking her into his arms.

And from now on, dancing and stolen kisses in the shadows were probably going to be as close as she would ever get to experiencing the sensual pleasures of sexual intimacy with a man. She had not entirely given up hope that one day she might meet a man who could deal with all of her, including her psychic side, but she had to be realistic. She might be alone for the rest of her life.

She got into her prim, calf-length white cotton nightgown and used the small steps to climb up into the imposing four-poster bed. Settling back against the pillows, she contemplated the red wallpaper and furnishings. She liked the color red, but a room full of it was a bit much. The suite resembled the Hollywood version of an expensive bordello. Not that she had ever seen a real bordello, but it wasn't difficult to imagine what a movie set of one would look like.

She leaned over and turned off the lamp. For a time she listened to the strange stillness that was settling on House of Shadows. It was certainly an unfortunate name for a personal residence. Names were important. They had power.

It was not the silence that made her uneasy—it wasn't really all that quiet, because the muffled rumble of the waves on the beach below the cliffs was an ever-present background noise. But the house somehow *felt* silent.

She was letting her imagination run wild. She was exhausted. It had been a very long day, and she had done little more than toss and turn the night before. Every time she had started to slide into sleep, she had snapped awake on the edge of panic. She probably wouldn't sleep well tonight, either.

She wondered how soundly Jack would sleep. She did not need her talent to know that he suffered from more than just the occasional nightmare. What monster walked through his dreams? She had done a lot of readings over the course of her career as a psychic. If there was one thing she had learned, it was that the scariest monsters were not the ones in the movies. The mummies and vampires created by Hollywood could not begin to compete with the real-life monsters—the monsters you knew.

She did not expect to sleep, so she was surprised when she awoke from a dream in which she was standing over the unconscious Tapson. His eyes were open but empty.

"You murdered me," he said.

A small wave of panic washed over her. She managed to suppress it and push aside the covers. She sat up on the edge of the bed, her pulse still beating uncomfortably fast, and reminded herself to breathe.

After a moment, her nerves back under control, she used her toes to find the bed steps. She got to her feet and started toward the bathroom, intending to get a drink of water.

A floorboard creaked in the hall outside her room. She froze. Another creak. The stairs this time. After a moment she tiptoed to the door and listened. She could hear a faint clicking but she could not identify the sound.

Cautiously she opened the door. The clicking was sharper now, more distinct. She realized she was listening to the sound of typewriter keys. She stepped out onto the balcony and looked down.

The light was on in the library.

After a while she went back to bed. At some point the clicking ceased, but there was no more creaking on the stairs or in the hallway. She remembered the sofa in the library and knew that Jack was spending the night in the only room in which he felt comfortable.

Chapter 16

Jack looked up from the crime tree he had been working on all morning and watched Prudence pluck a volume off a shelf. She was standing in front of the bookcase that he reserved for works dealing with metaphysics and the paranormal. It was the smallest collection of research materials in his library, but ever since the Bonner case, it had become the section where he spent the most time.

She looked good here in his library, he thought. She had looked good at breakfast, too. He had awakened cramped and stiff from a night spent on the sofa and gone upstairs to shower, shave, and dress. Midway through the process it had dawned on him that he had never considered the problem of breakfast. He was not much of a cook, but any way he looked at the situation, he was responsible for feeding his houseguest.

When he had come back downstairs, he had been greeted with the fragrance of toast and freshly brewed coffee. Enthralled, he had followed the aromas into the kitchen and discovered Prudence, an apron around her waist, frying eggs. *Yet another role*, he thought—the Modern Housewife Enjoying the Convenience of the Modern Electric Stove.

He had been savoring the unfamiliar frisson of delight at the realization that he was going to share breakfast with another human being when he noticed the morning edition of the *Burning Cove Herald* on the table. He and Prudence were on the front page. Reality had slammed back. The plan, such as it was, had been launched.

"The interesting thing about the dream reading business is that no one can prove the reader is a fraud," he said. "When you think about it, one person's interpretation is as good as another's."

Prudence opened the book and studied the first page. "Why are you so concerned with proving I'm a fraud? You've already made your decision."

He could see the cover of the book she had selected. *The Study of Dreams* by Rachel Jones. It had been published by a small press connected to a little-known and mysterious group named the Arcane Society. With the assistance of the head librarian at the Burning Cove Public Library, he had been searching for more publications from the press. Thus far they had not been able to come up with any. He reminded himself that for a few weeks Prudence had worked in the new paranormal research library at Adelina Beach College.

"Are you familiar with the publisher?" he asked.

"Hmm?" She flipped to the copyright page. "Oh, yes. The Arcane Society. It's extremely difficult to find their publications. I'm impressed that you tracked down *The Study of Dreams*."

"I found it in an antiquarian bookshop." He hesitated. "To be clear, I haven't concluded you're a fraud. It would be more accurate to say I'm curious."

She gave him a suspiciously bright smile. "You want to prove I'm a fraud, but you can't think of a scientific way to do that. Unfortunately, it looks like you've painted yourself into a corner."

He decided to ignore that. "It's a fundamental problem with the current state of research into the paranormal. Assuming that sort of energy exists, science lacks the technology needed to detect it. You can't measure what you can't detect."

"It's a problem, all right, for both of us."

"I understand why it's a problem for me, but why is it a problem for you?"

She snapped the book shut. The small action was sudden and fierce. "I'll tell you why it's a problem for me. Knowing that people like you think I'm a fraud is annoying, but it's hardly the worst thing that can happen to people like me."

He frowned. "What's the worst thing?"

"Knowing that some people, including many members of the medical profession, believe that those who claim to have paranormal abilities belong in an asylum."

He contemplated that briefly and shook his head.

"People who hallucinate obviously need treatment. But psychics and fortune tellers never get locked up."

Prudence gave him a triumphant smile. "Because people like you prefer to conclude that we're frauds and con artists or entertainers—not real psychics. Why do you think the women in my family have always made our livings in the dream reading business? No one thinks it's a crime. Or, at least, most people don't think it's a crime. We are among the lucky ones."

"And the unlucky ones?"

"Those with other, more disturbing talents are often perceived as mentally unstable. And perhaps some are made unstable by their abilities because they don't know how to control them. My friend Maggie Lodge spent a few months in a psychiatric hospital because her family was convinced her nerves were so fragile, she could not deal with normal life."

He clenched his hand around the pen. "What happened to her?"

"She learned how to control her abilities." Prudence paused and gave him another one of her very cool smiles. "She also learned how to conceal them from people who cannot accept her talent."

He heard the distant chimes and knew he was getting very close to something important. He also sensed that what he was picking up was as important to her as it might be to him.

"What is your friend doing now?" he asked.

"She's not in a hospital, if that's what you're wondering. She's on her honeymoon."

"Does her new husband know about her, ah, *talent*?"

"Yep." Prudence gave him another meaningful look. "Unlike some people we could mention, he's not worried about it."

He felt himself redden. "Can you blame me for being curious about your claim to possess paranormal talents? By now most of California knows I'm playing host to a psychic who is supposedly giving me private, personalized readings."

She put the book on a side table and walked across the room. When she reached his desk, she flattened her palms on the surface. The sunlight sparked briefly on the clear crystal pendant she wore around her throat.

"But you are not playing host, are you?" she said. "Luther Pell is paying you to investigate my case and protect me in the process. It would be more accurate to say you are working undercover."

He decided not to tell her that the last time he had worked undercover, two people had nearly died and he had been cursed with nightmares and a mask of scars.

He looked away from the pendant and focused his attention on the copy of the *Burning Cove Herald* on the desk. The photo on the front page had been taken from what had become his very bad side. He looked like he had been hit by a truck, but Prudence was glamorous and mysterious in black. He had glanced at the photo several times during the day because something about the way she gripped his arm almost made it look as if they shared an intimate connection. Almost. Probably just his imagination.

She was not wearing dramatic black today. Instead,

she was casually dressed in stylish hunter-green trousers and a tailored white blouse. Her near-black hair fell in waves to her shoulders, framing her fascinating eyes and strong features. She did not need a veiled hat to make her appear mysterious and rather dangerous.

Luther had called to say that the pictures had gone out over the wire and were in the San Francisco papers.

Prudence glanced at the stack of manuscript pages on his desk. "You are curious about my former profession because you're trying to figure out what sort of criminal I am and where I belong in your book."

"No. Damn it."

Her eyes heated. "Hah. I don't believe you. You are wondering how to fit me into your method for predicting criminal behavior. Admit it."

"I told you, I'm just curious."

She watched him for a long moment. "All right, here's my answer. I don't know if I'm a fraud when it comes to reading dreams."

He stilled. "You don't *know* if you're a fraud?"

"I know what I sense when I listen to someone describe their dreams," she said. "I rely on my intuition for the analysis, but the truth is, I have no idea if I'm right or wrong. What's more, I'd rather not know."

"Huh." He sat forward and selected a perfectly sharpened yellow number two pencil from the round container. He tapped the eraser end against the steel side of the sturdy Underwood typewriter. "Aren't you curious to know if you have some genuine paranormal sensitivity?"

"Does it matter? I'm no longer in the psychic dream reader business."

"You're evading the question," he said.

"I answered your first question. I said I did not know if I was a fake dream reader. Here's your problem, Mr. Consultant: I don't care."

"You must know if you are relying on something more than mere intuition when you claim to be interpreting a dream," he said.

"The line between intuition and psychic ability is invisible as far as I'm concerned, at least when it comes to reading dreams. I don't see how trying to define it would assist you in your investigation. What's more, I'm not inclined to answer any more questions today, not unless they directly impact my case. I'm a client, not a research subject."

"The more information I have, the faster I'll be able to resolve your case."

"Oh, no, you don't," she said. "I'm not falling for that line. You want to use me so that you can add a chapter on 'The Mind of the Fake Psychic Criminal.' Or something. Admit it."

That irritated him. "I never said you were a criminal."

"A con artist."

"No, damn it."

"Ah. Perhaps you've concluded I'm delusional."

"You're twisting my words."

"I've got news for you," she shot back. "It isn't hard to do. You took my case because you want to study me—admit it."

"I took your case because Pell is paying me a lot of money to take it."

"And because you think I'm an interesting specimen of a particular criminal type. It's hard to study fake psychics, because we don't leave many clues at the crime scene, do we? All that's left is a satisfied customer." She paused and gave him another icy smile. "At least that's all that's left if one is a very good fake psychic."

"This is a pointless argument. Let's change the subject."

"Excellent idea, but let me be very clear, Jack Wingate: I do not want to end up as an example in your manual of criminal analysis."

"Don't worry," he said, aware that his voice was tightening. "I can guarantee you that your name won't appear anywhere in my book."

"I don't think I trust you. I'm going to buy a copy of your book when it comes out and read it. If I see my name or anything that points to me, I will sue."

"I doubt if you'll ever see a copy. Assuming it does get published, it will be sold as a textbook to law enforcement agencies and serious academics who study the criminal mind."

She flattened her palms on his desk again and leaned forward with a menacing air. "Until a few days ago I was a librarian. Before that I was a psychic. Turns out the skills needed to excel in both careers overlap. I know how to find out stuff. I will locate a copy of your book and I will go through it page by page. If I see a single word or phrase that looks like you used me as an example of a fraudulent psychic, you will hear from my lawyer. Is that clear?"

"Yes," he said. "Can we change the subject now?"

"Fine." She swept her hands out to the side in a grand gesture of dismissal. "Let's talk about your talent instead."

He went still. "I am a serious researcher trying to design a methodology for observing and analyzing the evidence at crime scenes that can be used to track killers. My goal is to produce a useful tool for law enforcement. I do not have a paranormal talent."

"Well, well, well." The energy in her eyes belied the innocence of her smile. "That is so interesting."

He watched her warily. He knew he should not ask the next question, but he could not stop himself.

"Why do you find it so interesting?" he asked softly.

"Because it appears we have something in common, Jack Wingate. I read dreams. You read crime scenes."

He stopped breathing for a beat and then reminded himself that she was deliberately trying to provoke him because she was annoyed. Just a difficult, exasperating client. She could not possibly know about the questions that haunted him.

He took a deep breath and pulled hard on his control. "I don't see any comparison. I deal in facts. You deal in dreams. By definition there are no facts involved."

She picked up the heavy paperweight and held it in both hands so that it caught the sunlight streaming through the window. She studied the crystal as if she could see omens and portents inside. He could have sworn her pendant glowed with an inner fire. A trick of the light, he thought. But he could not ignore the icy shock of intense awareness that flashed through him.

"You're right," she said. She did not take her eyes off the crystal paperweight. "Maybe I should write a book on how to read dreams. After all, my theories are as valid as anyone else's."

"Given the current popularity of dream analysis, I'm sure your book would sell very well."

"I'll keep that in mind." She set the paperweight down on the stack of manuscript pages. "When did you first realize you could deduce something about criminals by studying the scenes of their crimes?"

The question caught him off guard. It shouldn't have, he thought. It was a logical question. Nevertheless, it stopped him cold for a beat.

"I can't remember exactly," he said. "I've always had a knack for being able to predict how people are likely to act under certain stressful conditions, provided I had enough information about them."

"Perhaps you should have been a psychiatrist," Prudence suggested.

"No," he said. "That way lies madness, at least for me."

"Why?"

He hesitated, not certain how to explain the singular fact that had cast a shadow over his life for as long as he could remember. It was something he almost never talked about. On the rare occasions when he had attempted to do so, he had discovered that no one understood.

"I can't contemplate a profession that is focused on healing the mind because I don't know how to fix people who are broken in that way," he said. "All I can do is come up with a fairly accurate guess about what they will do next. That is not always helpful."

"Because you can't change the circumstances or their behavior."

"Right."

She watched him in silence for a long moment. The energy of battle faded from her eyes. It was replaced with a disconcerting look of *knowing* that told him she understood all too well what he had just said.

"Why do I have the impression that you consider your ability a curse?" she said. "I would think it would be quite useful to know how someone will react under stress."

He heard a sharp crack and looked down at the pencil in his hand. It was now in two pieces.

"There is a very high price attached to the ability to predict the behavior of others," he said.

"All talent comes at a cost." Her eyes heated again, this time with something that looked like genuine sympathy. "What price do you pay for yours?"

"I live alone and I work alone for a reason," he said.

"I see. I'll bet your talent . . . complicates relationships."

"Do you have any idea what it's like to realize that a colleague you thought you could trust is about to stab you in the back? That the researcher you admired is likely to falsify the results of his study? That your fiancée no longer loves you and is going to end the engagement? And you know all this before it happens?"

"I've got news for you, Jack: Everyone has to deal with occasional betrayals and disappointments."

"I'm aware of that. But being able to predict them in advance is surprisingly—" He broke off, searching for the right word. "Unpleasant."

"You are not much of an optimist, are you?"

"I prefer to think of myself as a realist."

"My grandmother, who taught me everything I know about dream reading, said that if you send negative energy out into the world, you will attract negative energy in return."

"That sounds like something a psychic would say."

"Yes, it does, doesn't it? Especially a fake psychic. But think about the logic here."

"What logic?" he said.

"Everyone knows that if you go looking for trouble, it's easy to find. In the process of searching for it, you will intentionally or unintentionally ignore everything that *isn't* trouble. Do you see what I mean?"

"No."

"It stands to reason that if you make a habit of anticipating that all relationships will fail, you may consciously or unconsciously select potential friends and lovers who will fulfill your lowest expectations and, in the process, overlook a relationship that has positive possibilities."

"That is absolute nonsense," he said.

She tipped her head to one side, apparently giving his comment close consideration. Then she brightened.

"You're right," she said. "That was my grandmother's theory, not mine. I gave it a try. It didn't work out."

"Are you referring to your marriage?"

"Yep. Talk about misplaced optimism. It was a disaster. You know what? I'm tired of this conversation." She glanced at the manuscript. "I'd like to read your book."

Startled, he looked at the stack of typed pages anchored by the crystal ball. "It's not finished."

"I know. You still have to write the chapter on the fake psychic criminal mind. What's the title?"

"The Wingate Crime Tree: A Scientific Approach to Observing and Analyzing Crime Scenes."

"Bad title," she said, scrunching up her nose.

He glanced uneasily at the manuscript. "It's a working title."

"I'm good at marketing, thanks to my grandmother. Let me read your book and I'll come up with a much more exciting title."

He tapped the end of the broken pencil against the typewriter. "I hate to say it, but that makes a truly horrible kind of sense. Help yourself. But whatever the hell you do, don't lose a single page. That's my only copy."

"I will be very, very careful," she promised.

She moved the crystal ball aside and scooped up the manuscript. She went briskly across the library and paused in the doorway.

"By the way, we need to go grocery shopping today," she said.

"Why? I've got plenty of food on hand."

"I know. I checked. I regret to inform you that you have a very demanding houseguest. I'm afraid you can't feed her canned lima beans, Spam, and fruit cocktail. Those eggs I cooked this morning were the last ones in your refrigerator. Your bread is stale. Also, you don't have any tea."

"I drink coffee."

"Well, I drink tea." She glanced at her watch. "Let's go to the grocery store in an hour. We'll both need a break by then."

She disappeared out into the hall.

He sat quietly for a time, trying to figure out what had just happened. Eventually he gave up and went back to work on the crime tree.

After a while he picked up the phone and dialed the number for Kirk Investigations. He needed more information.

Chapter 17

I t's no secret that your mother has been displaying some very odd behavior in recent weeks," Ella Dover said. "But I worry that Clara has become positively unhinged by Gilbert's death."

Rollins Dover watched his wife crumple the delicate veil onto the brim of the stylish black hat. They were in the back of the limo on the way to the Dover mansion in one of San Francisco's most fashionable neighborhoods. Gilbert's body had been brought back to the city on the train yesterday. The small funeral had been held graveside that morning. The circumstances of the murder had convinced Clara that an elaborate event would only bring more potentially embarrassing publicity.

Always anxious to please her demanding mother-in-law, Ella had been careful to remain in black for the family meeting. She looked spectacular in mourning, Rollins thought, but then, she looked beautiful in anything she chose to wear.

She was the last of a New York family that had been destroyed in the Depression. After watching his fortune disintegrate overnight, her father had put a pistol to his head and pulled the trigger. Ella and her mother had been left alone to cope as best they could. And then Ella's mother had passed and Ella had gone to live with an aunt.

To escape the oppressive household of her relatives, Ella had taken the train west to San Francisco. Her East Coast sophistication combined with her polished manners and remarkable beauty had enabled her to thrive in society. He had been enthralled with her from the moment they were introduced. Unfortunately, his mother had made it clear that she held a different opinion.

Back at the start Clara had privately declared Ella a gold digger, but she had grudgingly accepted her new daughter-in-law because she hadn't really cared who her second son married. Rollins had understood that all that was required in his wife was a woman who would not embarrass the family in San Francisco society. Ella met that requirement.

But now Gilbert was gone and Clara was dealing with the destruction of her vision for the future of her precious empire. In addition, she had been humiliated by the circumstances of the murder. She was taking out her rage on everyone around her, including Ella—the wife of her second-best son.

"Everyone knows that Gilbert was Clara's favorite,"

Rollins said. "She needs time to get past the shock. She had convinced herself he was the future of the Dover bloodline."

"I know." Ella reached across the seat and lightly touched his hand. Her eyes and her voice warmed with sympathy and understanding. "I realize she takes that psychic nonsense very seriously. Gilbert's death has crushed her ridiculous dreams of having grandchildren she was sure would inherit her so-called paranormal talent."

Rollins grimaced. "She's convinced she gets her keen sense of business from messages she receives in her dreams. What I don't understand is why she thought Gil had inherited her talent. He never exhibited any sign of interest in Dover Industries. I'm the one who has done the day-to-day work of managing the company for the past few years. I'm the one who knows how to guide it into the next decade. War is coming, and thanks to me, Dover is well positioned to take advantage of the government contracts that will be going out to big industrial firms. But all my mother could see was Gilbert at the helm."

"He was her firstborn," Ella said gently. "She was obsessed with him because she had invested so much of herself in him."

"While she packed me off to boarding school as soon as possible."

"I understand." Ella patted his hand again. "But she will learn to see you in a different light now. Do you have any idea why she asked us to pay a call this afternoon?"

"Mother does not make requests," he said. "We

were summoned. When she telephoned, she said only that she had family business to discuss."

Ella brightened. "Maybe she has finally come to her senses and realized that you are now the rightful heir of Dover Industries. Whatever else you can say about Clara, she is not a stupid woman. She knows she can no longer pretend Gilbert is destined to be her heir."

"Don't count on it."

"She doesn't have any choice, Rollins. Gilbert is gone. She has to face reality. It's time for her to step down and let you take control of the company."

Rollins groaned. "You still have a lot to learn about my mother."

"What else can she do?"

"I prefer not to ask that question." He managed a wry smile. "I don't want to know the answer."

Ella was quiet for a moment.

"Do you think your mother will ever really accept me?" she asked finally.

It was his turn to offer reassurance and support. He gripped her hand and gently squeezed her fingers. "Yes, of course she will. As you just pointed out, she no longer has much choice. It is time for her to face reality."

Clara had become the power behind the throne of Dover Industries approximately twenty-four hours after she married Copeland Dover. He had never had any interest in the business and had been content to let her run the company while he played the man-about-town and indulged his notorious sexual tastes in the few brothels that would accept him as a client.

It wasn't long before everyone in the San Francisco

business community understood that Clara was the one running the fast-growing empire. When Copeland had dropped dead five years into the marriage, leaving a widow and two small sons, there had not been so much as a ripple of anxiety in the financial world. Everyone who mattered had understood that Clara was no longer standing behind the throne—she was sitting on it, scepter in her gloved fist.

Rollins had spent a lifetime observing Clara. He had realized early on that the key to her success was a remarkably keen intuition for sizing up and exploiting the strengths and weaknesses of Dover's competitors and customers alike. During the crash and the long Depression that had followed, Dover had not only remained afloat while other firms drowned; it had flourished.

The limo came to a halt at the front steps of the big house. The chauffeur opened the door. Ella stepped out of the vehicle with her customary grace. Rollins followed, took her arm, and went up the steps with her.

The housekeeper greeted them with an appropriately somber air. Maud Hollister had served in the household since Rollins and Gilbert were boys. She had watched them grow up. There had never been a Mr. Hollister, but at some point everyone had begun referring to her as Mrs. Hollister.

As a child Rollins had thought her quite pretty and had wondered why she always looked so grim and unhappy. She was in her mid-forties now, and whatever beauty she had once possessed had long ago disappeared, leaving behind the husk of an embittered woman.

Maud's most impressive attribute was her unquestioned devotion to Clara. As far as Rollins knew, he was the only one who had ever figured out why she had remained while so many others had come and gone.

Maud was still on the staff for a very simple reason— she had a son who had been locked up in a private asylum when he was in his early teens. She was blackmailing Clara and had been for years.

Rollins had discovered the truth when he had found Clara's private ledger years earlier. The generous checks routinely made out to Maud were for amounts significantly greater than her salary. Intrigued, he had done a little sleuthing and discovered that Maud, in turn, was writing checks to an expensive psychiatric hospital where her son was doomed to live out his days. Before that, she had used the money to pay for an expensive East Coast boarding school. As Clara was not known for her charitable inclinations, the expenditures had raised interesting questions.

He had established a habit of regularly perusing Clara's private ledger, which she kept in her dressing table drawer. There were other entries of interest. Over the years, several checks had been made out to employees who had quit their posts in the household due to mysterious accidents. There were also a number of payments to various charities that claimed their mission was to rescue prostitutes from the streets.

Rollins knew the household accidents had been caused by his brother, who had delighted in terrorizing the staff. As for the charities, they were actually brothel managers demanding compensation for the damage Gil had done to the unfortunate women who had been forced to take him as a client.

But the payments to Maud were the only ones that had aroused his curiosity. There was only one reason why Clara would have made the payments for so many years, and it wasn't because she felt sorry for Maud's institutionalized son.

So yes, Maud's loyalty to the family was unquestioned, and he knew precisely why she had remained while so many others had left.

"Mrs. Dover and Dr. Flood are in the blue room," Maud said.

Rollins groaned. "Flood is here? Again? I thought this was going to be a family business meeting. Why does she need that quack?"

"Mrs. Dover's nerves have been under a great deal of strain lately," Maud said.

She did not bother to hide the strong note of reproof in her tone. He smiled.

"We all know Mother has nerves of steel," he said.

Maud's jaw clenched. He ignored her. He and Maud went back a long way together. They had never liked each other, and neither of them felt obliged to conceal that fact. Years ago, Clara had turned over the day-to-day work of motherhood to Maud, who, in turn, had proceeded to adopt her employer's attitude toward her youngest son. Nothing Rollins did would ever be satisfactory. Second best was always second best.

Maud had focused most of her attention on Gilbert, covering up for him when he destroyed Rollins's favorite toys, making sure Rollins took the blame when a dead rat turned up in a pot of soup and again when Gilbert lost his temper and went after the kitchen maid with a butcher knife. The girl had needed stitches, but she had survived. She had immediately quit her post. Rollins had been blamed and sent back to boarding school before the end of summer vacation.

Yes, Maud had kept a close eye on Gilbert and had gone to the extreme of helping Clara protect him from the consequences of his violent temper, but Rollins didn't think it was because she was fond of Clara's firstborn. He was sure Maud had hated Gilbert. Maud, however, was devoted to Clara, so it followed that she looked after Clara's favorite.

And now Gilbert was gone. Things were about to get interesting.

"It's just as well that the doctor is here," Ella said quickly, stepping in, as usual, to try to smooth the hostile atmosphere. "Mrs. Hollister is right. Your brother's death has had a dreadful effect on your mother's nerves. She does seem to respond very well to Dr. Flood."

Poor Ella. One of these days she would finally realize there was no point trying to ease the brittle tension between Maud and him.

He snorted. "My mother doesn't need a doctor to

help her get through a family business meeting. Let's go. Might as well find out what the hell she's up to now."

He started across the marble entryway, heading for the blue room.

Ella fell into step beside him, her eyes shadowed with worry. He knew she had come to the same conclusion he had: It was unlikely that Clara had summoned them to inform him that she was handing the reins of Dover Industries to him. She was not the type to abdicate. Clara intended to die on the throne.

Maud followed them into the blue room. Clara, dressed head to toe in black and ensconced in a massive blue-and-white silk-cushioned chair, awaited them. She was not alone. Harley Flood, wearing a somber dark suit and a black armband, hovered discreetly in the corner.

Flood always seemed to hover, Rollins thought. Something to do with his slightly hunched shoulders and deferential air. His medical satchel was on the carpet at his feet. The only items inside were several bottles of the privately concocted nerve medicine he administered to Clara.

Rollins knew the contents of the satchel because he had managed to get a look inside. That had happened shortly after Flood had appeared in Clara's life. Clara had awakened in the middle of a nightmare and suffered a panic attack. That was extremely unusual for her. Panicked, Maud had telephoned Rollins. Reluctantly, he had climbed out of bed, dressed, and driven his Jaguar roadster to the mansion.

When he let himself in the front door, he discovered

that Flood was already there, trying to calm Clara, who was hysterical. Rollins had taken advantage of the confusion to examine the satchel. The vials of medicine were unlabeled.

Harley Flood was probably thirty at most, but with his gold-rimmed spectacles and funeral-director attire, he looked as if he was practicing for middle age. He did a good job of acting, but Rollins knew a quack when he saw one. Clara usually did, too. The fact that she had invited Flood into her tightly controlled world had been confounding at first. But it wasn't long before Rollins realized there was, in fact, no mystery about it at all. Clara was now addicted to whatever Flood kept in the glass vials. That was, Rollins had concluded, an amusing turn of events—and one he could use to his advantage.

"It's about time you two showed up," Clara said.

Rollins checked his Rolex. "We are right on time, Mother."

"The traffic was dreadful," Ella said quickly. "How are you feeling, Mrs. Dover?"

"Much improved," Clara said. "Thanks to this."

She picked up a newspaper and snapped it open to reveal the headline on the society page.

NOTORIOUS SOCIETY PSYCHIC
APPEARS IN BURNING COVE

Below the headline was a photo of a stylishly dressed woman in an evening gown and a tiny veiled evening hat. Her gloved hand was tucked under the arm of a dark-haired man in an evening jacket. The photo had been taken from a few feet away, but the woman's companion had turned his head, apparently to speak to her. In so doing, he had revealed the left side of his face. At first Rollins thought the image had been marred somewhere along the line during the printing process. It took a couple of seconds to realize he was looking at a network of scars.

The caption for the photo read, *Madame Ariadne and private client seen at nightclub in Burning Cove.*

Rollins felt his insides tighten. Ella cast him a worried glance. Before either of them could think of a response, Clara made her announcement.

"This is the woman who murdered Gilbert," she said. "Her real name is Prudence Ryland. She worked as a psychic named Madame Ariadne here in San Francisco. Gilbert was unable to communicate the exact location during the séance, but now I know where she is. I will be leaving for Burning Cove first thing in the morning. Maud and Dr. Flood will accompany me."

Rollins heard Ella's sharp, startled gasp. He was feeling queasy, too. The situation was spinning out of control. He glanced at Maud. She looked uncharacteristically anxious. Uncertain. Harley Flood watched his patient with an air of grave concern.

Rollins pulled himself together and strove to find a calm, reasonable tone of voice. "What are you going to do, Mother? You won't be able to convince the police to arrest her. You might have that kind of power here in San Francisco, but you won't have it in Burning Cove. Not unless you have some proof that Prudence Ryland is connected to Gilbert's murder."

"It will not be necessary to waste my time with the police," Clara said.

"Why?" Ella asked cautiously.

"Because I had a vision last night," Clara said. "Gilbert spoke to me. He told me that the woman who calls herself Madame Ariadne will soon die by fire. I am going to Burning Cove because I must be there to witness her execution."

Chapter 18

This is madness," Ella said. She stormed into the bedroom, sat down at the mirrored dressing table, and stripped off the black gloves. "Your mother is unstable, Rollins. Surely you can see that now."

"*Eccentric* is the term we prefer in society," Rollins said dryly. He closed the bedroom door and turned the lock. The last thing they needed was an unexpected intrusion from the maid. "And we don't use even *that* word around Mother."

"That is not amusing." Ella unpinned the black hat and hurled it onto the bed. "Where did she get the notion that Gilbert's fits of bizarre behavior were the result of his so-called psychic sensitivity?"

"From the psychic she consulted years ago when it became impossible to ignore his dangerous temperament and unpredictable moods," Rollins said. "For obvious reasons, she was afraid to have Gil examined by a real doctor."

"That so-called psychic told Clara what she wanted to hear."

"Don't we all? It's the only pragmatic thing to do with dear Mother. She could never bring herself to admit that her favorite son and designated heir belonged in a locked ward in a hospital for the criminally insane."

Ella met his eyes in the mirror. "I'm worried about her, Rollins."

"So am I," he admitted. "Something has changed in recent weeks. Flood is responsible. I'm certain of it."

"It is unnerving to think that the future of Dover Industries is in her hands."

Rollins walked into the sitting room that adjoined the master bedroom. The windows overlooked a park, San Francisco Bay, and the spectacular new Golden Gate Bridge. "Trust me, I am aware of the risks."

"You are now the heir to the family business," Ella said. "Clara will have to accept that."

"She won't have any choice." He went to the lacquered drinks cart and picked up the bottle of expensive whiskey that the staff was always careful to make available. "But we can't rush things, not with Mother. We need a plan."

"I don't think we have any time. You heard her. She's headed for Burning Cove tomorrow because she thinks she had a vision, a message from Gilbert. Something about Prudence Ryland dying by fire. Clara is getting worse, Rollins. She is obviously hallucinating now. We can't let this get out of hand. Who knows what will happen if she attempts to confront Prudence Ryland?"

"In case you haven't noticed, there's not much we can do to stop Clara."

"There is one way to control her." Ella appeared in the doorway between the two rooms. "You know what you have to do, Rollins."

"Forget it. I can't risk trying to get her committed." He splashed whiskey into a glass. "Even if I were successful, which is unlikely given that I probably won't be able to convince a doctor that Clara Dover, the head of Dover Industries, needs a rest cure, we simply can't afford the scandal. Not right now. Putting Clara in a psychiatric hospital would cause the Feds to panic, to say nothing of the impact on the business world. Rumors of insanity can easily destroy a company like Dover."

"Women get sent away for rest cures all the time, especially inconvenient women. No offense, but Clara qualifies as inconvenient."

"I couldn't agree more, but this isn't just any inconvenient woman." Rollins took a healthy swallow of the whiskey. "She owns one hundred percent of Dover Industries, and she controls the company. Our customers and suppliers know that she is the one who was responsible for building the business into the powerful manufacturing giant it is today. She's the one who pays off the politicians, city officials, and judges who quietly make Dover's problems go away. The only charity she never fails to support is the police department's Widows' and Orphans' Aid

Association. My mother doesn't just own Dover Industries, Ella. She owns a big chunk of this city."

Ella let out a long breath. "In other words, money talks."

"Always has, always will." He turned to look at her. "You are such an innocent, my dear."

"All right, I believe you. But we've got to do something."

"Don't worry, I'll clean up Gilbert's mess. I know how to deal with my mother. I've been handling her for years now."

"I know." Tears glistened in Ella's eyes. "I've tried so hard to please her, but today I realized I won't ever be able to do that."

"It was never even a remote possibility, my love," Rollins said. "No one can please Clara Dover."

"We're going to Burning Cove, aren't we?" she said.

"We don't have any choice."

Chapter 19

The following afternoon Prudence was in the kitchen arranging coffee and tea things on a tray when the phone rang in the library. It only rang once because Jack picked up immediately. It didn't take any psychic insight to know he was expecting news from either Luther Pell or Raina Kirk, the private investigator he was using to track down information.

She picked up the tray and carried it toward the door. Jack's manuscript was on the breakfast table. She was over halfway through and riveted. The subject was interesting in its own right, but what fascinated her was what she was learning about the author. She wondered if Jack had any idea how much of himself he was revealing in the pages of *The Wingate Crime Tree*.

She carried the tray along the hallway and into the library. Jack was at his desk, the phone in one hand, a pencil in the other. There was a notepad at the ready.

He glanced up when she set the tray on a nearby table, but he spoke into the phone.

"Who accompanied Dover?" he asked.

He started making notes on the pad of paper.

Prudence poured one cup of coffee and one of tea.

"Her personal doctor?" Jack asked. "Why? Her nerves? That's interesting." He made another note. "Anyone else? Yes, I want the names of the chauffeur and the housekeeper. I need everything I can get on everyone in that household. Thanks."

Prudence set the coffee on the desk. She had not bothered to add sugar or cream to the tray. After two nights and nearly three days of living in the very quiet household, she had discovered that Jack did not use either in his coffee.

She had learned a few other things as well, such as the fact that he did not get a lot of phone calls. The man evidently did not have many friends or business associates. She had been unable to determine with absolute certainty if there was a lover in the picture, but her intuition told her the answer was no. She was sure there had been some lovers in the past and there would be more in the future, because underneath that invisible suit of armor Jack wore, there was a man of strong passions. For some reason he appeared to be doing his best to bury them.

She sat down with her own cup and saucer, crossed her legs, and waited for the end of the conversation.

"Got it," Jack said. "I really appreciate this, Raina.

Yes, I'll give her your best. Yes, I will make sure you meet her soon."

He set the receiver in the cradle and looked at Prudence, his eyes heating with an unfamiliar intensity. The hunter in him had been aroused, she realized. This was the kind of work he had been born to do.

"Clara Dover arrived in Burning Cove by car this afternoon," he said. He noticed the coffee in front of him and picked up the cup. "She's not alone. In addition to her housekeeper and her chauffeur, she was accompanied by her personal doctor. They are renting a house on Sundown Point."

She had been about to take a sip of her tea. She paused the cup halfway to her mouth. "Clara Dover brought a doctor with her?"

"According to Raina, yes." Jack glanced at his notes and then looked up, very curious now. "Dr. Harley Flood. Apparently he specializes in various types of nervous conditions. Does that surprise you?"

"I'm not sure." She put the cup on the saucer while she considered the question. "Remember, I haven't had any contact with Clara for several months. She was one of the reasons I left San Francisco."

"Because she was pressuring you to marry her son and threatening to destroy your business if you didn't."

"Yes. Judging by what I knew of her then, I'd say she's the last person in California who needs a doctor for her nerves. That woman could face down a charging rhinoceros. But—"

"What?"

"She was obsessed with Gilbert. His death may have affected her nerves."

"Maybe, but Dr. Flood appears to have come on the scene before Gilbert died." Jack glanced at his notes. "A few weeks ago, in fact. That is, of course, very interesting."

He set the cup on the saucer, opened the wide center drawer of his desk, and took out a long rolled-up sheet of heavy paper that looked as if it had been torn out of an artist's sketchbook. He unrolled the page and anchored one corner with the crystal paperweight. He used various Bakelite desk accessories to pin down the other three corners.

Curious, she put down her tea and got to her feet. She stopped on the opposite side of the desk and studied the chart he was creating. As she watched, he uncapped a pen and used a ruler to draw a large square box. He inserted the words *Harley Flood. Nerve Doctor* into the box.

"You're making a crime tree, aren't you?" she said, intrigued.

"Yes," he said. He did not look up from the chart.

"I read your instructions for creating one in chapter two of your book," she said.

Jack drew another box and wrote in *Maud Hollister. Housekeeper.* "But it goes beyond family members. It's a chart of all the individuals who appear to be closely connected with Gilbert Dover."

"Your list of suspects," she said. "I understand. But are you sure the killer will be someone who is close to the family?"

"I told you back at the start that this case feels as if it turns on a revenge motive. Nothing about it is random. That suggests a killer who either is inside the

Dover household or has an intimate history with it. Someone so obsessed with his goal that he went to the extremes of kidnapping you and setting up that elaborate scene in the honeymoon suite at the Pentland Plaza." Jack capped the pen, sat back in his chair, and studied what he had drawn. "It suggests someone who is close enough to the Dover household to know how and when to lure Gilbert to Los Angeles. That individual also knew how to get close enough to murder him."

She shivered. "I see what you mean. When you think about it, there were a lot of logistical problems involved, weren't there?"

"Yes. The killer had a great deal of inside knowledge about the family."

"What else does your crime tree tell you?"

Jack studied the chart. "Not enough. Not yet. But we are dealing with a very organized killer, one who had everything planned out to the last detail. Your escape from the honeymoon suite ruined those plans. Now everything is in chaos, as far as he is concerned, and that is bound to have rattled him. Things are still spinning out of control. Clara Dover is in Burning Cove instead of San Francisco. You are here, too. The killer has to be unnerved."

"Do you think he will panic?"

"Not immediately. First he will try to come up with a new plan, but he no longer has the luxury of time. He will make mistakes."

Understanding made her smile. "You've set your own stage. It's a trap."

"That's the idea."

She studied the crime tree more intently and saw that some of the other squares were partially filled in.

"You've got a square for me." She braced her palms on the desktop and leaned forward to get a better look. "And there are notes. Let me see."

"The crime tree is still in its very early stages," Jack said. He started to move the desk accessories aside, obviously intending to roll up the chart.

She planted one hand on the crystal paperweight so that he could not move it and used her other hand to pin the opposite corner of the chart. "I want to see what you wrote about me."

Resigned, Jack leaned back in his chair and gripped the arms very tightly.

Prudence scrutinized the notes in the square marked with her name. *"Marriage annulled?"* She looked up. "Why is there a question mark after that entry? There's no question about it. I am no longer married. Why is my marriage even on your chart? It has nothing to do with this case."

"I need context and information on everyone involved," he said.

Prudence ignored him to read off the rest of the notes. *"Last dream reading client dead. Circumstances?"* She looked up again. "What are you implying with that question mark after circumstances?"

"Just that I'd like more information on Tapson's death."

She narrowed her eyes. "Natural causes, remember?"

"I remember," Jack said.

She went back to the chart. *"Librarian. Paranormal*

research. Fired. Psychic?" She looked up again. "Another question mark? Why didn't you just write *fraud?*"

"I told you, I'm not concerned with whether or not you are a fraud," he muttered.

"Yes, you are, you just won't admit it." She straightened. "Never mind. Did you give me my very own square on your crime tree because you think I'm a suspect in the murder of Gilbert Dover?"

"No, damn it." Jack was suddenly on his feet. "You've got a place on the chart because you are at the center of this case."

She pursed her lips. "The center? I thought I was just a pawn."

He watched her with a wary expression. "You started out as a pawn, but things have changed because the pawn—that would be you—didn't play the part the killer assigned you to play. You are now the key to this case."

"I am?"

"I keep coming back to the fact that you were not chosen at random to play the role of the Killer Bride."

"Hmm."

He watched her. "What?"

She began to pace absently around the room. "When you think about it, the killer had every reason to believe I could be used as a pawn."

"Why do you say that?"

"It makes sense when you think about what the killer assumed would happen if I had been arrested. I have no close family who might have made a fuss or paid for a good lawyer to keep me out of the gas chamber. I was not socially connected to powerful people who could pressure the police or demand an investigation. My job at the library did not make me invaluable to anyone. Just the opposite. My boss wanted to get rid of me. He could not have cared less if I got arrested for murder. I just don't—"

She stopped because Jack had picked up his pencil and was making more notes. He glanced up when she went silent.

"Go on," he urged.

"Why?"

"Because you are giving me more information, and I need that."

"Is that all you do with your life?" she asked. She swept out a hand to indicate the shelves of books that surrounded them. "Acquire information and use it to fill in charts?"

The question evidently caught him by surprise. He shook his head. "No. I'm writing a book, remember?"

"A book about how to acquire information and use it to fill in charts. Forget it. We have more immediate problems—namely me and my case."

"Exactly," he said, clearly pleased that she had arrived at that conclusion.

"All right, Clara Dover and members of her household staff are in town," Prudence said. "What are we going to do now?"

"We give Clara a golden opportunity to make the next move."

Prudence winced. "Do you think she will try to kill me herself? She's a very determined woman, but I can't imagine her pulling out a gun and shooting me dead. From what I know of her, she would be more likely to hire someone to do that."

"She wants revenge for the death of her son, but she didn't travel all the way from San Francisco with a doctor, a housekeeper, and a chauffeur to shoot you dead."

Prudence swallowed hard. "That's a relief."

"It's possible she might resort to using a gun if all else fails."

"Thanks for that upbeat thought."

"But I doubt it," Jack said. "She appears to have a very strong instinct for self-preservation, and she cares about Dover Industries. She won't want to get arrested for murder."

She took a breath. "Okay, any thoughts on what she is likely to do?"

"No, but I don't think we'll have to wait long. From everything we know about Clara Dover, she is a woman of action."

"You're right. Well, as it happens, I'm a woman of action myself. I do not intend to sit around this very big house and wait for Clara to make her move."

"Got a better idea?"

She smiled. "I believe I do."

He looked wary again. "What is it?"

She told him.

"Huh," Jack said. "That just might work." He reached for the phone. "We'll have to hurry if we're going to get your schedule for tomorrow into the morning edition of the local paper."

"What if Clara Dover doesn't read the newspaper while she's in town?"

"She's looking for you, and you tend to make headlines. Also, she doesn't have any resources here in Burning Cove. She's an outsider. Doesn't know the local power brokers. Trust me, she'll be reading the *Burning Cove Herald*."

"Who are you calling?" she asked.

"Luther. We need a few strings pulled, and in this town, he's the one who pulls them."

$$\boxed{\text{Chapter 20}}$$

Maud Hollister moved into Clara's bedroom and set the breakfast tray with its perfectly poached egg, toast, orange juice, and coffee on the small table near the window. In addition to the meal were a copy of the morning edition of the *Burning Cove Herald* and an envelope.

Clara, dressed in a robe and slippers, her gray hair secured in bobby pins, closed the door and turned around. Her eyes were feverish with excitement. The strange glitter made Maud uneasy. Clara had been prone to fits of nerves in the past few weeks. Her odd turns had become decidedly worse since she had learned of Gilbert's death. Last night she had awakened in another panic attack. It had taken some time and another dose of medication to get her calmed down.

"Well?" she said. "Any news of the creature?"

Maud picked up the morning paper and handed it to her. "There's a mention on page three in the Visiting Celebrities column. Madame Ariadne has an early-afternoon appointment at a local spa."

"Call the spa. Find out when she is due to check in. When you are sure of the time, tell Henry to have the car ready."

"I know you are set on confronting Prudence Ryland face-to-face, but I don't think doing so in such a public place is a good idea."

"I don't care what you think," Clara said, practically vibrating with the energy of her anticipated revenge. "Gilbert made it very clear in the vision last night. She must know what is coming. She is a witch and she will die by fire. I am to witness her punishment."

"It was just a dream, Mrs. Dover. You should not take it seriously."

"Normal people do not take their dreams seriously, but I am not a normal dreamer. My dreams have meaning. They are the means by which I access my paranormal senses. I cannot and will not ignore them."

Maud sighed. "I will make sure Henry has the car ready at the proper time."

When you worked for Clara Dover, you learned early on that once her mind was made up, there was no talking her out of a plan. You also learned that there was no point delaying bad news. Maud took a deep breath.

"Rollins phoned before you woke up," she said.

"He was at a gas station. He informed me that he and Ella are on their way here to Burning Cove. They got on the road early this morning and expect to arrive midafternoon."

"What?" Anger flashed in Clara's fever-bright eyes. "He intends to interfere with Gilbert's plan. That is so like Rollins. He was always jealous of his brother. Now he cannot abide the knowledge that Gilbert is able to contact me from the Other Side."

"For the last time, Gilbert is dead," Maud said. "There is no plan to punish Prudence Ryland. Your sleep has been very disturbed of late. You are—" She managed to stop herself before she let the word *hallucinating* slip out. Any reference to mental instability was guaranteed to drive Clara into a fury. "I believe that you are misinterpreting your dreams."

"Visions," Clara said. "Dr. Flood has made it very clear that what I am experiencing are visions, not ordinary dreams. Thanks to his medicine, the door to my psychic senses has been fully opened."

"You are having nightmares, Mrs. Dover. Anxiety attacks."

"Only because I am going through an adjustment period as I learn how to control my enhanced paranormal senses. Never mind. Whatever you do, you must not breathe a word of my intention to confront the witch at the spa to Rollins or his wife. I will not be stopped."

"I understand, Mrs. Dover."

"They can't stay here. I won't have that woman underfoot."

"Mr. Dover said he had booked a room at a local hotel," Maud said.

Poor Ella. Doomed to be *that woman*, never a unique individual in her own right. Sometimes Maud wondered if her employer had actually forgotten the name of her second son's bride.

It wasn't that Clara disapproved of the marriage, although that was probably what Ella believed. The truth was, Clara had very little interest in her. Yes, she was certain Ella had married Rollins for his money, but Clara didn't hold that against her. The same would have been true of any woman who moved in society. Marriages in those circles were always made for fortune and position. Clara had married Copeland Dover for those very reasons.

Aside from assurances that Ella had the manners and demeanor required to move in upper-class circles, Clara had been content to ignore the woman her younger son had chosen for his bride.

Maud picked up the coffeepot and filled a cup. When she set the pot down, she paused for a moment to contemplate the view from the second-story window. It was so very different from the scene she saw every morning when she drew the curtains in Clara's bedroom in San Francisco.

It was the same ocean, but the Pacific took on a much different aspect here in Burning Cove. In San Francisco, the waters of the Bay were often gray and choppy or layered in fog. Here in Southern California, the waves sparkled in the morning light. Both versions were equally deceptive, she thought. Both concealed the dangerous currents that seethed and swirled below the surface.

She picked up the envelope and held it out to Clara.

"I'm afraid there has been another letter. I found this when I went into the kitchen to prepare your tray."

Clara eyed the envelope as if it were a cobra. "The blackmailer followed me to Burning Cove?"

"So it appears."

"Let me see that."

Clara snapped the envelope out of Maud's fingers and glanced at the front. Her name had been spelled out in letters that had been cut from a magazine. She tore open the envelope and took out the note. Her face tightened with disgust.

"This is outrageous," she whispered. "The extortionist is demanding twice as much as last time. It says instructions for delivery will follow. That means the monster is *here*, Maud, right here in Burning Cove. He followed me."

"So it would appear."

"This is beyond belief. In the first note, the bastard said there would be only one payment." Clara crumpled the paper in one hand and began to pace the room. "Now there have been two more. What a fool I was to think it was finished. They say blackmailers never stop. Evidently that's true. I would give anything to find out who has been sending these damned extortion notes."

Maud said nothing. It was not the first time she had listened to Clara vent her fury. The blackmail threats had begun arriving a few weeks ago. Each of the demands had been larger than the one before.

Clara reached the far end of the room, swung around, and paced back across the space. "I shall arrange to have the money wired to that account because I can't be bothered with this nonsense. Not now. I have other priorities here in Burning Cove. But I have had enough, Maud. It's clear now that the blackmailer will bleed me forever. When we return to San Francisco, I shall hire a private detective to track him down."

"Yes, Mrs. Dover," Maud said.

"I can't believe it has come to this," Clara whispered. "Gilbert is gone. Rollins is all that I have left. I can only hope that, although the talent did not manifest in him, it may show up in his offspring. After all, he is my son."

"Yes," Maud said. "He is your son. He is of your bloodline."

Clara straightened her already rigid shoulders and raised her chin. "In hindsight, I should have paid more attention to the business of getting him a wife, one who showed some indications of a sixth sense. Now he is stuck with that weak, insipid little mouse."

"Yes, Mrs. Dover."

"Well, we both know there are ways to get rid of an inconvenient spouse, don't we, Maud?"

Maud twisted a hand in her apron. "Yes. We do."

"We shall worry about Ella some other time. Right now I must stay focused on making certain the vision I received last night is fulfilled."

"Are you sure a face-to-face confrontation with Madame Ariadne is a necessary part of that vision?"

"Yes, Gilbert made it quite clear. There must also be witnesses. So you see, a spa setting is ideal."

Chapter 21

I t was two in the afternoon, and almost every padded lounger in the pool room of Spa Elegance was occupied when Prudence was shown into the humid space. She was draped in a fluffy white robe, her hair bound up in a towel turban, her feet protected by white slippers. She was no longer wearing her signature black, but the attendant made certain everyone in the space knew who she was.

"Please relax, Madame Ariadne," the woman said, pitching her voice a little louder than necessary as she indicated an empty lounger. "I will bring you a pot of herbal tea."

Prudence tried not to wince. She reminded herself that her appearance at the spa was part of a master plan to draw out a killer. She had left Jack sitting in the shade of the small sidewalk café across the street, a cup of coffee on the table, a fedora angled over his left eye to partially conceal his scarred face. His job was to watch the entrance of the spa.

If today's plan did not work, they intended to follow up with a well-publicized dinner at the Burning Cove Hotel restaurant, followed by another night at the Paradise. Part of her was secretly hoping the spa setup failed, because the thought of another night of dancing with Jack held a lot of appeal.

The attendant arrived with the tea. Prudence reclined on the lounger and took stock of her surroundings. On any other day—specifically on a day when the obsessed Clara Dover was not in town—she would have enjoyed spending the afternoon in a first-class spa. She knew very well she would not be here today if Jack hadn't called Luther Pell and asked him to make the arrangements. Pell had been happy to oblige.

The interior of Spa Elegance looked as if it had been inspired by the legendary spas of Europe. The blue-and-white-tiled walls of the high-ceilinged room gleamed. Women wrapped in large fluffy towels clustered around the edges of the three crystal-clear pools. Attendants dressed in aqua-blue uniforms padded about delivering tea and fresh slices of cucumber for the eyes. It was as if she had stepped into a Hollywood movie, Prudence thought.

Yes, she would definitely have been enjoying herself if it were not for the fact that someone wanted to kill her—possibly two people, if Jack was right.

She was reaching for the cup of herbal tea when the woman on the neighboring lounger spoke in low tones.

"I beg your pardon," she said, "but I couldn't help overhearing the attendant address you as Madame Ariadne."

"That's right," Prudence said. "And you are?"

"Mildred Ashwood," Mildred said. "From San Francisco. I read in the papers that you were in town. I must say, this is quite exciting. I followed your case very closely."

Prudence froze. "My case?"

"That business of your last client dropping dead. Oh dear, I suppose that's not quite the right way to put it, is it?" Mildred said, chuckling.

"No," Prudence said. "It isn't."

"Oh dear, I have got this all muddled. I meant to say I followed the stories in the papers that appeared after the, uh, *incident* in which you were involved several months ago." Mildred glanced around and then leaned across the short space that separated the loungers. Her voice sank to a whisper. "The one in which the papers called you the Nightmare Psychic."

"Oh, *that* incident," Prudence said, drumming her fingers on the cushion of the lounger. "It was unfortunate that Mr. Tapson suffered a stroke while visiting my reading room, but he certainly did not die there. He expired in the hospital. The reading had nothing to do with his death."

At least I don't think it did, she added silently.

"I never for a moment intended to imply otherwise." Mildred cleared her throat and continued speaking in whispery tones. "Between you and me, no one mourned Thomas Tapson, not even his family.

I'm sure his relatives were quietly relieved by the news of his death."

Okay, this was getting interesting.

"Is that so?" Prudence said.

"There were rumors about him, you know."

"No, I had no idea. What sort of rumors?"

"My brother and Tapson attended the same private school in San Francisco for a year. I remember that William and the other boys were absolutely terrified of Tapson. He tormented the younger children and did horrible things to small animals. The school authorities were finally forced to expel him after a rather mysterious fire in the gymnasium."

"What happened to Tapson?"

"He more or less disappeared. We never saw much of the Tapson boy after that. We didn't know he was back in the city until we saw the news of his death. Do you mind if I ask what you've been doing since you left San Francisco? You vanished overnight, according to the papers."

"I've been traveling," Prudence said vaguely.

"According to the local paper, you are working for a private client here in Burning Cove. But do you still do outside readings? If so, I would love to book one. I have the most interesting dreams."

"I'm a little busy at the moment."

"But surely you could manage an outside reading?"

"I don't think that will be possible." Prudence drank some tea and set the cup and saucer on the table. "Readings are exhausting, and I feel I must save my energy for my private client."

"I see." Mildred's tone chilled. "He must be paying you very well."

"He is," Prudence said.

Mildred narrowed her eyes. "You do realize that after you left San Francisco there was a great deal of, shall we say, *speculation* about you in certain circles."

"Is that right? I had no idea."

"It was not the sort of talk that enhances a lady's reputation," Mildred said.

"In that case, I'm surprised you would want to take the risk of having a woman of doubtful virtue read your dreams—"

The swinging doors at the far end of the pool room crashed open. Every head turned to watch Clara Dover sweep into the room with the force of a petite hurricane. She was never less than an intimidating presence, Prudence reflected, but today, dressed in black from head to toe, Clara appeared even more menacing than usual.

"Where is the creature?" she demanded in a voice that rang off the tiled walls. "Where is the woman who murdered my son?"

The effect on the pool room was dramatic. Prudence realized that no one, including herself, was moving. Even the water in the three pools appeared to have gone still.

Prudence took a breath, sat up on the edge of the lounger, and stood. "Are you looking for me, Clara?"

Clara's head swiveled until she located Prudence among the white-robed women. When she spotted her, she strode forward.

"How dare you?" Clara said in the voice of a

woman who has come to pronounce doom. "I offered you the opportunity to become one of the Dovers of San Francisco. I chose you to be the mother of my grandchildren, the heirs to Dover Industries. How did you repay me? You murdered my son."

"No, Clara, I did not murder Gilbert," Prudence said quietly but firmly.

"Don't lie to me. I know that you killed him."

"You can't possibly prove that, because it did not happen."

"I might not have the sort of evidence that can be used in a court of law," Clara said. She clenched her hands into fists at her sides. "But I know it's true. *Gilbert told me.*"

"What?" Prudence took a step toward her. No one else moved. "That's impossible. Gilbert is dead, Clara."

"He communicates with me through visions," Clara rasped.

"That can't be true," Prudence said. "You are an intelligent woman, Clara. I understand that you are grieving, but you can't go on like this. You must face reality."

But Clara was beyond reason now.

"You will pay," Clara shrieked. "I saw it in a vision."

Prudence took another step closer. "Are you going to be the one who tries to murder me? Is that why you are here in Burning Cove?"

"I will not kill you. Your fate has been sealed. You will die by fire. A proper ending for a witch. I am in Burning Cove because Gilbert said I must witness your punishment."

Her message delivered, Clara whirled and swept toward the exit. Two members of the spa staff managed to break free of their paralysis and turned to open the swinging doors.

For the first time, everyone in the chamber, including Prudence, noticed that the doors were already open. Jack loomed in the entranceway.

There were several yelps of outrage and dismay from the crowd in the spa. Women scrambled to make sure they were adequately covered in robes and towels.

Jack ignored the outcry and stepped aside to allow Clara to storm past. She did not pay any attention to him. *Why would she?* Prudence thought. Clara Dover was accustomed to people getting out of her way.

Prudence met Jack's eyes across the room. "I'm finished here. I'll be out in a few minutes."

He nodded once, turned, and disappeared. Prudence exhaled the breath she did not know she had been holding, tightened the sash of the white robe, and threaded a path through the loungers, heading toward the changing room.

She knew from the shock on the faces of the spa staff that there would be news of another scandal involving Madame Ariadne and her new client in the next edition of the *Burning Cove Herald*.

Chapter 22

S he said you are going to die by fire," Jack said. He did not take his eyes off the winding road that hugged the edge of the cliffs above the ocean. "She was very specific, wasn't she?"

"Yes," Prudence said. "It's not the sort of wording that is open to vague interpretation. Do you think it's important?"

They were on their way back to House of Shadows. Jack was at the wheel. The top of the Packard convertible was down, and she found the brisk breeze clarifying. She needed to marshal her thoughts into a coherent report. Jack craved logic. Facts. Details. He needed to know that his conclusions and deductions were based on hard evidence, not speculation or, horror of horrors, *psychic talent*.

Unfortunately for him, she relied on impressions,

sensations, and intuition. She worked the way artists did. She was pretty sure now that Jack did, too, at least to some extent, but he did not want to admit it. No, she decided, he was *afraid* to admit it. He was desperate to believe that he took a scientific approach to crime solving.

"Of course it's important." He flexed one hand on the steering wheel. "It's a critical bit of information. I wonder if Clara Dover has some history with fire."

Surprised by the comment, Prudence glanced at him. "What makes you say that?"

He was silent for a moment. "Fire leaves an impression on a person. You never forget a dangerous fire."

This was important, she thought. It was personal for Jack. She was suddenly sure there was a connection between fire and his scars.

"How long were you standing there in the doorway?" she asked.

"Long enough. I followed Clara because it occurred to me that I might have miscalculated when I told you I didn't think she would resort to using a pistol at this stage."

"Really?" She looked at him. "You were actually worried that you might have miscalculated?"

"There's no such thing as one hundred percent certainty in my business, Prudence."

"Gosh, now you tell me."

"Let's get back to Clara," he said, refusing to rise to the bait.

"You heard her," Prudence said. "You now know as much as I do. She thinks she is having visions in which Gilbert is communicating with her from the Other Side."

"*Vision* is a precise word, too," Jack said. "It's not the same as *dream*. Did she ever consult you or your grandmother about visions?"

"No. When she consulted my grandmother and, later, me, she always used the word *dreams*. She never claimed to have visions."

"She also called you a witch," Jack said. "Did she ever mention witchcraft or magic?"

"No. I would have remembered."

Jack downshifted for a curve. "Something has changed in her world."

"Her designated heir is dead. Gilbert Dover's death has apparently pushed her to the edge of a nervous breakdown. Maybe over the edge. She's hallucinating, Jack. She thinks she's having *visions*. That is not the Clara Dover I knew in San Francisco."

If Jack caught the sharp note of frustration in her voice, he chose to ignore it. He concentrated on his driving.

"When we get back to the house, I'll add this new information to the crime tree," he said. "It's important."

"Fine. I'm going to take a walk on the beach. I need to think."

"Not a good idea."

"Me trying to think is a bad idea?"

"I didn't mean it that way."

"I need to take a walk, Jack. Having someone tell you that you're going to die by fire is oddly stressful."

She did not add that she was not looking forward to returning to the echoing silence of House of Shadows.

"I'll go with you," he said.

She glanced at him, briefly surprised. Then understanding struck. Jack wasn't any more eager than she was to return to the big empty house on the cliffs.

Chapter 23

"Y ou were right when you predicted that Clara Dover would show up in Burning Cove," Prudence said.

"It wasn't a prediction," Jack said. "It was a logical assumption with a high probability of being correct."

Prudence laughed. "Like I said, a prediction."

He thought about arguing the point and decided it wasn't worth the effort. He had other priorities at the moment. At first he had assumed a walk on the beach was a waste of time. He needed to get back to the crime tree. But to his surprise, the walk was turning out to be a good idea. The tangy breeze felt good, and the waves were rolling in, crashing, and retreating in a rhythmic pattern that was refreshing. Stimulating. Energizing.

The waves and the breeze were not the only elements energizing the atmosphere, he thought. Prudence had a similar effect on him. Refreshing. Stimulating. Energizing. Very energizing. He had a sudden urge to reach for her hand and had to make a conscious effort to suppress the impulse. What would she do if he did try to link his fingers with hers? he wondered. Would she be shocked? After all, she was his client, not a lover. But who knew how she would react? This was Prudence. He had never encountered anyone like her. There were still a lot of unknowns when it came to Prudence Ryland. But he knew he liked being here on the beach with her. He liked it a lot. She made everything in his life feel . . . different.

She gave him a speculative look. "Can you always calculate what other people will do in a given set of circumstances?"

"No. When it comes to human beings, there is never enough information available to ensure a hundred percent certainty."

"It's the same with dream reading."

"Is it?" he said, keeping his tone neutral. He did not want to argue with her. Not now. Priorities.

"Yes," she said. "There's such a thing as knowing too much about someone else, isn't there?"

"I hadn't thought about it in that way, but yes."

"That's why I never liked dream reading," she said. "I can do it for real, but I can also fake it. Mostly I faked it. So, in a sense, you're right. I am a fraud."

"Why fake it if you've actually got a talent for it?"

"Because I really don't want to know that much about other people. The process of reading someone's dreams is very . . . intimate. Unpleasantly so. It's like flying into a terrible storm. You don't know what might be lurking in the center, and you really don't want to know. You can see just enough to realize you should not be there. You don't belong there. Worst of all, you're pretty sure that if you hang around too long you might get trapped in someone else's nightmares."

He exhaled slowly, stunned by the sense of relief that was washing over him. She understood.

"Sometimes I feel that way at crime scenes and when I'm working on my crime trees," he said. "I start to see the world the way the killer does, and I don't like the sensation."

"I told you, what you can do with crime solving and what I can do with dream reading are very similar. Do you want me to explain your talent to you?"

"You mean give me your opinion of my observational and analytical skills? Why not?"

"Okay, here goes," she said. "You have the kind of intuition that allows you to assemble facts and observations and use those things to get inside the minds of the bad guys. When you do that, you sense the killer's most horrible, most uncontrolled desires. You see the monsters inside. You also comprehend that you can't fix such people. But you are compelled to try to stop them. You have found a way to do that by consulting for law enforcement."

Somewhere in another dimension, chimes clashed gently. The music of truth. Jack tried to decide how he felt about the unsettling insight. Part of him was relieved to be able to acknowledge the truth to someone who understood. But at the same time, it was unnerving. He was learning that a sense of disorientation was becoming a normal experience when he was around Prudence.

"I agree that intuition plays a role in what I do," he said, choosing his words carefully.

She smiled. "Face it, Jack. Your intuition is off the charts when it comes to analyzing crime scenes. That makes you psychic, whether you want to admit it or not."

"What makes you so sure?"

"It's all there in the case studies you use to illustrate *The Wingate Crime Tree*—the way you make the leaps between clues and tie them all together. Your process in the course of the Cordell Bonner case is especially interesting."

"That case ended in disaster," he said.

"Because Bonner died in the explosion in his lab and took his secrets to the grave?"

"The FBI was desperate to question him about the experiments he was conducting. In the end, they got nothing. Bonner died in the blast. The fire afterward destroyed the chemicals he was working with and his notebooks."

"I understand that not every case ends the way law enforcement would prefer, but your analysis of the criminal mind was correct. It led the authorities to Bonner and his lab."

He shook his head, a little dazed. "You picked all that up from my manuscript?"

"Yep." She swept out both hands. "No psychic dream reading required. I just paid attention to the words on the page. I'm almost finished, by the way. I'm working on some ideas for a new title."

"What's wrong with the one I've got?"

"It feels stodgy. Old-fashioned. The word *tree* has to go. It will make people think of an ancestry chart. You need a title that sounds more modern."

"Let me know if you come up with something better."

They reached the end of the beach. Jack glanced at his watch. He did not say anything, but Prudence gave him an amused look.

"I know," she said. "You need to get back to your crime tree. I understand."

"I'm concerned with the personality change that you noted during the confrontation with Clara Dover," he said.

They walked back across the beach and started up the cliff path.

"You did more than consult on the Cordell Bonner case, didn't you?" Prudence said.

The question caught him off guard. He had been thinking about the information he intended to add to Clara Dover's square on the crime tree. He tried to refocus.

"What?"

"You were the undercover man the FBI sent inside Cordell Bonner's lab."

"How did you figure that out?"

"Intuition," she said lightly.

He groaned. "You're right. I was able to use information collected at the crime scene to identify Bonner as the most likely suspect. The Feds needed someone to go inside his operation and find the evidence required for an arrest."

"You made the classic mistake of volunteering, didn't you?"

"It wasn't as if there were a lot of options. The job required someone who could go into a sophisticated drug lab, recognize the various chemicals and processes, and figure out what was going on. I was able to do that. But things got complicated. When Bonner realized he had been targeted, he set off the explosion. That caused a massive fire. And before you ask, yes, that's how I got the damned scars."

She glanced back at him. "I wasn't going to ask."

"Because you already knew the answer? You being a psychic and all?"

"Of course not. I made a logical deduction based on careful observation of the available facts."

"Right."

Prudence reached the top of the cliffs and stopped abruptly, her attention fixed on the house.

"Uh-oh," she said.

"My keen intuition tells me that does not sound promising," he said.

He reached the top of the cliffs and saw the Jaguar convertible parked in the drive. The rumble of the breakers on the beach had masked the noise of the vehicle's arrival.

A well-dressed man in a pale linen jacket, dark blue trousers, and a fedora lounged against the fender of the car. He was smoking a cigarette. The top of the convertible was down and the passenger side door was open, revealing a woman in fashionable trousers and a pullover sweater. She was sitting on the saddle leather seat, one foot braced on the ground.

Jack heard the chimes again and got a rush of anticipation. "This is going to be interesting."

Prudence shot him a quick, searching glance. "Not friends of yours, I take it?"

"No. Something tells me we are about to meet the other members of the Dover family."

Chapter 24

The man in the fedora spotted them and straightened away from the vehicle. He dropped the cigarette and ground it out with the heel of a polished leather shoe.

Prudence watched him carefully as he approached. He held himself with the arrogant confidence that was the birthright of the very wealthy—those who had barely noticed the economic havoc the Depression had wreaked upon the country. Jack was right. There was, indeed, a high probability that they were about to meet Rollins Dover.

He was smiling politely, but when he got closer, he saw Jack's scars. There was a flash of barely concealed morbid fascination followed by equally brief and barely concealed revulsion before he recovered. He made a point of fixing his gaze on Jack's eyes.

"Jack Wingate, I presume," he said. "I'm Rollins Dover."

"Dover," Jack said.

The handshake was perfunctory, over almost before it began. Rollins turned toward her. The sunlight sparked briefly on a wedding band . . .

. . . and on a gold signet ring on the little finger of his left hand.

She stopped breathing. *It's just a signet ring*, she thought. A lot of men wore them as symbols of family heritage or affiliations with clubs and fraternal organizations. *Just a signet ring. Don't jump to conclusions.*

But she knew she would not be able to rest if she did not get a close look at the engraving on Dover's ring.

Rollins smiled. "You must be Miss Ryland," he said. "I've heard a lot about you—or, rather, I should say I've heard about Madame Ariadne."

She pulled herself together with an effort. *Just a common signet ring.*

"Mr. Dover," she said.

She had to make an effort not to stare at his left hand. *You can do this. You can act.*

"My wife, Ella." Rollins glanced at the woman who was walking toward them. "Ella, this is Miss Ryland and Mr. Wingate."

Ella Dover smiled graciously and stopped beside her husband.

"A pleasure," she said. "But I do regret the unfortunate circumstances that bring us here today."

"Mrs. Dover," Prudence said.

Jack inclined his head. "Mrs. Dover."

Ella's charming smile flickered off for only an instant when she noticed Jack's scars. Startled horror flashed in her eyes, but she recovered as smoothly as her husband had.

"Mr. Wingate," she said.

"We arrived in town a couple of hours ago," Rollins said. "We checked into our hotel and then immediately drove out to the villa Clara is renting. The only one at home was her doctor, Harley Flood. He told us Mother had gone out with her housekeeper and the chauffeur. We did not realize what had happened at the spa until Clara returned. That's when she announced that she had confronted you and informed you of her ridiculous vision."

"I can't believe she conducted what must have been a dreadful scene in a fashionable spa, of all places," Ella said. "I'm afraid we must all brace ourselves for embarrassment in the press."

"Miss Ryland, we can't begin to apologize for what Clara did today," Rollins said. "We are rather stunned, to put it mildly."

"Forgive us for dropping by unannounced like this," Ella added. "We should have telephoned. It's my fault. When we discovered what had occurred at the spa, I told Rollins we had to see you immediately. Mrs. Hollister, Clara's housekeeper, said that according to the local paper, you were staying here with Mr. Wingate. I believe the residence is known as House of Shadows."

Prudence glanced at Jack. He did not say anything, just stood there, waiting. If he had ever learned the rules of polite behavior, he either had forgotten them or was choosing to ignore them. Prudence suspected the latter. She thought about nudging him but decided that would look even more odd. It was time to take charge. This was, after all, an opportunity for him to employ his keen powers of observation. Also, she needed to get a closer look at Rollins's signet ring.

"I appreciate the gesture," Prudence said, slipping into her smooth, professional psychic voice. "I do realize that Mrs. Dover was in a rather strange mood today. Let's go inside to discuss the situation. There is iced tea in the refrigerator."

Ella looked grateful. "Thank you, but please don't bother with the tea. We won't be staying long."

Rollins grimaced. "We just want to explain a few things."

Jack frowned but did not raise any objections. Prudence led the way into the house.

"Please sit down," she said when they reached the living room.

Ella looked around with a mix of amazement and barely concealed disapproval. "My, what interesting décor. Very much in the modern style."

Prudence smiled. "Very much in the Hollywood style. The former owner was a movie star. Jack purchased the house furnished. He hasn't had time to redecorate, have you, Jack?"

"What?" Jack surveyed the large room as if he had not seen it before. He shook his head, clearly impatient with the direction of the conversation. "No."

"I see," Ella said. She managed a sympathetic smile as she perched on the gold velvet cushions of the gilded sofa. "The Hollywood crowd is known for its rather flamboyant taste, isn't it?" She nodded toward the arched windows. "You do have a lovely view, though."

Rollins sat down beside Ella and gave Jack an approving look. "Can't go wrong with waterfront property."

"I've heard that," Jack said.

Prudence sat down across from Rollins and tried not to stare at his hand.

Jack took up a stance near the window, the left side of his face turned away. "What is it you thought we should know about Clara Dover?"

Rollins exhaled heavily and focused on Prudence. "Mother is not herself these days. She has been failing for weeks now. I'm afraid the shock of my brother's death has completely shattered her nerves."

"Her demeanor this afternoon was certainly different than it was when she met with me in San Francisco," Prudence said.

"She is under the care of a doctor, Dr. Flood," Ella said. Her mouth tightened. "Supposedly he has some new methods for treating conditions of the nerves, but we fear he may be doing Clara more harm than good. In the past few weeks she has become convinced that she is having visions. Since Gilbert's death, she has begun insisting that he is visiting her from the Other Side. We fear she is hallucinating."

"Unfortunately, she insists that Dr. Flood is the only medical expert who understands her," Rollins said.

"What do you know of Flood?" Jack asked.

Rollins grimaced. "Not much, to be honest. He showed up in Clara's life a few weeks ago, and almost immediately she hired him as her private doctor. My personal opinion is that he's a quack and a fraud, but my mother has decided that he's brilliant. I can tell you from long experience that once she sets her mind on something, there's no changing it."

"Why is your mother convinced that Flood is an excellent doctor?" Jack asked.

"To understand her interest in Flood, you have to know a few things about my mother," Rollins said. "It's no secret that she is a believer in the paranormal. Just ask Miss Ryland. She'll vouch for that."

"It's true," Prudence said.

"Clara is also convinced that she herself possesses a powerful psychic talent," Rollins said.

"To be honest," Ella said with a wry smile, "given her success as a woman in the business world, one could make a case for that belief."

"Mother believes my brother possessed a similar talent," Rollins continued, "although I certainly never saw any indications of it." He grimaced. "Unfortunately for me, she thinks the gift, whatever it is, skipped me entirely."

"Clara also mentioned to me that she was certain Gilbert had some psychic ability," Prudence said.

Rollins snorted softly. "You mean when she tried to convince you to marry Gilbert. She was very keen on stabilizing his so-called paranormal talent. Thought marriage would do the trick."

"In my opinion you had a narrow escape, Miss Ryland," Ella said quietly. "I knew Gilbert for only a few months, but that was long enough to realize he had a brutal temper."

"And absolutely no interest in managing Dover Industries," Rollins added.

Jack stirred a little. Everyone looked at him.

"What sort of talent did Mrs. Dover believe her eldest son possessed?" he asked.

"Some version of her own intuition for matters of business, I believe," Rollins said.

Ella smiled at Rollins. "My husband is the one who possesses the common sense and the talent for business it takes to run a firm the size of Dover. Clara does not realize how fortunate she is to have him as her son and heir."

"To be quite frank, the incident at the spa today has convinced me that my mother needs more medical expertise than her private quack can provide," Rollins said. "We are looking into the option of having her sent away for a rest cure at a very discreet clinic. But we naturally want to handle things in a manner that does not hurt Dover Industries."

"I understand," Prudence said.

"As I said, I'm sure Flood is a quack, but Mother insists he's the only one who can treat her," Rollins said. "In hindsight, Miss Ryland, Clara was far more calm and reasonable when she was seeing you for those dream readings."

Prudence gave him a sharp smile. "But you think I'm a fraud, don't you?"

Rollins winced. "I don't mean to offend you. You're nothing like Flood. But I admit I'm not a believer in the paranormal. I don't think there is such a thing as a psychic talent."

"You are certainly not the first person to conclude

that I'm a fake psychic," Prudence said. She gave him one of her shiniest smiles. "There are a number of people who do not give any credence to the various theories of the paranormal. As has been pointed out to me, it's hard to accept the reality of a form of energy that science is not yet equipped to measure and record."

Out of the corner of her eye she saw Jack's expression harden. She kept the smile in place and pretended not to notice.

"Thank you for your understanding," Rollins said. "I apologize if I sounded rude. I have always felt that Clara's interest in consulting psychics was a harmless pastime. It never interfered with her ability to steer Dover Industries from one success to another. But things are different now that Flood is living in the same house with her. He's giving her some sort of medication. We have no idea what it is."

"I'm afraid Clara trusts her housekeeper more than she does Rollins," Ella said. "Maud Hollister approves of Dr. Flood. She encourages Clara to depend on him for treatment."

"That is true," Rollins said. "Hollister claims Flood is the only one who truly understands my mother's condition." He glanced at his watch and got to his feet. "We have intruded long enough. We should be on our way. Once again, we apologize for my mother's erratic behavior this afternoon. We hope you understand the position we are in."

Rollins was right-handed. He wore his signet ring on the little finger of his left hand. His watch was on his left wrist. When he checked the time, Prudence got another quick look at the ring. She still wasn't close enough to make out the engraving.

Ella rose and gave Prudence another gracious smile infused with remorse and regret. "This is an extremely delicate time for Dover Industries. Rollins tells me an important government contract will soon be negotiated. Naturally we are hoping to avoid a scandal."

"Miss Ryland is hoping to avoid being murdered," Jack said.

Rollins stared at him, shocked. "I assure you, my mother would never go so far as to attack Miss Ryland."

"I don't know about that," Jack said. "From the sound of it, the woman is unhinged."

"I promise you she is incapable of genuine violence," Rollins said. He turned back to Prudence. "Please don't worry, Miss Ryland. You are not in any serious physical danger."

"I hope you are right," Prudence said.

"I'm sure I am," Rollins said.

He took Ella's arm and started toward the door.

Frustrated by her failure to get a good look at the signet ring, Prudence jumped to her feet and hurried across the room to get ahead of Rollins and Ella. She reached the door first and wrapped her fingers around the knob. The couple stopped, waiting politely for her to open the door.

"Thank you for taking the time to stop by and explain," she said.

"It was the least we could do," Ella said. "Rest assured we will keep an eye on Clara. We want to avoid another awkward scene as badly as you do, believe me."

"Thank you," Prudence said. Unable to think of anything more subtle, she turned to Rollins. "I couldn't help but notice your unusual signet ring, Mr. Dover."

"What?" Rollins paused and glanced at his left hand and held it up to display the ring. "Old boarding school memento. No good memories, to tell you the truth. I wear it as a reminder that I survived. The school did not."

She finally got a good look at the top of the ring. It was engraved with a key. It took everything she had to keep her smile fixed in place.

"How interesting," she managed. "What school was that?"

"The Bennington Academy," Rollins said. "I'm sure you've never heard of it. It was a private boarding school in Northern California. Burned down years ago. Now you must excuse us. We really do need to be on our way. I have some business calls to make from the hotel. Dover Industries never sleeps."

"Of course," Prudence said.

She yanked open the door and followed Rollins and Ella outside. Jack left his post at the window and moved to stand beside her. Together they watched the Dovers get into the Jaguar and drive toward the main road.

Jack did not speak until they were alone. Then he looked at Prudence, his eyes cold and knowing.

"Why is the ring important?" he asked.

She inhaled slowly and let the breath out with control. Her pulse was skittering wildly.

"Tapson, the client who collapsed on the floor of my reading room in San Francisco, wore an identical ring."

"Did he?" Jack said very softly. He glanced in the direction of the departing Jaguar. The car had already vanished. "That is interesting."

"Okay, we should not jump to conclusions," she said. "San Francisco society is a relatively small community. The people who inhabit it belong to the same clubs. Go to the same parties. Shop at the same stores. They send their offspring to the same schools. This business with the signet rings could be a coincidence."

"No."

"Coincidences do happen, Jack."

"Not in a murder investigation." He turned and walked back into the house. "I need to make a phone call, and then you and I have to have a chat about what the hell happened to Tapson in your reading room in San Francisco."

"I was afraid you were going to bring up that subject again." Prudence hurried to follow him into the house. "Who are you going to call?"

"Raina Kirk. We need some more professional investigation work."

She trailed after him as he went into the library. "I thought you were my assigned investigator."

"How many times do I have to explain to you that I'm your consultant?" Jack sat down behind his desk and picked up the phone. "My job is to collect information and then find the connections."

She dropped into the big reading chair, crossed her legs, and gripped the padded leather armrests with both hands. "No offense, but that really does sound like a job description for a private investigator."

"Maybe, but there's one big difference between a private investigator and me."

"What?"

"I charge a lot more."

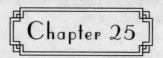

Chapter 25

"Thanks, Raina," Jack said. He kept an eye on Prudence while he spoke into the phone. "I'll take anything you can get on that private school. As for Tapson, I'd really like to know where he was before he arrived in San Francisco and proceeded to collapse in Madame Ariadne's reading room. No, that's all for now. I appreciate the help."

He hung up the phone and folded his arms on top of his desk. Prudence had not moved during the course of his conversation with Raina. Instead, she had watched him steadily. He knew she had been trying to decide just how much to tell him.

"Everything, Prudence," he said.

She raised her brows in silent inquiry.

"All the stuff you left out when you told Luther and

me that Tapson was alive when the ambulance took him to the hospital. I want to know everything."

"The problem with telling you the truth is that I doubt very much if you will believe me," she said.

"Try me."

She drummed the fingers of both hands on the arms of the chair, and then she started to talk.

"Tapson was mad," she said. "Dangerously so. I knew that as soon as he touched the crystal bowl I occasionally used in my readings."

"You saw his madness in the bowl?"

"No, I sensed it. I was touching the bowl, too, you see."

"The bowl makes a difference?" he asked.

"Crystal is an excellent conductor of psychic energy if you know how to use it." She raised her fingertips to the pendant at her throat. "I can pick up dream energy when I touch someone physically and open my senses, but I don't like to do that."

"The intimacy problem," he said.

"Yes." Her eyes darkened. "It's a very . . . disturbing experience."

"I understand," he said. Because, he realized, he did understand. Whether or not he wanted to comprehend her meaning was another question. He had never believed in the old saying that ignorance was bliss, but lately he had begun to wonder if it might be true, at least in some cases. "Go on."

"I realized immediately that he intended to murder me."

She stopped and waited. He knew she expected

him to tell her she was either lying or a victim of an overactive imagination. What she did not realize was that he had known she would say something like this, and he was prepared to believe her.

"I know how it feels to be very certain that someone is going to commit murder," he said.

"Right. Because of your crime tree method." She hesitated and then started talking in a cool voice that made it clear she did not expect him to believe her. "I used the crystal to reverse and destabilize the currents of Tapson's dream energy. That's when he collapsed. I called for an ambulance. He was unconscious but alive when they took him to the hospital. I found out later that he died sometime during the night. And that is all I can tell you."

"But you believe you caused him to collapse," Jack said, wanting to be certain. "Tapson did not keel over from a very convenient stroke?"

"No," she said. Ghostly shadows appeared in her eyes. "I'm very certain that I'm the one who sent him to the hospital. But I don't know if I killed him."

That evening Jack poured two glasses of wine and watched, fascinated, as Prudence used a large wooden spoon to lightly pound the fresh abalone steaks into the desired state of tenderness. There was a pile of fresh asparagus on the tiled counter, waiting to be washed and trimmed. A loaf of fresh bread stood at the ready.

"You look like you know what you're doing," he said.

She paused her pounding to pick up her wineglass. "Does that surprise you?"

"Everything you do surprises me, Prudence."

"My grandmother taught me how to cook," she said.

He smiled. "Did she warn you that you might never get married if you didn't learn how to cook?"

"Nope. She taught me because she said food was a source of pleasure and should be treated with respect. She wasn't worried about me snagging a husband. The women in my family don't do well with marriage. Something about our talent."

He watched her, unable to decide if she was teasing him. She sounded so matter-of-fact about it. *No news here, just the way things are.*

"Are you serious?" he asked.

"That was my grandmother's theory. She said sooner or later women like us scare men. Sure, they start out thinking we're a curiosity. They're weirdly fascinated or intrigued. Sometimes they see us as a challenge." She set the wineglass down, picked up the wooden spoon, and waved it around in a dramatic fashion. "But eventually they start to get uneasy, and the next thing you know, they panic and that's the end. They run off with another woman or they disappear or"—she paused for a beat—"they file for an annulment."

His insides turned to ice. "Is that what happened with your marriage? Your husband filed for an annulment because he decided your psychic talent scared him?"

"Well, that was part of it." Prudence began to dredge the abalone steaks in some seasoned flour. "But to be fair, he had every reason to panic. And it was my fault."

"How was it your fault?" he asked. He realized he was feeling dazed and disoriented, and not because he'd had a little wine. This was his life with Prudence these days.

She floured another abalone steak, apparently unaware of her effect on him. "I told you earlier that I have a problem with physical contact when my psychic senses are wide open. I didn't realize that would be an issue when it came to, uh, marital relations."

"Marital relations." For some reason it took him a couple of seconds to realize she was talking about sex. "Huh." He couldn't think of anything else to say, so he drank some more wine instead. "Huh."

"The marriage and the annulment were my fault from start to finish. I was very lonely after Grandma died. Julian was a client and he was—is—a very nice person. Warmhearted. Easy to talk to. Kind. Great sense of humor. Loves dogs, loves to dance, loves to go to the movies. Wanted to start a family. All in all, ideal husband material. So I decided to marry him. In hindsight, that was very unfair to Julian. He never stood a chance."

"Because he was fascinated and intrigued by your dream reading talent?"

"That was part of the reason it was so easy to convince him to marry me." Prudence sighed. "But the other part was that he was desperate to rebel against his domineering father. I think Julian saw me as a way to prove to himself and his parents that he was a man and capable of making his own decisions. When he introduced me to his family, everyone was horrified. They were convinced their son should look much higher than a professional psychic who had to be a fraud. I did not come from the right social circles."

"So you engineered a runaway marriage?"

"In my defense, I would like to point out that Julian was quite enthusiastic about the idea of going to Reno. He bought the train tickets and surprised me with them. I was starting to have my doubts, but the poor man was determined to prove he could make his own decisions. He convinced himself and me that he loved me. I felt guilty for having seduced him with my psychic talents, so I went along with his plans. I told myself we could make it work. But things went very badly on our wedding night. We both agreed we had made a mistake. The only question at that point was how to get out of the situation."

"How did you obtain an annulment?"

"Julian's father handled everything. He knew a very good lawyer. Naturally, the family did not want the scandal of a divorce."

"What grounds?"

Prudence's smile got very bright and shiny. "Fraud. Apparently I used my skills as a clever con artist to convince Julian that a spirit guide on the Other Side had directed him to marry me."

"Julian went along with all this?"

"Reluctantly." Prudence stopped smiling. "He knew it wasn't true, but I insisted. We all wanted the quickest, cleanest way out. The annulment was handled quietly. I'm sure there was some gossip in certain social circles, but nothing appeared in the papers, so my business was not affected."

"What happened to Julian?"

Prudence's light laugh sounded rueful but also real. "He is now married to a woman from his world. I hope he is happy."

"Have you seen him since the annulment?"

"No. We never moved in the same social circles. The only reason we met in the first place was because he came to me for a dream reading. I've got a hunch he does not patronize psychics these days."

He watched her finish dredging the abalone steaks.

"It wasn't your fault, Prudence," he said. "You didn't somehow use your psychic talents to coerce Julian into marriage."

"That's easy for you to say." She washed her hands in the sink and reached for a dish towel. "You don't believe I actually possess any psychic abilities."

"I told you, I'm keeping an open mind."

"I'll take your word for it. Want to help me trim the asparagus?"

"Okay. But just so you know, I have never trimmed asparagus in my life."

"It's easy. I'll demonstrate." She picked up a stalk of asparagus and snapped off the end. "After you do a couple you'll get the feel of it."

He set his wine aside, washed his hands, and went to stand in front of the pile of asparagus. Experimentally he picked up a stalk and gently bent it. He snapped off the end.

"You're right," he said. "You can feel the break point." He reached for another stalk. "Think you'll ever risk marriage again?"

She picked up her wine and watched him work on the asparagus. "After the disaster with Julian, I decided I was not cut out to be a wife. My plan is to be a professional committed flirt."

He blinked and started to laugh. "Is that an actual career?"

"I see it as a hobby or a pastime, like golf or tennis. My *career* goal is to open a bookshop focused on the literature of the paranormal. I was working in the Adelina Beach College library to get some experience and develop my knowledge of the field. What about you? Think you'll take another chance on marriage?"

He was trying to deal with the concept of flirting as a hobby or a sport. Her question caught him by surprise. *Should have seen it coming.* After all, he had just asked her the same question.

"I don't think marriage is in my future," he said. "Not with this face."

"You don't get to use your scars as an excuse, not with me." She smiled. "I'm psychic, remember? I know perfectly well that the real reason you're afraid of marriage is because of your talent."

"I'm not afraid of marriage. I've studied the odds and they are not good, at least not in my case."

"Uh-huh."

"And I don't have a *talent*. I have a certain ability to observe the actions of others, and I am able to interpret what I observe in ways that allow me to assign a statistical probability to the actions an individual is likely to take under certain stressful situations."

"What's the difference?"

He thought about that as he snapped off the bottom of the last stalk of asparagus. "Damned if I know."

Chapter 26

Raina called back later that evening. Jack was at his desk. He reached for the phone.

"This is Wingate."

"This is Raina, Jack. I've got some information for you."

"Terrific," he said. He picked up a pencil and opened his notebook. "I'm listening."

Prudence was curled up in the big reading chair in the library, working her way through *The Wingate Crime Tree*. She was almost finished, he noticed. She lowered the page she had been reading and waited.

By the time he hung up a few minutes later, the chimes were clashing so loudly he was amazed Prudence did not hear them.

"As Rollins Dover told us, the Bennington Academy was a small private boarding school," he said. "What he did not mention was that it was a school for the troubled youth of the wealthy."

"Troubled youth?" she repeated. "That covers a lot of territory."

"It does. Apparently Bennington was known for its strict discipline. The boys were locked in their dormitories at night."

"It sounds like a prison."

"Yes, it does. The academy was located in a small rural town in the mountains. Raina managed to track down the former sheriff. He remembered the school very well. It was the source of his biggest problems. Some of the boys were known to be violent, and occasionally they escaped the dorms. He confirmed the place burned to the ground years ago. The headmaster died in the fire. Evidently he was locked in his office and unable to escape."

"*Locked* in his office?"

"The fire was considered suspicious, although no one could prove arson. The sheriff told Raina he always believed one or more of the boys set the fire and made sure the headmaster was trapped."

"Judging by their signet rings, Tapson and Rollins Dover were both students at the Bennington Academy," Prudence said. "That's a connection, isn't it?"

"A very strong connection. The school records were destroyed in the fire, but Raina says Tapson and Rollins are the same age and would have been in their teens at the time of the fire."

"Okay, this is getting very scary." Prudence held up a page of the manuscript. "Your criminal analysis method emphasizes the critical importance of identifying the links between individuals. We now have two men from the same social circles in San Francisco who were together at a boarding school that sounds as if it was designed to be a classy reformatory for the offspring of the upper classes."

"Raina had some additional information on Tapson. Evidently he did not spend the last several years hunting big game and climbing mountains. When he turned twenty, his family had him quietly committed to a private psychiatric hospital. He escaped shortly before he appeared in San Francisco and booked that appointment with you."

"Why me? There are a lot of psychics working in San Francisco. I can't believe he picked me out of the phone book."

"We both know the connection here is Rollins Dover," Jack said.

"But that makes no sense. I never even met Rollins until today."

"It makes a lot of sense if you consider that back in San Francisco he may have perceived you as a threat. Clara had chosen you as Gilbert's future bride. The mother of her gifted grandchildren. Rollins had every reason to think that you would leap at the opportunity to marry his brother."

"Following your logic, Gilbert was the threat, not me."

"As long as his older brother showed no interest in

assuming responsibility for Dover Industries or marriage, Rollins had no reason to take the risk of murdering anyone. But if you had married Gilbert, that would have changed everything. It might or might not have caused Gilbert to settle down and take up his position at the company. But it certainly had the potential to complicate the inheritance situation. If something happened to Gilbert, you, as his wife, might have wound up controlling a chunk of Dover Industries. And if you'd had any offspring—"

"I see what you mean," Prudence said. She was quiet for a moment. "I can't believe we are discussing the possibility that Rollins Dover might have convinced his insane schoolmate to murder me because I threatened his control of Dover Industries."

Jack studied his crime tree and made a note. "We don't know for certain that's what happened, but I'm going to assign a high probability to that possibility."

She gathered up the manuscript pages and tapped them on the end to neaten the stack. When she was satisfied, she set the pile aside and picked up her after-dinner brandy.

He watched, telling himself to keep his mouth shut, but in the end he could not resist. He had to ask the question. "What do you think?"

"About the manuscript?" She glanced at the stack of pages. "I'm certainly not an expert on the subject, but so far your method makes sense. It provides a logical way of examining and mapping a crime scene. The writing is clear and crisp."

"Tell me the truth—is it boring?"

She looked surprised by the question. "No, not at all, at least not to someone who is interested in such things. And I am interested." She paused. "But—"

He braced himself. "What?"

"You are trying to quantify and describe your methods and techniques, and I'm sure that will be very helpful to the law enforcement community. But you are overlooking a key factor in your own success."

He grimaced. "Is this where you tell me that I am a successful consultant because I possess a psychic talent for the work?"

She gave him one of her flashbulb-bright smiles. "Why don't we call it *intuition*, hmm?" She glanced at the clock on the wall. "It's getting late. I'm going to go to bed. Do you mind if I take your manuscript with me? I'm almost finished."

"Help yourself," he said.

She finished the brandy, gathered up the manuscript pages, and walked toward the door.

"Good night," she said just as she was about to step out into the hallway.

He sat forward abruptly, suddenly needing more answers.

"Prudence?" he said.

She stopped and gave him an inquiring look from the other side of the door.

"Yes?" she said.

He lost his nerve. He wasn't sure yet if he wanted answers to the questions that haunted his dreams.

"Never mind," he said. "It's not important. Good night."

She disappeared out into the hall. A moment later he heard her footsteps on the stairs. A door closed. The house settled for the night.

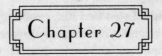

Chapter 27

The muffled sound of shattering glass brought Prudence out of a restless, dream-ridden sleep. A second explosion followed before she could get oriented.

No, not a second explosion. Someone had just slammed open the door of the suite.

She came fully alert on a wave of nervy energy, opened her eyes, and saw the figure of a man looming over the bed. He was silhouetted in the pale glow of the light she had left burning in the bathroom. He ripped the covers aside.

She opened her mouth to scream but her throat was too tight. No sound emerged. Frantic now, she tried to roll away to the opposite side of the bed. Jack stopped her.

"Prudence, it's me," he said. He yanked back the

quilt and hauled her out of bed. "The house is on fire. We have to get out now."

She struggled to focus on the word *fire*.

"Slippers," he ordered. "Protect your feet."

"Right," she said. "Slippers."

The command steadied her, enabling her to concentrate. He released her hand and went toward the door. She hopped down from the high bed and shoved her feet into the slippers.

"My robe," she said. "It's in the bathroom."

"No time," he said. "The main staircase is already blocked. We'll take the back stairs. Follow me."

He went out into the hall. Prudence realized she could smell smoke now. She grabbed the stack of manuscript pages off the bedside table and rushed after him.

She followed him along the corridor. When they reached the landing, she looked down and saw the flames leaping out of the library, starting up the main staircase. The fire moved with terrifying speed, consuming everything it touched.

There was no time to take in the horror of what was happening. Clutching the manuscript with one hand, she hoisted the long skirts of her nightgown and ran after Jack. He had reached the end of the hall and was opening a stairwell door.

"Good," he said. "No smoke in here."

He moved inside and toggled the light switch. Wall sconces came on, illuminating the two flights of steps.

"Go," he ordered, standing aside.

She grabbed the railing with her free hand and plunged downward. Jack closed the door, briefly blocking the smoke, and followed her.

The rear stairs ended in the utility room off the kitchen. Jack got the back door open and together they raced out into the firelit night.

"The car," Jack said. "We need to get to a phone to report the fire."

She hurried after him. When she felt the gravel under her feet, she was suddenly grateful for the slippers.

The Packard was in the detached garage behind the house. Jack backed it out into the driveway. Prudence yanked open the passenger side door and jumped into the front seat. Jack turned on the headlights but paused before he put the car in gear.

"Listen," he said.

She heard it, too—the sound of a heavy car engine accelerating away into the night.

"We'll never catch him," Jack said.

He put the vehicle in gear and went around the side of the burning house, heading toward the lane that would take them to Cliff Road.

An apparition appeared in the headlights. A ghostly figure in a long white robe. Her shoulder-length gray hair was a chaotic mane around her face. Her eyes were stark and wild.

Jack slammed on the brakes. "What the hell?"

"Meet Clara Dover," Prudence said.

Chapter 28

S he's gone mad," Jack said. He opened his door and got out.

"You'd better let me handle this," Prudence said.

She put the manuscript on the floor, jumped out of the car, and went forward.

"Clara, what have you done?" she said, pitching her voice to be heard above the roar of the flames.

"No," Clara screamed. "You can't be alive. You're supposed to die by fire. Gilbert said you would burn in hell tonight for what you did."

"Clara," Prudence said. "Listen to me. You're hallucinating."

"No," Clara shouted. In the flaring light of the blazing house, her face was a mask of horror and disbelief. "I came here to witness your death by fire.

You're supposed to die in that house. Why aren't you dead?"

She whirled and stumbled toward the cliffs.

"Clara, stop," Prudence called. "You'll fall."

Prudence started forward but almost lost her balance when one of the slippers slid off her foot. She braced a hand against the fender to catch herself.

"Stay where you are," Jack said. "I'll get her."

He was already running after Clara.

But it was too late. With a scream of rage and anguish, Clara vanished over the side of the cliff. Jack stopped at the edge and looked down. Turning, he loped back to the car, leaned into the passenger seat, and took a flashlight out of the glove box.

"Is she—?" Prudence asked.

"I don't know."

Jack headed back to the edge of the cliff and switched on the flashlight. Prudence hurried after him and watched as he swept the beam of light back and forth. Clara was sprawled midway down the rocky path that led to the cove.

"Here, take the flashlight," Jack said. "I'll get her."

Prudence held the beam steady as Jack descended and crouched beside Clara.

"She's alive," he announced. "Looks like she hit her head. I'll bring her up. We'll take her to the hospital."

He collected Clara and carried her up the path. When he brought her into the glow of the headlights, Prudence saw the blood matting the gray hair.

"Her robe is too dirty to use as a bandage," Prudence said.

She leaned down and tore a strip off the bottom of her nightgown.

Jack watched her put the makeshift bandage on Clara's bleeding head. "The woman just tried to murder both of us and now we're trying to save her life. Don't know about you, but I find this situation extremely irritating."

"Stop grumbling. You know we have to do what we can."

"Also, we need answers," Jack said, visibly cheered by that logic.

She was securing the ends of the bandage when sirens sounded in the distance.

"Someone driving past on Cliff Road must have seen the fire and reported it," Jack said. He watched the flames leap into the night sky. "Probably visible for miles. That will save us having to waste time trying to find a phone."

He eased Clara into the rear compartment of the vehicle, closed the door, and went around the hood to get behind the wheel. Prudence got into the front seat, then turned and knelt to lean over the back so she could keep an eye on her patient. Jack put the car in gear and continued on to Cliff Road.

"Clara," Prudence said gently. "Can you hear me?"

Clara stirred and opened her eyes. She stared at Prudence as if seeing a ghost.

"You were supposed to die in the fire," she managed, her voice trembling in confusion and dismay. "Why are you alive?"

"Who told you I was going to die, Clara?"

"Gilbert. He came to me in a vision. He said you would die tonight."

"Clara, that's impossible. Gilbert is dead. You buried him."

"His spirit visits me."

"Keep the questions specific," Jack said, not taking his eyes off the road. "Try to get her to deal with facts."

Prudence leaned farther over the seat and touched Clara's hand. She was startled by how cold the woman felt.

"When does Gilbert visit you?" she asked.

"At night."

The sirens were very close now. Jack braked to a halt and flashed the headlights. The first truck stopped.

"I'll be right back," Jack said.

He climbed out of the seat and went forward into the headlights to explain the situation.

Prudence touched the crystal pendant at her throat and tightened her grip on Clara's hand. She steadied her nerves for the jolt that was coming and cautiously heightened her senses.

She was braced for the disturbing storm of energy, but she was shocked by how chaotic it was.

"Tell me about your last vision of Gilbert, Clara," she said.

"He spoke to me tonight," Clara moaned.

"Were you in bed when he appeared?"

"Yes. He told me the time had come."

The door opened. Jack got behind the wheel. He

started to speak but stopped when he realized Clara was talking. Without a word he drove toward the lights of Burning Cove in the distance.

"How did you get to the fire?" Prudence asked.

"Good question," Jack said very softly.

Clara struggled for a moment. "I can't remember." She suddenly became agitated. "Why can't I remember?"

Prudence glanced at Clara's slippered feet. The soles of the shoes were scuffed and dirty, but they did not appear to be badly damaged.

"Did you walk?" Prudence asked, battling the headwinds of Clara's wild dream energy to hold the focus.

"No." Clara sounded very certain.

"Did you drive to the scene of the fire?" Prudence asked.

"I haven't driven in years."

"Did your chauffeur drive you to the fire?"

"No, Henry didn't drive me." Again Clara sounded very sure of her answer. "Henry's gone. Quit. No notice. So typical of workers these days. No sense of loyalty or gratitude for a steady job."

"Who drove you?" Prudence said.

"I can't remember," Clara shrieked in frustration. "Why can't I remember? Maybe it was Gilbert. Yes. Yes, it must have been Gilbert."

"Gilbert is on the Other Side," Prudence said gently. "He can't come through the veil to drive a car."

"Or start a fire," Jack muttered.

"Car," Clara whispered. "I was in a car."

Her dream energy surged alarmingly. The storm

got worse. Uncertain what was happening, Prudence intuitively countered the churning currents with a quiet, soothing pulse.

"Why can't I remember?" Clara whispered, her voice breaking.

She collapsed into a deep sleep.

Prudence released her hold on Clara's hand, turned around, and sat down.

"I'm not going to ask what you just did to her, but please tell me if you learned anything," Jack said.

Prudence thought about Clara's stormy energy. "I'm not sure, but something has definitely changed. Clara's energy is distorted and erratic. When I was doing readings, I occasionally had clients who were on drugs. Their currents had the same weird sense of chaos and distortion."

"Rollins Dover said Clara's new doctor was giving her some medication for her nerves."

"Yes, he did say that, didn't he? But I think there is more to it. I almost got the feeling she was reading from a script. There would be fire. She was supposed to witness my death. Even if she wanted me dead, where did the details come from? And why the memory problems when it comes to the issue of how she got to your house?"

"Hypnotic suggestion," Jack said, very grim now. "Maybe whoever drugged her gave her the script and then told her to forget certain elements of it."

"I don't know, Jack. It all seems so bizarre. First Gilbert Dover's murder and now this fire."

"I've decided that when it comes to this case, no theory is too far out of bounds."

"It's hard to imagine anyone drugging and manipulating Clara Dover. She is such a strong-willed woman."

"Everyone has a weak point," Jack said. "With her, it was her son Gilbert and her dream of establishing a dynasty of psychically gifted descendants. Rollins Dover is looking like the one with the most powerful motive, but if he's behind this, where does Harley Flood fit into the picture? And then there's the faithful housekeeper."

"I understand your suspicion of the doctor. He's new in the household and we don't know much about him. But why are you suspicious of Maud Hollister?"

"She appears to be the one employee who has remained on Clara's staff when everyone else quit or was fired."

"You're questioning Maud's loyalty?"

"No, her loyalty is a fact," Jack said, turning in to the hospital driveway. "But I would like to know the reason for it."

Chapter 29

I never did like that house," Jack said.

"But you got a very good deal on it," Prudence said.

They were in one of several private villas scattered around the lush grounds of the glamorous Burning Cove Hotel. It was nearly three in the morning. They had checked in a short time ago. Luther Pell had phoned ahead to alert the front desk. If the staff had questions about a disheveled unmarried couple arriving in the early-morning hours with no luggage, they had kept those questions to themselves. The hotel catered to Hollywood royalty and the rich and often infamous. It had a long-standing reputation for discretion.

It also had excellent service, Prudence thought. When she and Jack had pulled up in front of the main entrance, they had been met by a gracious member of the housekeeping department who was holding a spa robe. The robe had been quickly draped around Prudence, and she had been discreetly whisked off to the villa like any self-respecting woman intent on embarking on an illicit liaison. Jack had stayed behind for a few minutes to handle the formalities at the front desk.

Two small overnight kits containing a few emergency essentials had been waiting in the room. She had opened the one labeled *Hers* and discovered to her delight a toothbrush, toothpaste, a comb, a nail file, and a note advising her that suitable clothing would be delivered in the morning.

When Jack walked through the door a short time later, he had glanced inside the kit marked *His* and disappeared briefly into one of the bedrooms with it. When he had rejoined her, she had not been sure how to read his mood. She had handed him a glass of brandy that she had poured at the well-stocked drinks cart. He had taken it without comment and immediately swallowed a healthy dose. She had done the same with her own whiskey.

Until now Jack had been focused on each crisis as it arose—escape the burning house, rescue Clara Dover, explain the situation to the authorities. Then he had made the phone call to Luther Pell from the hospital lobby pay phone informing him that they needed a room for the night and why.

Now he was standing at the closed French doors, contemplating the darkened patio and deep shadows

of the small private garden. The lights of the lobby
and the wings of the main part of the sprawling hotel
sparkled through the foliage. The muffled music
of the dance orchestra, still going strong, could be
heard in the distance.

This was, Prudence realized, the first time Jack
had stopped moving forward since the firestorm
at House of Shadows had started. He had to be
exhausted.

He could have been killed tonight, she thought. Because of her.

She set her empty glass down on the coffee table
next to the manuscript and walked across the terra-
cotta tiles to join Jack at the window. They stood
side by side, not touching, and looked out into the
night.

"It really was a spectacular house," she said, trying
to find the right words. "Very striking décor."

"It never felt right."

"Because you bought it for a different future than
the one you got."

To her surprise his hard mouth quirked in a
flash of bemused amusement. "Is that a psychic
insight?"

"Nope. A conclusion based on the evidence." She
took a breath and concentrated on the shadows looming on the other side of the glass panes. "You almost
got killed tonight. You lost your home. Your library.
All your stuff. Because of me. That's not right. I'm so
sorry you got dragged into this."

"You didn't drag me into anything. Luther Pell

hired me to consult on your case. I'm getting paid, remember? You are a client. Your case is a job."

"That may be true, but it wasn't supposed to include risking your life to save me from a burning house. If it hadn't been for me, you would still have a roof over your head."

He glanced up at the ceiling of the villa. "This one will do."

"Damn it, Jack—"

He turned to confront her, his eyes still smoldering a little with the embers of the fierce energy that had been driving him for the past few hours.

"Would you mind very much if we saved this argument until morning?" he said. "I've got other things to concentrate on at the moment."

She felt the heat rise in her face. "Yes, of course. I'm sorry. I was just trying to apologize for putting you in harm's way."

"Don't."

She took a breath. "Okay. Can I at least thank you for saving my life tonight?"

"You're welcome. Now do me a favor and don't raise the subject again."

She sniffed, not sure why she was suddenly close to tears. Shock, she decided. She had been through a lot tonight. So had Jack. A person's nerves could take only so much. She nodded once, very crisply took a step back, and turned to head toward the bedroom—the *other* bedroom. Not the one Jack had chosen earlier. She did not want to make that mistake. That would be a very dumb thing to do. Also humiliating.

"I'll leave you to your consulting," she said.

"What is that?" he said, his voice sharpening.

She stopped and looked back to see what he was talking about. She realized he had turned away from the window and was staring at the typed pages of *The Wingate Crime Tree* on the coffee table.

"Oh, that's your manuscript," she said. "It was on my nightstand when you came to my room to tell me that the house was on fire, so I grabbed it."

He looked at her with utter disbelief. "You saved my manuscript?"

"You did say it was your only copy. I realize you could reconstruct the book if necessary, but you've obviously put so much work into it already. It just seemed a shame to leave it behind."

Jack walked toward the coffee table, reached down, and picked up the stack of pages. He looked at the title page and slowly shook his head.

"You were running for your life," he said. "You could have grabbed something valuable. Your handbag. A few of your new clothes. But you saved my manuscript? What were you thinking?"

Her temper sparked. "Your manuscript is valuable."

"To me. Not to you."

"Look, the damn thing was just sitting there on my nightstand. I did not put either one of us at any additional risk by picking it up on the way to the door. It happened to be convenient to save your manuscript, so I did."

"Thank you," he said quietly.

She blinked. "You're welcome."

He winced and put the manuscript back down on

the coffee table. "This is another stupid argument, isn't it?"

"Yes, but we've been under a lot of stress tonight. We're probably not thinking clearly."

"Probably not, because I want to kiss you, and I know that would be the wrong thing to do. Probably."

She stilled. "You want to kiss me because I saved your manuscript?"

"That and other reasons."

"Why would that *probably* be the wrong thing to do?" she asked.

"You took a risk when you agreed to move into the house of a man who lived alone, a man who was a complete stranger."

"To be fair, you did come with Luther Pell's recommendation."

"The point is, you took the risk of moving under my roof because you didn't have much choice," he said. "I can't betray your trust."

"Okay, I took the risk. And it's true I didn't have a lot of options, but if you're afraid to kiss me because you are worried you *probably* would be taking advantage of me, you can relax."

He watched her warily. "Yeah?"

"Yep." She stretched her arms out wide in a grand see-for-yourself gesture. "The circumstances have changed."

"How do you figure that?"

"Simple." She gave him what she knew was a very smug smile. "We are no longer in your house; therefore, we don't have to abide by your rules. Instead, we are

currently shacked up at the famous and quite notorious Burning Cove Hotel, which is well-known for pro-
viding discreet accommodations and opportunities for
shacking up."

"Shacking up?" he repeated, his voice a little too
even.

"I believe that is the technical term, yes."

"And you don't have a problem with that?"

"Nope." She rested her hands on his shoulders.
"Everyone knows the rules are different in a hotel like
this. Places like this are made for illicit affairs and
clandestine liaisons."

He cradled her face between his palms. "Why do I
have the feeling I'm being manipulated?"

"I'm trying to flirt with you, not manipulate you. I
believe I mentioned that my goal is to become a professional flirt."

"Right. I almost forgot."

"I haven't had a lot of opportunities to practice.
How am I doing?"

"You are doing a great job of flirting." He drew her
closer. "I'd say you have a natural talent for it."

"Thank you." She seized handfuls of the front of
his shirt and smiled. "You're not doing bad yourself.
The strange thing is that back at the start, I was sure
you would not be any good at flirting."

"Too serious?"

"That was part of it. But I told myself that for
you, the real problem with flirting was that you
would be too busy fretting about how the relationship
would end. You wouldn't be able to enjoy the
moment."

"Just to be clear, I don't fret. I make deductions and conclusions and assign probabilities to specific outcomes."

"Whatever you say."

"I don't fret," Jack repeated. He paused for emphasis. "And I don't flirt."

"I might be able to teach you," she whispered.

"No."

She closed her eyes, her heart sinking. She had let the high-wire excitement and emotions of the night lead her down a treacherous path. What she had done was not fair to Jack.

"My apologies," she said. "I should not have led you on."

"I may not be any good at flirting, but I still want to kiss you," he said, his voice rough and edgy.

Her eyes flew open. She was shocked by the intensity in his voice. The fires in his eyes were no longer banked. Elation swept through her senses. Her mouth went dry. She shivered, not from cold—from excitement and anticipation.

"I want to kiss you, too," she said.

There was no time to say anything else. His mouth came down on hers in a heavy, desperate, hungry kiss that sent shock waves through her.

When he finally raised his head, she could hardly breathe.

"Do you want to stop?" he asked.

She had survived a fire intended to kill her tonight. She could survive a few more passionate kisses with Jack.

"No," she said. "No, I don't want to stop. But it's

only fair to warn you that at some point I will have a panic attack and ruin everything."

"What the hell are you talking about?"

She swallowed hard. "I'm trying to explain why I've made the decision to become a flirt. I found out on my wedding night that my nerves can't handle the paranormal energy of sex."

He moved his hands to her waist and lifted her off her feet. She gripped his shoulders to steady herself. His eyes burned.

"You discovered this little problem with your nerves on your wedding night?" he asked.

"Yes. Exactly." She struggled to catch her breath. "But I'll be okay up until, you know, the actual act. And then I'll have a panic attack, during which I might, ah, hurt you."

"Hurt me?"

"Accidentally," she said quickly. "Not intentionally."

"Right. Not intentionally. How will you hurt me?"

"You'll have a panic attack, too—or, to be more accurate, my panic attack will slam into your nerves and trigger one. It's the close physical connection that does it, I think. You'll be sensitized, and after that, every time we touch each other there will be a rebound effect, and it will get worse and, oh, I really, really do not want to talk about this. Not now. I just want to kiss you and flirt as long as I can."

"Life is never dull around you, Prudence Ryland. I'll tell you what. Let's see how far we get before we both have panic attacks."

"You're sure you want to take the risk?"

"I have never been more sure of anything in my life."

He carried her into a darkened bedroom—his bedroom.

So much for teaching Jack how to flirt, she thought. He was a natural.

Chapter 30

S omeone entered the darkened room.

"Gilbert?" Clara Dover struggled to focus on the footsteps. It wasn't easy. She had a pounding headache. "Is that you? She's alive. How can that be? You said she would die in the fire."

"It's unfortunate that Miss Ryland survived, but it's a complication, not a disaster," Maud Hollister said. She moved to stand over the bed. "The main goal was achieved."

Not Gilbert. Clara stared up at the shadowed face of the woman whose unfailing loyalty and silence had been purchased years ago on the installment plan.

"What are you talking about, Maud? I don't understand. Where am I?"

"The Burning Cove hospital. After you set fire to

Mr. Wingate's house, you tried to throw yourself off a cliff into the sea. You have a severe concussion."

"I did not cause the fire," Clara said, annoyed by the inaccuracy. "I was there to witness the death of that witch. Where is Dr. Flood? I must speak with him about my last vision. Something was wrong with the interpretation."

"He is back at the villa talking to Rollins and your daughter-in-law. He is explaining to them that you need to be committed to a psychiatric hospital."

"*No.*" Panic shot across Clara's nerves. "They can't do that. I won't allow it."

"You tried to murder two people by setting fire to the house in which they were sleeping. The choice your family faces is whether to let the police arrest you for arson and attempted murder or have you quietly put away in a private asylum and hope that Jack Wingate doesn't press charges. I'm sure Rollins will be able to purchase Wingate's silence. Everyone responds to money. It's just a matter of finding the right number, isn't it?"

"Stop talking like that."

"Just think about how many people you bribed and paid off over the years," Maud said. "And we all kept quiet, didn't we? Don't worry, I doubt you'll go to prison. Regardless of whether or not Wingate takes the money, I'm quite sure you will end up in an asylum, and that's what matters."

"Shut up. This has gone far enough. Tell Rollins I want to see him. Immediately."

"Rollins and Ella were here earlier," Maud said. "You do remember who Ella is, right? She's the woman who married Rollins. Poor thing. She's tried so hard to please you. I could have told her she was wasting her time."

"I insist on talking to Rollins now."

"He's busy deciding where to send you for your so-called rest cure."

Clara moaned, trying to think clearly. "I must speak with Rollins about the company."

"He's going to have his hands full trying to save your empire after word gets out that you had to be institutionalized."

"They can't put me away. I am not insane."

"Always a difficult thing to prove," Maud said.

"Damn you. Call Rollins immediately and tell him to come back to the hospital. I must speak with him. He doesn't know how to handle the press. I have to tell him what to say."

"Don't worry, your son already knows what he has to do. Over the years he paid much closer attention to Dover Industries than Gilbert ever did."

"He doesn't have Gilbert's talent."

"Gilbert never had any talent," Maud said. "He was a spoiled, violent little boy who grew into a spoiled, violent man. He died a well-deserved violent death. The world is better off without him. No one misses him except you."

"That dream reader murdered him."

"And you tried to murder the dream reader," Maud said. "But you failed, and now you will spend the rest of your life in an asylum for the insane."

"You hate me so much? After all I've done for you?"

"I hate the entire Dover family. I have dreamed of

vengeance all these years, and slowly but surely I am seeing my dream come true. That monster you married died first. Yes, I know I did you a favor when I put the poison in Copeland's soup, but I took pleasure in my revenge. We stood over him and watched him die. We made sure he knew that both of us had murdered him and that no one would ever find out. Remember how he pleaded with us to send for a doctor?"

"Yes, yes, I remember. He deserved it. Copeland was a brute."

"So was Gilbert. Like father, like son. But he's gone, too. Now you will die in a madhouse."

"You're the one who's insane," Clara gasped.

"Maybe," Maud said. "Who knows? But the good news for me is that no one cares enough to have me committed. I'm just the housekeeper. I'm not standing in the way of anyone's inheritance."

"I told you I would take care of everything in my will."

"It will be interesting to see if you kept that promise. By the way, before I say goodbye, I've got a secret to tell you."

She leaned over the bed and whispered into Clara's ear.

"No," Clara gasped. "No, that can't be true."

"It's the truth," Maud said. She turned away from the bed and started toward the door.

"Come back here," Clara whispered. "You can't do this to me, Maud. We are friends. All these years—"

"No, we have never been friends," Maud said.

She went out into the hall and closed the door.

Clara tried to ignore the pain in her head. She had

to escape the hospital room. She reached for the bed rails, intending to get to her feet. But she could not move her hands. There was something wrong. She looked at her wrists.

Horror swept through her when she saw the leather restraints.

She screamed, but she knew she managed little more than a croaking cry.

The door opened. A figure appeared, silhouetted against the hallway light.

"It's about time you showed up," Clara said. "Get me out of these restraints."

But her late-night visitor did not free her. The next thing she knew, there was a heavy pillow coming down over her face, muffling her attempt to scream. She could no longer breathe.

The killer explained quite clearly why she was being murdered. Clara's last conscious thought was that everything she had built would soon be in ruins.

Chapter 31

Prudence was still trying to deal with the exhilarating rush of sensation igniting her senses
when Jack came down on top of her, crushing
her gently into the luxurious bedding. She reached up
to wrap her arms tightly around him and silently
vowed to savor every second, every element, every
aspect of the experience—right up to the point where
the panic attack kicked in.

"Prudence," Jack said against her mouth.

Her name sounded as if it had been dredged up
from the bottom of a very dark pool. It was a question,
a plea, and a statement of fact.

"Yes," she said.

He did not try to talk after that. Neither did she,
because she knew they had moved too far beyond the
safe zone. Retreat was no longer an option. She was

committed, not for the future but for right up until the moment when her nerves shattered.

When he moved his mouth down her throat to her breasts, she clenched her fingers into the sleek muscles of his shoulders. His body was furnace hot. Knowing that he wanted her with such fierce intensity filled her with an intoxicating sense of her own power.

Everything about him fascinated and excited—the sleek power in his shoulders, his granite-hard erection. But most of all it was the raw, elemental energy resonating between them that dazzled and seduced her senses. It was all so different from her wedding night.

At some point he rolled away from her long enough to grab the overnight kit off the nightstand. She watched him take out a small tin and sheathe himself in a condom.

He rolled back and gathered her close. "They really do have first-class service here at the Burning Cove Hotel."

"Yes, they do," she said.

She levered herself up on one elbow, leaned over him, and kissed him. And then she kissed his scars. He tensed. She ignored his reaction and moved her lips to his throat. He groaned. Another kind of tension replaced the flash of uncertainty. His warm hand slipped down her back to her hip. His fingers clenched gently. She continued her exploration.

He drew a sharp breath and abruptly changed positions. Then he took his time learning every inch of her body. By the time he settled onto his back again, she was soaking wet and consumed with the need for release.

He pulled her astride his thighs.

"Is this the point at which you have a panic attack?" he asked, his voice raw.

"Any minute now."

"I've been warned. I'm willing to take the risk. How about you?"

She drew a deep, steadying breath. "Yes. Just promise me you won't blame me afterward."

"Don't worry. If this doesn't work out, I'll blame myself."

He began to thrust into her, going deep. She yelped and flinched when she felt the sharp pain. Her hands became claws on his chest as she dug her nails into him.

Jack went utterly still. "Pru? What?"

"Not a panic attack," she gasped. "Not yet. Just give me a minute."

"Take your time," he growled. "I'm not going anywhere."

Her body began to adjust to his. Experimentally she started to move. He responded, pushing gently into her and then slowly withdrawing. She tightened herself around him. After a time, he moved two fingers to the sensitive place between her legs.

Everything inside her clenched until she thought she would shatter, but not from a panic attack.

"Is your necklace glowing?" he asked in a hoarse whisper.

"Just a trick of the light," she said.

And then the impossible, unbearable tension was

released in a cascade of thrilling waves. In the next moment, Jack's climax pounded through him. She hung on for dear life.

Jack emerged from the dimly lit bathroom, sprawled beside her on the bed, and reached out to draw her close.

"I hope that wasn't your definition of a panic attack," he said. "Because if it was, I apparently suffer from the same problem with my nerves."

"Oh, shut up," she said.

"Okay."

He closed his eyes and promptly fell hard into sleep. She rested her head on his shoulder and waited. The panic attack might have been delayed. She would stay awake for a while, just in case. If she felt it coming on, she would escape to her own room.

Chapter 32

The phone rang, dragging Jack out of the first deep, untroubled sleep he'd had since the Bonner case. Reluctantly he opened his eyes. He wanted to stay right where he was and savor the incredibly intimate feel of Prudence's soft frame cuddled against him.

The phone blared again.

"Damn."

With a groan, he eased away from Prudence, rolled out of bed, and grabbed the robe he had found on a hook in the bathroom. He padded barefoot toward the door, tying the sash.

"Jack," Prudence yelped.

Startled by the shock in her voice, he turned quickly. She was sitting bolt upright in bed, clutching the sheet to her throat. Her eyes were wide with something between bewilderment and disbelief.

"Don't worry," he said. "I'll get the phone. It's probably Luther Pell."

She did not appear reassured by that news. Instead, she continued to stare at him in consternation. It was not an illogical response, he thought. A morning call from Pell was probably not going to bring good news.

He continued into the living room and seized the receiver just as it gave another blaring ring.

"This is Wingate."

"Clara Dover died sometime last night," Luther said.

"Natural causes?"

"That's what it looks like. The doctor says it's not a big surprise, given her age and the nature of her injury. Head wounds are always unpredictable."

"How is the family handling it?"

"Evidently Rollins Dover was making arrangements to have his mother transferred to the care of a private psychiatric hospital. He was planning to tell the press that Clara was going away for an extended voyage. Now he'll be arranging to have his mother's body transported back to San Francisco for a funeral."

Jack thought about that. "Death from natural causes is a much less damaging story for the company. Instead of trying to conceal the fact that his mother was being sent away to an asylum, he'll be telling everyone that she died in an accident and he will be taking the reins of Dover Industries."

"He still has to deal with the fact that it looks like

Clara Dover burned down your house, but he may be able to finesse that," Luther said. "After all, with Clara dead, there's no one to arrest. Viewed from a certain perspective, his mother's death simplifies his life."

"His life might be simplified, but we've still got a problem, because Clara Dover did not burn down my house last night."

"You're sure of that?"

"Positive." Jack summoned up his memories. "She was hallucinating. It's possible she was the person who actually threw the firebomb through the window, but I doubt it. Even if she did, I guarantee you someone else constructed the device, drove her out to House of Shadows, and made sure it went through the window. Prudence and I heard a big car on the main road. It was moving very fast."

"Think it was the same individual who killed Gilbert Dover and tried to pin the murder on Prudence Ryland?"

"Possibly. Regardless, that makes three members of the Dover family who are dead."

"Three?"

"Copeland Dover, Clara's husband, died years ago, remember? The anointed heir, Gilbert, was killed a few days ago, and now Clara Dover is dead."

"Well, the good news is that your list of suspects is shrinking rapidly," Luther said. "By the way, I drove past what's left of your house this morning. I'm sorry to tell you there's very little worth salvaging."

"The library?"

"Destroyed."

"Prudence saved my manuscript," Jack said. "She grabbed it on the way out the door."

"That was quick thinking. Glad to hear it. Call me when you've got more information."

The phone went dead. Luther Pell did not linger over goodbyes and pleasantries.

Jack replaced the receiver in the cradle and turned to find Prudence watching him from the hallway that led to the bedroom. She was enveloped in her robe. Her hair fell in heavy, tangled waves around her shoulders. She was still staring at him as if she was not sure she recognized him. A pang of anguish twisted his insides at the realization that she might be regretting last night.

"Clara Dover died," he said, hoping to distract her before the conversation went down a grim, dispiriting, depressing road. "Natural causes."

The tactic worked. Prudence blinked a couple of times and refocused. "That changes things, doesn't it?"

"Yes, it does. It means Rollins is now the last member of the Dover family still standing. He just inherited the company and everything that goes with it."

"After being criticized, belittled, and mostly ignored by his mother all his life," Prudence said with a thoughtful expression.

"Because he lacked psychic talent," Jack concluded.

"So Clara believed. All she seemed to care about was the paranormal sort of talent. But Rollins has worked quietly in the head office of Dover Industries for years. He may not have any paranormal sensitivity, but that doesn't mean he doesn't have the ability to run the company."

"And maybe he got tired of his brother and his mother standing in the way," Jack said.

"Do you think he murdered his own mother last night?" Prudence looked truly shocked.

He sighed. "I hate to disillusion you, but it wouldn't be the first time a child has murdered a parent."

"That's a very unsettling thought."

"It's also a logical possibility. It will be interesting to get the name of Clara Dover's last visitor."

"You don't think her death was a result of her head injury?"

"I think her death is very convenient for Rollins Dover. But first I need a shower and breakfast, and then I have to re-create my Dover crime tree."

He had a plan. It was good to have one. Energized, he strode toward the hallway where Prudence stood. She stepped aside to let him go past, never taking her eyes off him. A chill went through him. Perhaps, in the intimacy of the bedroom, the scars had proven to be too much. Maybe she could no longer look past them. Or maybe she had not been attracted to what she had seen when she had looked beyond the ruins of his face.

He stopped. He had to know if she wished last night had never happened.

"Just say it." The words were acid on his tongue.

"I slept with you," she whispered. "I had sex with you and then I went to sleep."

"I remember. Is that a problem for you?"

"I didn't have a panic attack. Neither did you. We had sex and then we just . . . went to sleep."

"Is that what this is about?" An overwhelming

wave of relief swept over him. It was followed by a surge of outrage. She had put him through some very bad moments for absolutely no good reason. "You're wondering why you didn't have an attack of nerves last night?"

"Well, yes."

He took a step closer to her. Whatever she saw in his eyes evidently alarmed her, because she took a quick step back. But there was no room to run in the confines of the hallway. She came up against the wall.

He planted one hand on the unyielding surface behind her and leaned in a little. "You based your stupid fear of panic attacks on your experience with one man."

"It wasn't a stupid fear. It was based on experience."

"You married the wrong man. You knew it, but you told yourself a fairy tale. You were sure you could make it work, but deep down you realized it was a mistake. Your marriage was doomed from the start. You blamed the wedding night panic attack on your psychic sensitivity. You managed to convince yourself that the reason you couldn't consummate the marriage was because your talent caused you to have delicate nerves. Lady, I've spent the past few days with you, and I can tell you that you don't even know the meaning of *delicate nerves*."

"You don't understand. Julian also had a panic attack. I caused it."

"Sounds like Julian is the one with delicate nerves."

"You've got a lot of nerve lecturing me about delicate nerves. You're the man who convinced himself that his fiancée could not bring herself to marry him because of the scars on his face."

"That's the truth, damn it."

"I don't think so. I think you had a lot to do with the end of your engagement."

"What is that supposed to mean?"

"You said your ability to predict what others will do in certain circumstances has cost you all sorts of relationships. You can't let yourself trust other people because there's a chance they might betray you. Has it occurred to you that an attitude like that can become a self-fulfilling prophecy?"

That stopped him cold. "That's not true."

"Wanna bet? How do you think it makes people feel when they realize you're just standing around watching them, waiting for them to disappoint you?"

"That's not how it is."

She gave him a steely smile. "Maybe yes, maybe no. But the good news for us is that you think you already know the truth about me. I'm a fraud, remember? So you don't have to wait for me to disappoint you. Neither of us is under any illusions about the other. By your own flawless logic, that would seem to indicate we are a perfect couple. At least for now."

"What the hell?"

"Think about it. You don't have to pretend that you believe I've got some actual psychic talent. I, in turn, know that for some reason you are scared to admit to yourself that you might possess something more than very good intuition. You could say we have a unique understanding of each other. Sounds to me like the basis of a great relationship."

"A great relationship?" he echoed.

"For now," she said.

"For now?" He was trying desperately to stay afloat in the riptide of her ridiculous logic. But he was floundering. Badly.

She reached up with one hand and gently patted his scarred face. "Think, Wingate. Use your amazing powers of reason. I'm a professional flirt. You don't trust anyone, so you will never be able to make a commitment. Don't you see? We're a perfect couple. No illusions."

He stared at her, frustrated and outraged. Unable to think of any reasonable verbal response, he resorted to action. He covered her mouth with his own and kissed her with a force that shocked both of them.

She responded immediately, throwing her arms around his neck. The kiss got hotter, wetter, and more intense.

The sound of the doorbell broke the spell. He raised his head, dazed.

"Oh, good," Prudence said. She ducked under his arm and headed toward the door. "That will be our new clothes. I can't wait to see what the hotel management thinks is suitable fashion for a lady conducting an illicit liaison here at the Burning Cove Hotel."

Dumbfounded, he managed to get his mouth closed. He decided he should probably go take a shower. A cold one.

Chapter 33

Hotel management delivered two garment bags and two boxes. The bag marked *P. Ryland* held a fashionable pair of waist-defining trousers in a rich coffee-brown color and a bronze silk blouse detailed with a flowing self-tie at the throat. The accompanying box contained a pair of sporty loafers and some dainty undergarments. There was a note in the box. *Please contact the front desk immediately if you require other sizes or styles. If there are any problems with the fit, the hotel will be happy to send a seamstress to the villa.*

"I could get used to living like this," Prudence said. "I can't wait to see what's in your garment bag."

But there was no response. Jack had already vanished into the bathroom. She could hear the shower running. She took the bag labeled *J. Wingate* and the box into his bedroom and left both on the bed.

By the time she emerged from the bath, showered and dressed in the stylish new outfit, her washed, still-damp hair clipped behind her ears, she was in good spirits. Energized. Invigorated. Jack might be having difficulty coming to terms with what had happened between them last night, but she viewed it as a major turning point in her life, one that had changed her perspective on the future.

The living room was empty. The French doors stood open, allowing the fresh morning air off the sea into the room. Breakfast had arrived while she was in the shower and had been set up on the patio. There was a pot of tea and one of coffee. Jack was at the table, dressed in a crisply pressed shirt and trousers. He had a sheet of paper in front of him and several sharpened pencils. A cup of coffee sat close at hand.

She reminded herself that she was a modern, sophisticated woman, the sort of woman who could engage in an illicit liaison in a glamorous hotel without a second thought. She took a breath, summoned a breezy smile, and went briskly out onto the patio. Jack looked up from the sheet of paper.

"Beautiful day, isn't it?" she said. She sat down and reached for the teapot. "How is the crime tree going? I imagine you have all sorts of new insights to add now."

Jack watched her warily, apparently not sure what to make of her mood. But after a beat he took refuge in the job at hand.

"I contacted the hospital while you were in the shower," he said. "They don't keep logs of visitors, but the nurse on the late-night shift remembered that the

Dover housekeeper came to see Clara after Rollins and Ella had left. Evidently Maud Hollister was in the room for some time. The nurse didn't know for how long or if anyone else went into the room after that, because she got called away to an emergency in another room."

"So Maud Hollister stays on your list of suspects."

"Yes." Jack glanced at the crime tree. "I want to talk to her because no one was more devoted to Clara Dover."

"You want to know why."

"Yes."

Prudence thought about that while she nibbled on a triangle of toast. "The psychic circuit might have some background on that relationship. I can make a few calls after breakfast."

"That would be helpful," Jack said, excruciatingly polite. "Thank you."

Prudence smiled. "You don't have to act like you're walking on eggshells. As you pointed out, I am hardly a delicate flower."

He looked more wary than ever. "I shouldn't have said what I did about your marriage."

"Annulled marriage."

"Right. I shouldn't have said those things about your annulled marriage. It's none of my business."

"Nope. But don't worry. After all, it's clear now that you were right."

He frowned. "I was?"

"Obviously I had a panic attack while attempting to be a proper wife to a man I sensed I shouldn't have married. I developed a phobia about sex. I convinced myself it had something to do with my psychic sensitivity. Last night made it clear that I don't have a nervous disorder after all, at least not when it comes to normal sexual exercise."

"Sexual exercise," he repeated a little too evenly.

"Exactly."

The phone rang. Jack shot to his feet, clearly relieved by the interruption. "I'll get it."

She watched him move into the shadows of the living room, and then she lifted the silver lid that covered the platter of scrambled eggs. She was surprised to discover that she was quite hungry. She usually preferred a light breakfast. Not this morning. Evidently escaping a burning house and having panic-free sex with the most interesting man she had ever met had a marked effect on a woman's appetite.

She was finishing another slice of toast when Jack returned. He no longer looked like a man who was trying to deal with an awkward morning-after conversation. Energy shivered in the atmosphere around him.

"Who was that?" she asked.

"Rollins Dover." Jack reached for the coffeepot. "He and his wife would like to meet with us again. This morning."

"He probably wants to apologize for what happened to your house last night and convince you not to sue or tell the press that his mother was a firebug."

"Yes." Jack poured some coffee and set the pot down. "We are not going to mention that we don't think Clara was alone last night."

"Why not?"

"The first rule in dealing with suspects is to make sure you don't give them any more information than necessary to get them to talk."

She dusted toast crumbs off her hands. "Got it. Speaking of collecting information, I should start making those phone calls to my old colleagues on the San Francisco psychic circuit."

"We want any information on Maud Hollister that goes back to the start of her employment in the Dover household. There must have been a reason for her steadfast loyalty to Clara Dover."

Chapter 34

"Zorana? It's Prudence Ryland. Madame Ariadne. Remember me?"

"Of course I remember you, dear," Zorana said. "It's so good to hear from you. I read all about your new career path in the papers. Congratulations on landing that private consulting job in Burning Cove. We've all been wondering what you've been doing since you left San Francisco."

Zorana had a real name, but she had worked for so long as Zorana, Psychic Guide, that no one used it. Prudence gripped the telephone a little more tightly, aware of a twinge of homesickness. When she had disappeared from San Francisco, she had left long-time friends and a community of psychics—some real, some fake—behind.

"I've been busy," Prudence said.

"Obviously." Zorana chuckled. "How is business? Does the private consulting work pay better than a storefront operation?"

Prudence glanced across the living room. Jack was at the table laboring on his crime tree, but she knew he was listening to every word of her side of the conversation.

"Private consulting has a few drawbacks," she said.

"I can imagine. You're at the beck and call of the same client twenty-four hours a day. Sounds stressful. Is the money significantly better, though?"

"Sadly, there isn't much in the way of actual income," Prudence said. "At least not yet. But all expenses are covered, including wardrobe, travel, and lodging. And here I am in Burning Cove, playground of the stars. The private work is turning out to be more of a free vacation than a long-term career path, so I won't be able to afford to do it for long."

Jack looked up from his crime tree, frowning.

"I understand, dear," Zorana said. "We must be practical about business. A woman on her own in the world needs to consider her future."

"Yes, I know. I've got long-term plans. I'm going to open a bookshop. But in the meantime, I've run into an old client of my grandmother's, Clara Dover, here in Burning Cove."

"A rather difficult client," Zorana said. "Years ago she was one of my regulars. Haven't done a reading for her in over a decade."

"I did a few for her after Grandma died." Prudence hesitated. "The thing is, she died last night. Accidental fall."

"Oh my," Zorana said. "That will certainly send a shudder through the business world here in San Francisco. There was nothing in the morning papers, but I'm sure there will be in the afternoon edition. I expect it will be front-page news. This is a rather astonishing turn of events for Dover Industries. First the eldest son is murdered in a bizarre manner, and now the woman who built the company into what it is today is dead. Was she vacationing in Burning Cove?"

"No. She came here to find me. She thought I had something to do with the murder of her son."

"Nonsense. Why on earth would you kill Gilbert Dover? And even if you did decide to do that, you certainly would not have made such a dramatic mess of things."

"Thanks. I think."

"I suppose this leaves the other Dover boy in charge of the company."

"Yes. And he's not a boy. Rollins Dover and his wife are in town at the moment. But I called because I have some questions about Mrs. Dover's longtime housekeeper, Maud Hollister."

"I remember that poor woman. She often accompanied Clara to the readings."

"*Poor* woman?" Prudence said.

"Not in the financial sense. She has been employed in the Dover household all these years, including during the worst of the bad times. But I always felt sorry for her. She was an unhappy, bitter woman."

"Because she had Clara Dover for an employer?"

"Well, I'm sure that was part of it. It can't have been easy working for that woman all these years. But I was referring to what happened to Hollister in the early days of her employment in the Dover household."

Prudence caught her breath. "What was that?"

"Mind you, the only reason I know the truth is because I did a few readings for Hollister on the side. At reduced fees, of course. I needed more information about Clara Dover, and I knew the best way to get some background was to do a reading for her housekeeper." Zorana paused. "Housekeepers know all the secrets of a household."

"Did Clara know you were consulting for Maud Hollister?"

"No, not unless Maud told her, which I very much doubt. Poor Maud was little more than a girl when she first went into the Dover household. Fourteen or fifteen, I think. That dreadful monster, Copeland Dover, raped her. Got her pregnant. As is so often the case in those situations, Maud was let go immediately."

"Do you know where she went?"

"The East Coast. Clara Dover bought the train ticket for her to make sure she left the city. I believe she gave Maud a little money to see her on her way. A very small sum, I might add. Clara has never been known for her generosity. I don't know how Maud survived financially. It must have been very hard. At any rate, she had the baby and raised him on her own until he was about five or six. At that point she packed him off to boarding school and returned to San Francisco. She was immediately hired back into the Dover household."

"Wait," Prudence said, stunned. "The child went to a boarding school? Don't you mean an orphanage?"

"No, I meant what I said. Someone paid the boy's boarding school fees for years, and I think it's safe to say that individual was Clara Dover."

"Clara is an excellent businesswoman, but as you said, she is not known for her generosity."

"No," Zorana said. "There is only one way to explain why Clara Dover would have paid for a fancy boarding school for her employee's illegitimate son, and it wasn't because she felt sorry for the girl."

"Clara paid for the school because she knew the son was Copeland's?"

"I'm sure she knew, but that would not have made her any more sympathetic. That sort of thing happens a lot. Wealthy men in society rarely acknowledge their illegitimate offspring. Remember, at first Clara just wanted to get Maud as far away as possible. Why do you think she paid for that ticket to the East Coast? I'm sure she forgot about Maud as soon as the girl was out of town."

"So why did Clara pay for boarding school and take Maud Hollister back into the household as an employee?"

"In the course of a reading, Maud let slip that she could *prove* the boy was Copeland's offspring."

"How? All Copeland Dover had to do was deny the child was his. There's no reliable way to prove paternity."

"Maud Hollister told me she could prove the boy was Copeland's because of an unusual birthmark. Evidently all three of Copeland's sons have the same mark, and it is distinctive. That sort of evidence would not have survived in a court of law, but the press here in San Francisco would have run wild with the story."

"So Maud threatened to reveal the truth about her son's parentage and provide proof that could not be disputed if Clara didn't pay for the boy's boarding school education?"

"Yes," Zorana said. "Clara was always keen to avoid scandal. By then she was already running the company, and she was determined to build an empire. She wasn't about to let Copeland's philandering stop her. When he conveniently dropped dead after Maud returned, there was, in fact, a lot of gossip in the psychic community to the effect that Copeland Dover's death was probably not by natural causes."

"What was the speculation?"

"Many of us, including your grandmother, were quite certain that Clara or Maud or both of them working together put something lethal in Copeland Dover's soup the night he died."

"They both had motive," Prudence said, thinking it through. Out of the corner of her eye she saw Jack watching her intently. "Maud probably wanted revenge. Clara wanted her brutal husband out of the way."

"Copeland Dover had a terrible temper. There's no knowing what went on behind closed doors in that house. Clara gave him an impressive funeral, but I doubt very much that she shed a single tear."

Prudence looked at her notes. "All right, I understand that Clara and Maud had an arrangement of some sort. But the child would be an adult by now, and Copeland Dover has been dead for years. It's hard to believe that Clara was still willing to pay for Maud's silence after all this time."

"Clara Dover stopped paying the boy's boarding school fees when he was in high school," Zorana said. A skilled storyteller, she knew how to pause for effect. "Because she had to start paying the other fees instead."

Prudence had been about to make another note. She stopped, the tip of the pencil hovering over the paper. "What other fees?"

"Those charged by a very expensive, very discreet psychiatric hospital. Copeland Dover's illegitimate son had to be committed before he was out of his teens. Gossip on the psychic circuit is that he murdered a roommate at that pricey boarding school."

Understanding slammed through Prudence. "Clara Dover would have paid any price to protect the Dover empire from rumors of insanity in the bloodline."

"Oh, yes," Zorana concluded. "Anyone in her position would have done the same."

"Thank you, Zorana. I appreciate this information."

"I'm glad I could be helpful. Don't be a stranger, dear. Your friends here in the city have missed you."

"I've missed you, too," Prudence said. "Goodbye, Zorana."

"Goodbye, dear. Enjoy your all-expenses-paid vacation in Burning Cove."

"I'll try to do that."

Prudence ended the call and twisted partway around in her chair to look at Jack, who had abandoned his crime tree and was waiting impatiently.

"What?" he said.

"Clara Dover has been paying Maud Hollister for her silence all these years. First because of a birthmark that could prove Maud's illegitimate child was Copeland Dover's son and then because that boy had to be committed. Gossip is, he murdered another boy at the boarding school he was attending. Clara feared that if the word got out, there would be rumors of insanity in the bloodline."

"That would have been a nightmare for Clara Dover. No wonder she allowed herself to be blackmailed."

"Exactly." Prudence tapped her notebook with the pencil. "There's more. Word on the psychic circuit is that Maud and Clara conspired together to poison Copeland Dover."

"Now, that does not surprise me."

Prudence wrinkled her nose. "Of course not. You are the all-seeing consultant. Regardless, it seems to me that Maud Hollister had no motive to murder Clara. That would have put a stop to the payments that kept Maud's son in a private asylum."

Jack looked amused. "You're getting good at this work."

She gave him a breezy smile. "Obviously psychic dream readers, librarians, and investigative consultants have a lot in common."

"Looks like it."

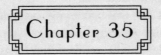

Chapter 35

Rollins and Ella Dover arrived at the hotel a half hour later and were promptly escorted to the villa. Prudence had ordered a fresh tray of coffee and tea from room service. She and Jack were seated on the shady patio with their visitors.

The Dovers looked grim, she thought, but she did not detect any hint of grief or sadness. If anything, there was an aura of relief about the pair, as if they had been able to put aside a heavy weight.

"I cannot begin to apologize for my mother's behavior last night," Rollins said to Jack. He looked and sounded earnest and sincere. "I insist on making financial compensation for the loss of your house."

"That won't be necessary," Jack said. "The house was insured."

Rollins nodded. "I'm relieved to hear that. Still, that

will hardly make up for Clara's actions. All I can tell you is that she was a very ill woman. When Ella and I called on you at your house, we told you that her mental state had deteriorated in recent weeks."

"I remember," Jack said.

"We knew she was becoming unstable but we had no idea she had entirely lost her grip on sanity," Ella said. "After last night, we could no longer ignore the situation. Rollins was making arrangements to have Clara committed for an extended rest cure when the hospital called with the news of her death."

"My condolences," Prudence said.

Ella gave her a weary smile. "Thank you. Under the circumstances, that is very generous. You and Mr. Wingate could have died in that fire last night."

Rollins looked at Jack. "I understand you rescued my mother after she tried to kill herself by jumping off that cliff."

"That's right," Jack said. "But I don't think she was attempting suicide. She was hallucinating, and in the darkness she could not see where she was going. I think the fall was an accident."

"We were told you drove her to the hospital," Ella said. "Thank you."

"Was she conscious?" Rollins asked.

"Part of the time," Jack said.

Rollins's mouth tightened. "Did she say anything coherent?"

Jack glanced at Prudence. It didn't require any psychic mind reading to know he wanted her to answer the question. She was oddly flattered.

"Nothing that made any sense," Prudence said smoothly. "As Jack said, Clara was hallucinating."

"I see." Rollins grimaced. "I suppose she told you Gilbert sent her to the house to witness the fire?"

"Yes," Prudence said.

"That damned Dr. Flood," Rollins muttered. "He's the one who put those ridiculous notions about Gilbert visiting from the Other Side in her head."

"Speaking of your brother," Jack said, "have the authorities made any progress in the investigation of his death?"

Prudence went still. Her mouth was suddenly very dry. She realized she was holding her breath.

"No," Rollins said, oblivious to her reaction. "I'm told the L.A. cops have hit a brick wall."

Ella lowered her cup into her saucer. "Rollins and I were hoping you could clear up a small mystery for us."

"What's that?" Jack asked.

"We can't understand how Clara managed to get to your house," Rollins said. "She doesn't drive."

"Good question," Jack said. "We've wondered about that, too. Do you think she might have ordered her chauffeur to drive her out to my place?"

"No," Ella said. "Henry, her driver, quit yesterday after the spa incident. Evidently he got a job at one of the hotels here in town. He told Mrs. Hollister, the housekeeper, that the pay was better and Burning Cove was a lot more fun than San Francisco."

Rollins grunted. "My mother was notoriously cheap. Seemed to think she was living in the last century when it came to wages."

Jack gave Rollins a considering look. "There are two other people living in the house your mother rented. Dr. Flood and Maud Hollister."

Ella and Rollins exchanged looks.

Rollins looked grim. "Ella and I talked about that. Maud never learned how to drive. But Harley Flood does drive. He could have driven my mother out to House of Shadows in the limo, but why would he do that? He had a very comfortable position as Clara's private doctor. Why risk it by taking a chance on having her arrested for arson and attempted murder?"

"Or on the chance that Clara might be committed?" Prudence added quietly. "Because that's what you were planning to do, isn't it?"

"Yes." Rollins shook his head. "It doesn't look like Flood had a motive. Clara must have called a cab last night. It's the only explanation."

Prudence caught Jack's eye and knew they were both thinking the same thing: Clara had been hallucinating wildly. It was very difficult to imagine her calling a cab and carrying out an obviously premeditated act of arson.

Ella got to her feet and looked at Rollins. "We should be on our way. We've got a long drive ahead of us."

"Right." Rollins stood and checked his watch. "We need to get on the road."

"You're leaving for San Francisco today?" Prudence asked.

"Yes," Ella said. "Rollins wants to return to the city as soon as possible to deal with the press and to re-assure Dover's clients. We packed this morning and made arrangements to have Clara's body transported home by train. The only reason we're still here in Burning Cove is because Rollins wanted to call on you to apologize for Clara's behavior."

"What about Maud Hollister and Dr. Flood?" Jack asked.

"Flood offered to drive Clara's limo back to San Francisco," Rollins said. "I took him up on it. Maud will pack Clara's things and drive home with Flood. And as soon as the car and my mother's personal possessions have been returned to the city, I intend to fire both Flood and Maud."

"Is that right?" Jack looked politely curious. "I know you don't think much of Flood's medical skills, but I was under the impression that Maud Hollister worked for your mother for years."

"She must be devastated by Clara's death," Prudence said quickly. "Everyone says she was devoted to her employer."

"She probably won't be quite so devoted when she discovers that my mother left her out of the will," Rollins said. "And I certainly don't intend to make up for that oversight with a check. I never did like Hollister, and I can assure you she feels the same way about me."

"You're aware of the contents of your mother's will?" Jack asked.

"No, but I know my mother very well," Rollins said. "Trust me, she was not the type to remember staff, no matter how faithful or devoted, in her will. Let's be on our way, Ella."

"Yes, of course," Ella said.

"I'll get the door," Jack said.

He saw Rollins and Ella out of the villa and returned to the patio. Prudence recognized the banked fires in his eyes.

"What are you thinking?" she said.

"I'm thinking that with the Dovers on the way out of town, the devoted housekeeper and the quack doctor will be alone in that rented villa."

"We're going to talk to them?"

"Yes."

"We'll have to have that conversation this afternoon. They will be leaving town tomorrow to drive the limo back to San Francisco and take Clara's things home."

Jack's eyes got a little hotter. "We will definitely talk to them today, but I don't think they will be rushing to leave town tomorrow. They have to know things are not going to go well for them when they finally do return to San Francisco."

"Because they know how Rollins feels about them."

"Yes." Jack looked down at his crime tree. "I've got a theory about Maud Hollister and Harley Flood. I'm curious to see if I'm right."

Chapter 36

"Mr. and Mrs. Dover left for San Francisco this morning," Maud Hollister said. "If you want to file a lawsuit because of what happened last night, you'll have to get in touch with them. I had nothing to do with it."

She stood in the doorway of the villa, blocking the entrance. She was trying hard not to stare at the side of Jack's face, but her eyes kept darting from Prudence to the scars and back again.

Prudence gave her a cool smile. "I'd like to offer you my condolences, Maud. I know you were very close to Clara Dover. But first let me introduce my client, Mr. Wingate. Jack, this is Clara's devoted housekeeper, Mrs. Hollister."

Jack tipped his fedora. "Mrs. Hollister. We would appreciate some of your time. We won't stay long."

"I don't have anything to say to you," Maud said. But she was starting to look uneasy.

"It might interest you to know that the Dovers came to see us at the Burning Cove Hotel on their way out of town," Jack said.

"That's none of my business," Maud said.

"They mentioned you," Prudence said. "And Dr. Flood, as well."

Maud reddened with sudden anger. "Did that bastard Rollins Dover tell you that I had something to do with what Clara did last night? Did he accuse me of helping her set the fire?"

"Not directly," Jack said. "But he does appear to be asking a lot of questions about how Clara got herself and a homemade firebomb all the way out to my place last night. Evidently his mother didn't know how to drive."

"Neither do I." Maud clutched the edge of the door. "I don't know anything about last night."

A man loomed in the shadows of the hallway. "What's going on here?"

"Mr. Wingate and Ms. Ryland want to talk to me," Maud said, her voice wooden.

"You must be Flood," Jack said.

Harley studied Jack's scars for a beat and then snorted. "It was your house Clara burned down last night. Rollins said you had a face that looked like it had been through a meat grinder."

Jack did not respond. He looked bored.

Prudence smiled. "Such elegant manners, Dr. Flood. Your mother must be so proud."

Maud drew a sharp, startled breath. She twisted one hand in her apron and stared at Prudence.

"Well, that settles one question," Prudence said to Jack. "Mrs. Hollister is Harley Flood's mother, just as your crime tree predicted."

"That means Dr. Flood is Copeland Dover's third son," Jack said, satisfied with his logic.

Maud's mouth fell open in shock. "How did you find out?"

"Mr. Wingate is very good at that sort of thing," Prudence said.

"It was the only conclusion that made sense," Jack said. "Why else would you let someone besides yourself get so close to Clara Dover?"

Harley's eyes narrowed with speculation. "You're Madame Ariadne, the psychic Clara wanted Gilbert the Golden to marry. According to the press, you give very interesting private readings. Have any more clients dropped dead since San Francisco?"

Prudence realized that Jack no longer appeared bored. He had gone dangerously still.

"I prefer to be called Miss Ryland," she said quickly, trying to take control of the situation.

Harley grunted. "Let them in, Maud."

Maud hesitated. "I don't think that's a good idea."

Harley looked as if he couldn't care less about her opinion. "I'm curious about why they felt the need to drive out here to see us," he said.

"You don't want to have this conversation on the front steps, Mrs. Hollister," Jack said. "Trust me."

"He's right," Harley said. "This will be interesting."

Without a word, Maud stepped back. Prudence moved into the hall. Jack followed. Harley led the way into the front room. Most of the curtains were closed, drenching the space in shadows.

Maud sat down slowly, moving in a stiff, awkward manner that made it clear she was not accustomed to sitting in a room that was generally reserved for the owners of a house and their guests.

Prudence took a chair across from her. Maud glared, her lips tightly pressed together.

Harley went to the drinks cabinet and picked up a bottle. "How about a glass of my half brother's excellent whiskey, Wingate?"

"No, thanks," Jack said. He did not sit down. "Does Rollins know you're his half brother?"

"Not yet. I'm sure he knows that good old Dad got Maud pregnant and that she disappeared to have the baby. I wouldn't be surprised if he knows that Clara paid for the bastard to be locked up in a private boarding school for *troubled youth* until the boy was in his teens. I don't know if he's aware that his mother paid even more money to have that young man locked up in a *fucking asylum for the insane at the age of thirteen.*"

Harley hurled the glass containing his unfinished whiskey against the wall. No one moved. Prudence watched, shocked in spite of herself, as the shards cascaded to the floor. She was aware that Maud appeared both frightened and anguished. The only one who seemed unfazed was Jack. *He probably saw that coming,* she thought.

Harley took a couple of deep breaths and then

poured himself another glass of whiskey as if nothing had happened. "I'm not insane. That's what made it all so intolerable, you see." He glared at Maud. "I was perfectly sane, but my mother had me locked up at the age of five, first in that school and then in the asylum."

"Looks like you escaped from the asylum a few months ago," Jack said.

"Yes." Harley snorted and gulped some of the whiskey. "Naturally the first thing I did was set out to find my long-lost mother. After all, I needed to give her a change of address so that she could send the money to me instead of the asylum. My time in the hospital was not entirely wasted. The institution was very modern. The doctors there are running all sorts of experiments with new medications for those afflicted with nervous disorders. I was one of their research subjects. When I left, I took several vials of the latest drug with me."

"That's what you used on Clara Dover," Prudence said. "You drugged her and then hypnotized her into thinking she was having visions."

"It was an amusing game. She wanted so desperately to believe she had astonishing psychic powers. The more I assured her that she did, indeed, possess paranormal talent, the more she trusted me." Harley winked. "And the more money she paid for my services. I started blackmailing her anonymously on the side, and that doubled my income. All in all, it's been a profitable venture."

"When are you going to inform Rollins that you are his half brother?" Prudence said.

It was Maud who responded. "After Clara's will is read," she said, very fierce now. "That's when I find out if she kept her word or if she lied to me."

Jack looked at her. "Clara promised to put Flood in her will?"

"We made a bargain all those years ago. She promised to see to it that my son would be looked after financially for the rest of his life if I kept the secret."

"She wasn't threatened by gossip about her husband having fathered an illegitimate child," Prudence said. "But she was terrified that word would get out that the boy had to be locked up at an early age because of mental instability."

"I had proof that Harley was Copeland Dover's son," Maud said. She clenched her hands into fists. "She knew she could not deny it."

Harley chuckled. "I have a very distinctive birthmark on my upper chest. Care to see it?" He started to unbutton the collar of his shirt.

"Don't bother," Prudence said quickly.

Harley laughed and shrugged. "Suit yourself."

"Gilbert and Rollins have the same mark," Maud said. "I watched them grow up. I saw them in swimming trunks many times. I saw the same mark on their monster of a father when he raped me. When I told Clara that I could prove beyond a shadow of a doubt that my son was her husband's child, she agreed to pay, first for that fancy boarding school and then for the asylum."

"But now she's dead," Jack said. "That's going to be

a problem for you if it turns out she didn't put Harley into her will."

"She promised," Maud hissed. "She swore to me Harley would always be taken care of. She knew I would destroy the Dovers and their business by telling the truth about the tainted bloodline."

"Shut up, Maud," Harley screeched. "You stupid woman. The bloodline isn't tainted. There is nothing wrong with me. I'm a sane man who was falsely imprisoned in that asylum. I never murdered anyone. It was an accident."

"What did happen to your roommate at boarding school?" Jack asked.

Harley made a visible effort and managed to get his temper under control, but Prudence could feel the currents of volatile energy sparking in the atmosphere. She knew Jack was aware of them, too. Harley Flood was a dangerously unstable man. There was fear in Maud's eyes as she watched her son.

"Harley," she said quietly.

He ignored her. Harley was fixated on Jack now.

"It was a fucking accident," he said. "He fell off the dock and drowned. But the school authorities claimed I slammed a rock against his head and pushed him into the water. They were looking for an excuse to kick me out. You're starting to bore me, Wingate."

Maud gave him another desperate, fearful look. "Harley, that's enough."

Jack ignored Harley. He studied Maud. "According to the hospital, you went to see Clara last night. Was she alive when you left her?"

"Yes." Maud was suddenly consumed with an anguished rage. She came up out of the chair with a jerky, panicky movement. "I didn't kill her. Why would I want her dead? I wanted her to suffer. I had just found out Rollins was finally getting ready to have her committed. I was thrilled. She was going to spend the rest of her life locked up in an asylum for the insane. I could not have wished for a more perfect revenge."

Prudence could have sworn that an electrified stillness had settled on the room. Jack, however, either was unaware of the strange tension or else he did not give a damn. She suspected the latter.

"Thank you for confirming my conclusions, Mrs. Hollister," he said. "I knew this was about revenge. I understand most of it now."

Harley scowled. "What exactly do you think you understand?"

"You and Maud intended to punish the Dovers and make them pay for what was done to Maud all those years ago. You both wanted to see Clara Dover locked up in an asylum, and you both wanted to force the family to give you what you considered your share of Dover Industries. But things went wrong last night, because Clara is dead. She won't be spending the rest of her life in an asylum. The only thing you can hope for now is that she did put you into her will. If I were you, I wouldn't hold my breath."

"Get out of here," Harley screamed.

"The only question left is, who murdered Clara Dover last night?"

"I didn't kill her," Harley roared. "Why would I do that? I was having too much fun playing games with her, making her believe she was getting visits from her precious Gilbert. I wanted her to get committed, too. She deserved to know what I went through all those years, first in that fucking school and then in an asylum."

Jack looked at Prudence. She got the message. She was already on her feet. She headed for the door, aware that Jack was following her. A shiver went through her when she realized he was covering her to make sure she made it safely outside.

Neither of them spoke until they were in the car.

"I believe Maud," Prudence said. "I think she did want Clara Dover to live and be sent away to an asylum."

"I agree," Jack said. He started the car, put it in gear, and drove toward the main road. "And that's probably what Harley Flood wanted, too. But he is a very volatile man. He's capable of long-range planning, but he can't control his temper."

"Do you think he is insane?"

"Not in the medical sense of the word. But he has an explosive temper and very little impulse control."

"Which describes most of the other men in the Dover family," Prudence said. "The exception being Rollins. I have a feeling that if it hadn't been for the Dover money and social status, Copeland and Gilbert would probably have wound up in prison. Sounds like the only reason Harley didn't get arrested for the murder of his roommate when he was a teen was because

Clara Dover was able to make him disappear into an asylum."

"I think it's time to examine the crime scene."

"Which crime scene?"

"House of Shadows."

Chapter 37

The house was no longer smoldering, but it had collapsed in on itself and was now in ruins. *Just like Cordell Bonner's lab,* Jack thought. He forced himself to push the memories back into the hellhole where they belonged.

"What do you want to bet my insurance policy contains a clause that says the company doesn't have to pay off if the fire was caused by arson," he said.

Prudence glanced at him. "When did you become a betting man?"

They were standing in the driveway, studying what was left of the big house. The water that had been poured on the blaze had soaked what little the fire had not destroyed.

"Once in a while I'll bet on a sure thing," he said. "Trust me, the policy will exclude arson."

"You're probably right," Prudence said. "So why didn't you take Dover up on his offer to reimburse you for damages?"

"Because he was trying to buy me off. That irritated me."

"I understand," she said.

"I never did like this house."

"You mentioned that. Do you want my advice?"

"I don't know," he said. "Depends on the advice."

"I think you should look at the positive side of this situation."

"There's a positive side?"

"Yes." She waved a hand at the ruins. "Think of this as giving you a clean slate. A fresh start. I know you didn't like the house, but you do like the property. The view is amazing. You've got a beach you can walk every day. There's plenty of privacy, but you're close enough to Burning Cove to take advantage of the library, the restaurants, the theater, and the shops. This is the California coast. Land of the future. Property values will only go up."

"Have you considered a career in real estate sales?"

"I'm serious, Jack." She raised a hand to keep her hair from blowing into her eyes. "You have to live somewhere. You'll never find a finer piece of real estate. You are now free to build the house of your dreams."

"I don't think I have a house of my dreams."

"Sure you do. Everyone does. You just haven't given the problem serious thought."

"Maybe because I just had my other house—the

one I didn't like—burn down. I'm still focused on that one."

"Okay, good point," she said. "You need time. But don't do anything rash like sell the property until you've had a chance to think over the possibilities. Time to focus on the future, Jack."

"Sure, I'll get right on that. After I figure out who tried to frame you for murder."

Prudence let out a long breath. "Okay. I agree we do have other priorities at the moment."

He surveyed the ruins. "I've got a rough outline of what happened here, but I need to fill in a few details."

"How are you going to do that?"

"Observation," he said. "No psychic insight involved."

"Uh-huh."

He ignored that and started walking around the perimeter of the burned-out house, studying the remains from various angles.

"It looks like some of the pots and pans survived," Prudence said when they went past what was left of the kitchen. "I think you could scrub off the soot."

"I don't need cookware that badly," Jack said.

They continued on around to what had once been the living room.

"I don't see anything there that is worth salvaging," Prudence said.

"No loss," Jack said.

He kept walking but stopped when they got to what had been a window in the library.

Prudence winced. "Unfortunately, books burn much too easily."

He contemplated the ruins of the library-office. The desk was a charred hulk. There was a large lump of blackened metal sitting on what was left of his typing table.

"I'll be needing a new typewriter," he said.

"Definitely." Prudence peered more closely through the empty window at the ash-covered items scattered on the floor. "Oh, look. I think your lovely paperweight survived."

He glanced at the rounded object covered in soot and ash on the floor. "I won't be needing a paperweight for a while."

"It's a very nice piece of crystal." She started to lean forward. "I might be able to reach it."

"Stop." He wrapped a hand around her upper arm and hauled her upright. "You can't reach it, and you're not going to walk into those ashes. The floorboards might give way. There could still be hot spots."

"You're right. I don't know what I was thinking."

He heard the chimes that told him he was missing something important. "You like crystal, don't you?"

"Yes." She hesitated and then made a small dismissive motion with one hand. "That paperweight is a rather nice piece, but it's not worth the risk of trying to retrieve it."

She could not reach it, but he might be able to if he had a tool.

"Stay here," he said. "I'll be right back."

"Where are you going?"

"To get the lug wrench out of the trunk of my car. I can use it to reach the paperweight."

He went around the house, retrieved the lug wrench, and returned to the empty window. He crouched, leaned forward a little, and managed to use the end of the wrench to propel the crystal through the soggy muck all the way out of the library and onto the ground.

Prudence started to pounce on it with a flimsy little handkerchief she had taken out of the pocket of her trousers.

"Wait," he said. "You'll need something larger."

He reached inside his jacket and produced a square of neatly folded white linen. She took it from him and used it to wrap the grime-covered crystal ball. He thought she looked ridiculously pleased. It was just a paperweight. Yes, it was a nice paperweight. But still.

"This is interesting," she said. She closed one hand around the fabric-wrapped paperweight. "It feels a little different. I wonder if the fire changed the energy in it. Fire is a very elemental force."

"Is that how psychics talk?" he asked.

She gave him a breezy smile. "Yep. Get used to it."

He got lost in her eyes for a second, and while he was sinking beneath the surface, he allowed himself a flash of a daydream, one that envisioned a future with Prudence in his life.

"I could do that," he said softly.

She blinked, breaking the small spell, and then gave him one of her overbright smiles. "I'll wash off your paperweight when we get back to the hotel."

"It's yours now," he said.

He turned back to the scene of the library and started cataloging more details and impressions. He infused them with his memories, building the picture in his mind. The sound of shattering glass. The smell of gasoline. The direction of the breeze off the ocean. The way the smoke had unfurled on the ground floor. The burn pattern. The firestorm that had followed.

And he listened to the chimes.

"The incendiary device was thrown through this window," he said, indicating a spot on what was left of the floor.

"How can you be sure?"

"The burn patterns. Fire behaves a lot like a storm. So we know the arsonist stood here. After that, he ran back to the main road, where he left the car."

"But we found Clara Dover on the other side of the house," Prudence said.

"Yes, we did," Jack said softly. "She certainly did not throw the device. The arsonist left her on the other side of the house, and then he came around to this side to throw the firebomb. He was running back to the car while you and I were on our way down the rear stairs."

"Still think Harley is the arsonist?"

"Yes, but we'll never be able to prove it. The question is, did he murder Clara in the hospital?"

"He said he wanted her to suffer in an asylum."

"I'm sure that's true, but he had to worry about what she might remember and what she could tell the police. And then there is his lack of impulse control. He would have been very excited by the fire. Euphoric, probably. And we know he hated Clara Dover."

"She would have been helpless in that hospital bed."

"Yes. I've seen enough. Let's go."

They walked back to the Packard. He got behind the wheel and started to turn on the ignition. But something made him pause. He studied the charred wreckage of House of Shadows, and then he looked out at the view of the sparkling Pacific.

"You're right," he said. "It's a beautiful property."

"Yes, it is," Prudence said.

She could have put the wrapped paperweight on the seat beside her or on the floor of the car. But she held it in both hands all the way back to the Burning Cove Hotel.

He spent the time connecting dots.

"I've got a plan," he said as he turned in to the long palm-lined driveway that led to the entrance of the hotel.

Prudence smiled faintly. "That does not come as a huge surprise. What is it?"

He glanced at the scrum of photographers hanging around the front of the hotel. Management had a strict policy when it came to the press—reporters and photographers were not allowed onto the grounds without special approval, but they were free to roam around outside. Several cameras were already being aimed at the convertible. The arson at House of Shadows was front-page news in town.

"I'll tell you when we get back in the villa," he said.

He waited until they were alone before he explained the scene he intended to stage.

"I don't like your plan," Prudence said when he had finished.

"I had a feeling you were going to say that."

Chapter 38

"Assuming your plan for tonight works, what happens next?" Prudence asked. She folded her arms and began to pace the front room of the villa, imagining all that could go wrong. Unfortunately, she reminded herself, she had a very vivid imagination.

"After that, we stay out of the line of fire," Jack said. He sank down onto the couch. "We're going to keep our heads down until we see who is still standing when the shooting stops."

She tensed. "Shooting?"

"Metaphorically speaking. I hope."

She threw him a stern glare as she went past the sofa. "That is not amusing."

"Right."

She stopped at the table to study the latest edition of the crime tree.

"Rollins Dover will be the last one standing, won't he?" she asked.

"There's a high probability of that, yes," Jack said.

She shuddered. "It means he murdered his own brother."

"I refer you to the story of Cain and Abel."

"It will be interesting to find out what is in Clara's will."

"We'll know soon. But from our point of view, this case is about finding the individual who kidnapped you and tried to frame you for Gilbert Dover's murder."

"Rollins Dover," Prudence said quietly.

"He certainly had motive for killing both his brother and his mother."

"Yes, but why the elaborately staged scene in the honeymoon suite? Why choose me to play the part of the Killer Bride?"

"Revenge. In addition to getting his brother out of the way, Dover wanted to punish Clara. She had spent years making certain he knew he was not the anointed heir to the throne. What better revenge than to humiliate her by making sure the bride she had hand-picked for Gilbert turned out to be the one who murdered him?"

Prudence reached the end of the room, stopped, and turned around. "You don't think Harley Flood was the person who kidnapped me and murdered Gilbert? He's obviously obsessed with revenge."

"It would be convenient to make him the killer, but I'm very sure now that he didn't do it."

"Why?"

"There was too much planning involved. Too many details. Harley Flood is driven by his mood and by impulse. He could pretend to be Clara Dover's nerve doctor for a few weeks because he enjoyed playing the game. But in the end, he acted impulsively by burning down my house in an attempt to kill you and have Clara blamed for the act of arson. It was sloppy work. The individual who murdered Gilbert possesses a very different temperament. He is someone who was able to wait patiently in the wings for years before trying to take control of Dover Industries."

"Rollins Dover."

Jack laced his fingers behind his head and leaned back against the couch cushions. "The only real question is, why did he wait as long as he did?"

"Because it took that long to work up the nerve to take the huge risk of murdering two members of his own family?"

"Yes." Jack contemplated the ceiling. "But why now?"

"Something pushed him over the edge. Is that what you're saying?"

"Some*one*, not some*thing*," Jack said. "Several months ago, the possibility that you would marry Gilbert set him in motion. He used Tapson to try to get rid of you. That failed, but you disappeared, so he assumed the situation was back under control, at least for a time. But then Harley Flood came on the scene, and things got complicated again. He knew Clara was falling under Flood's influence. She was becoming unpredictable. He had no idea what she would do. He could no longer bide his time, waiting for an opportunity. He decided he had to act."

"It all fits, doesn't it?"

"Yes," Jack said. "But Flood is a wild card."

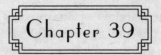

Chapter 39

"Do you collect crystal?" Jack asked.

Prudence took a bite of her pan-fried fish and put down her fork. Absently, she touched the pendant around her neck and got a speculative look. He knew she was trying to decide how much to tell him.

"Not exactly," she said.

She was doing it again, he thought. She wasn't lying to him, but she wasn't telling him the whole truth. He reminded himself that he had no right to dig into her personal life unless he believed it had some relevance to the case. Still, he could not resist probing just a little.

He glanced at the crystal paperweight on the coffee table. "You're attracted to it, aren't you?"

"Certain pieces interest me." Her hand fell away

from the pendant. "Your paperweight is a particularly intriguing piece. It feels old."

"It *feels* old?"

"Where did you get it?" she asked.

Another question neatly avoided, he thought. "I saw it in the window of an antiques shop a few months ago. I needed a paperweight. It looked like it would do the job. It wasn't very expensive. I bought it. There. I answered your question. How about answering mine? Why do you find crystal so intriguing?"

She smiled a slow, teasing smile. "Surely you know that psychics like to use crystal balls."

"No, psychics aren't known for employing crystal balls. Carnival fortune tellers like to impress their clients with crystal balls."

"Semantics."

"It's not semantics," he said. "You made it clear you were never in the business of telling fortunes or reading palms. Your specialty is interpreting dreams."

"I'm no longer in that profession, remember?"

"But it was your former career as a psychic that made you the target of a killer. I need to know more about that aspect of your life."

She hesitated, and then she eased her plate aside and propped her elbows on the table. She linked her fingers, rested her chin on them, and watched him with her riveting eyes.

"I come from a long line of women who made their living as psychic dream readers. We have a tradition of using crystal because it enhances the interpretation process."

"Do you really believe that?"

"Yes," she said. She narrowed her eyes a little. "I believe it because I've experienced it. Crystal makes it easier to focus psychic energy. That results in sharper, clearer readings."

She wasn't trying to fool him, he decided. She believed what she was saying. The last thing he wanted was an argument about the metaphysics of the paranormal. He had enough problems just trying to keep her safe.

"Okay," he said.

Now she looked amused. "Okay?"

"It's an interesting theory," he allowed.

She laughed. "Which you are not buying."

A thought occurred to him. "Can you do your dream readings without crystal?"

"Yes, but to get the same sharp focus, I have to have physical contact with the client." She gave a visible shudder. "I don't like doing that. It's much more disturbing than a crystal connection."

"Too intimate?"

"Yes. And too dangerous."

"For you or for the client?

"I think it depends on which one is stronger," she said quietly.

"You *think*?"

"It's not like I've had many opportunities to practice." She gave him a cool smile. "I told you, when I was in the business of reading dreams, I usually cheated."

"How does a dream reader cheat?" he asked, once again fascinated by the endless mystery of Prudence Ryland.

"I just asked people to tell me their dreams. That process can be excruciatingly boring, but it's not painful, not like making a true psychic connection. Frankly, there was rarely any point subjecting myself to the real thing, because the interpretations often fell into one of a handful of standard categories." She paused and gave him a wicked smile. "It was a lot like identifying, sorting, and labeling criminals using the Wingate Crime Tree method."

"What are the categories?" he asked, refusing to be sidetracked.

"In my experience, dreams frequently indicate that the dreamer is under some form of stress or worry. There are also dreams in which we try to rewrite the past. Dreams that involve sexual fantasies. Dreams that are absolutely meaningless."

He watched her carefully. "I've heard people claim that their intuition speaks to them in their dreams. They say they have awakened with answers to problems that haunted them."

"That's true." Prudence gave him a knowing smile. "But you don't believe in that sort of dreaming, do you? It would imply that our dreams allow us a form of perception that is not available to us with our normal senses. Horror of horrors, it might indicate a possible psychic sensitivity."

Jack considered that briefly and shook his head. "No, it would indicate a form of intuition."

"Haven't we already decided the border between intuition and psychic sensitivity is impossible to define?"

"Pru—"

He stopped because he did not know what to say, how to explain, where to begin.

Prudence watched him. Her eyes got deeper, more mysterious. She appeared to come to a decision. She straightened in her chair, lowered her arms, and stretched one hand across the table.

He hesitated because he suddenly knew what was going to happen next.

"I don't think this is a good idea," he said.

"You have a recurring dream that bothers you, don't you?"

"How did you—?"

"I've done a lot of dream readings. I know when clients are struggling with a nightmare. You want answers. I might be able to give them to you."

"That's what I'm afraid of," he said.

"The dream will probably plague you endlessly unless you find a way to understand it."

She was right. There might not be any answers in the mirror dream, but he had to know that for certain.

He reached for her hand. She threaded her fingers through his.

"Tell me your dream, Jack," she said.

Chapter 40

He tightened his grip on her fingers and started talking before he could change his mind.

"The dream always starts the same way," he said. "I'm in Cordell Bonner's lab. It's the moment after the explosion. There is a fire. It is spreading rapidly. I have just freed the two homeless men Bonner was using as subjects for his experiments. They run from the building. There's another explosion. Chemicals. Glass." He reached up with his fingertips to touch the side of his face and then lowered his hand.

"Is that how you got the scars?" Prudence asked. "An explosion of chemicals and glass?"

"Yes. I know I should run. Follow the two men I just set free. But I can't."

He paused because a shiver of intense awareness arced through his senses. He saw that Prudence was touching her pendant. He could have sworn the crystal was starting to glow. *A trick of the light.*

"Why can't you follow those two men out of the burning lab?" Prudence asked.

"The notebooks. I turn and go back for Bonner's notebooks. But it's too late. The fire is too intense now. In the end I give up and try to escape. In reality that is what I did. But in my dream there is always a mirror blocking my path."

"Was there a mirror in Cordell Bonner's lab?"

"No. Only in my dream. I know it's the only way out for me, but there are flames in the mirror, too. I can see a figure concealed in the fire on the other side of the glass. I can't tell if it's a man or a monster, but I know I have to identify him before I can escape. I can't make him out, though, so I'm trapped. That's the point at which I wake up."

He stopped talking. Prudence sat silently for a time, and then she released his hand.

"Well?" he said. He tried to sound casual, merely curious. He was pretty sure he failed.

"You go back for the notebooks," she said, "but it's too late. You can't get to them because of the fire. Then, when you give up and try to escape, the mirror blocks your path. You are trapped unless you identify the figure in the mirror."

"Yes. Well?"

"What do you normally see when you look directly into a mirror?"

"My reflection."

"Exactly," Prudence said.

"I don't understand."

"It's a mirror, Jack. That means you are seeing yourself, but you aren't sure it's a version of you that you want to see. Maybe it's a version that will scare you."

"Because I don't want to look at my scars?"

"No, because you don't want to acknowledge that something might have happened to you that day in Cordell Bonner's lab because of the explosion of those chemicals. You knew you had been exposed to whatever he was concocting in his lab. That's why you went back for the notebooks. You wanted to know what you had been hit with, but it was too late. You had no choice but to leave without the answers. You escaped. But one morning you woke up knowing something had changed."

He groaned. "You really are good at this dream reading business."

"What did change?"

"I see things differently now when I look at a crime scene. Details I would not have noticed before. And it's not just crime scenes. I find myself jumping ahead to conclusions about people and situations without making sure the facts add up."

Prudence smiled. "Welcome to the sixth sense club. Obviously you had some talent before you went into that lab, but now your sensitivity is even more acute."

He could not take his eyes off her now. "Maybe."

"Deep down you're afraid that whatever chemicals were released in the explosion and the fire in that lab might have opened a pathway to your psychic senses. And that's why you resist trying to identify the man in the mirror. You know that man is you, and you are afraid you are not the same man you were before the Cordell Bonner case."

He stopped breathing for a beat. "That's a little far-fetched."

"I don't think so. I'm certainly not infallible, but in your case I think I've got a clear read. My analysis provides the answer to a question I've had about you from the very beginning."

"You now know how I got the scars?"

"No. It explains why you agreed to consult on my case." She poured a cup of coffee for him and reached for the teapot. "Luther Pell said he assigned you to the investigation primarily because you had taken an interest in my situation. He seemed to think that was a rare and amazing thing."

"That's an overstatement."

She poured tea for herself. "Regardless, now I know why you took me on as a client." She set the pot down and picked up her cup. "You need to know if you've developed some genuine paranormal talent or if you're becoming delusional, maybe going insane. You took my case because you hoped I could give you the answer."

He watched her for a long moment, allowing himself to acknowledge the truth. "How did you come to that conclusion?"

"Simple." She took a sip of tea and lowered the cup. "You went back for Bonner's notebooks. On the surface, that appears to have been a reckless, even foolish decision. The lab was on fire. You had rescued the two men Bonner had imprisoned. Glass vials and beakers were no doubt exploding, sending unknown chemicals into the atmosphere. You should have been running for your life. Instead, you tried to retrieve the notebooks."

He was silent for a moment, and then he nodded. "You're right. I didn't know what Bonner was working on in his lab but did know that two of his other so-called research subjects went mad and died by their own hands."

"And after you recovered from your injuries, you realized you were changing. You wondered if you were becoming insane. No wonder you started having nightmares."

"I definitely see some things in a different light now," he said.

"Do you want the opinion of a possibly fake psychic dream reader who is known to cheat on occasion?"

"Yes," he said.

"Here's what I think is going on," Prudence said. "You always had a whisper of psychic talent, but you told yourself you possessed acute powers of observation and a logical mind. After the explosion in Bonner's lab, your abilities became even sharper, and that worried you. Maybe you did have some psychic ability or maybe you were becoming delusional. If you were delusional, you might be doomed, just as those poor research subjects were."

"I've figured that much out for myself. Just tell me what you think is happening to me."

She smiled her mysterious smile. "I could remind you yet again that the dividing line between intuition and psychic sensitivity is very murky. And that would be true."

"Or?"

"Or I could tell you another truth. I was raised in a family of genuine psychics, and in the course of my former career, I met a lot of frauds. I can tell the difference. Your new talents for observation and deduction are at least a couple of steps beyond ordinary intuition, and deep down you know it. The longer you refuse to acknowledge that simple fact, the more miserable and depressed you will become. The choice is yours, but you are not delusional."

"You're sure?"

"Yep."

He thought about that for a moment. "I told myself I was consumed by my work, but I think I have spent a lot of time being miserable and depressed."

"Yep."

He was shaken by the sense of relief that came over him. It was as if he had been walking through a dark cave and had finally found the way out into the sunlight.

He smiled. "In my own defense, I would like to point out that I was not miserable and depressed after we slept together last night."

She looked startled, and then her eyes got warmer and deeper. "Are you certain?"

"Positive."

"I'm glad. As you know, I did not have a panic attack."

"Sounds like a solid basis for a relationship."

"Yes, it does."

He wanted to get to his feet, walk around the table, pull her up out of the chair, and kiss her, but he suddenly remembered to check the time.

"It's going on eight o'clock," he said. "We need to get dressed for our evening at the Paradise Club." The new evening gown and a tuxedo had been delivered late that afternoon by the hotel's housekeeping department.

She winced. "I really don't like this plan."

"Trust me, it's got a very high probability of working."

Chapter 41

The waiting was always the hard part.

Jack was standing in the deep shadows behind the large padded reading chair in the darkened living room when the front door of the villa opened. The lights had been turned off earlier when he and Prudence had left to take a cab to the Paradise. Prudence was there now, safe in the hands of the club's excellent security personnel. He had returned to the hotel an hour ago and reentered the grounds via the service entrance.

The door widened, allowing the weak glow of the outside lights to slant through the opening. A figure moved through the entrance and was briefly silhouetted. A man.

The intruder shut the door and switched on a flashlight. There was a nervy excitement about his movements. The flashlight beam swept back and forth in frantic, jerky arcs, searching the shadows. Jack crouched behind the big reading chair.

The light landed on the drinks cart and abruptly stopped.

The intruder moved quickly across the room, stopped at the cart, and set the flashlight down so that the bottles and decanters were illuminated. Jack watched around the edge of the chair as the man reached inside his dinner jacket, took out a small bottle, and started to remove the cap.

Jack stood and switched on the floor lamp. "I was sure you would use poison, Flood. Something of a family tradition, isn't it? Odds are your father died that way."

Harley Flood whirled around and stared at Jack. The nervy excitement that had energized the atmosphere around him a moment ago blossomed into something very close to panic. But he relaxed when he saw that Jack was not holding a pistol.

"I realized this afternoon that you were going to be a problem, Wingate," Harley said.

"So you figured you'd get rid of me by dumping poison into the liquor bottles here in my room."

Harley put his hand back under his jacket and took out a pistol. Holding the weapon infused him with confidence. "I knew there would be a drinks cart in here. The Burning Cove Hotel is a classy establishment."

"Did you use that stuff to poison Clara Dover in the hospital?"

"No. I told you, I didn't want the old bitch dead. I

wanted her to end up in an insane asylum. I wanted her to go through what I did all those years. I wanted her to pay."

"Clara was hallucinating the night she showed up at my house."

Harley grimaced. "I used one of the drugs they gave us at the asylum. It makes people hallucinate. They'll see whatever you tell them to see. Believe anything you want them to believe."

"You made Clara believe her dead son was communicating with her from the Other Side."

"It was almost too easy to fool her. Everyone thought she was so smart. So sharp. A brilliant businesswoman. Maybe she was. She certainly built Dover Industries into an empire. But when it came to Gilbert, she was remarkably gullible."

"You didn't murder Gilbert Dover, either, did you?"

"No. I heard the scene in that honeymoon suite was a real mess. If I'd gotten rid of Golden Boy, I would have done it with this stuff." Harley motioned toward the bottle he had put on the drinks cart. "It's the same poison Maud and Clara used on dear old dad. It doesn't leave a mess. The results look like a heart attack."

"A gun is going to make another mess," Jack said.

"Unfortunately, you haven't left me any choice."

"How are you going to explain shooting me in my own hotel room?"

"I won't have to explain anything. There's a genuine Maxim Silencer on this pistol. Cost me a couple hundred bucks, thanks to the damned National Firearms Act tax, but worth it. By the time someone finds your body, I will be nowhere near this hotel. My alibi is solid."

"Because Maud Hollister will swear you were with her at the house on Sundown Point? That won't work, Flood. Hotel security saw you come in tonight. You were not stopped because management instructed the staff to be helpful. That's why it was so easy to find the right villa. I knew you would show up here."

"You're lying." Harley's voice quivered with rage.

Jack spread his hands. "Why the hell do you think I was waiting for you?"

"Shut up."

"You are very predictable," Jack said.

Harley jabbed the gun at him. "I said shut your mouth."

There was movement in the hallway that led to the bedrooms. Luther spoke from the shadows.

"Drop the gun, Flood," he said.

Harley, already unnerved, flinched and swung around to confront the threat, simultaneously pulling the trigger in a frantic, reflexive motion. The sound of the shot was muffled but not actually silenced. A bullet punched a wall.

"Shit," Luther muttered.

Harley tried to line up another shot.

Jack had already grabbed the crystal paperweight. He launched it at Harley. The small missile slammed into Flood's chest with enough force to make him grunt and stagger back, off-balance. He dropped the pistol. It rang on the tile floor.

Luther moved out of the hallway. "Hands behind your head, Flood."

Flood lurched back another step and came up against the drinks cart.

Luther started across the room, bending down to retrieve the gun.

"Stop him," Jack shouted, heading across the room toward Harley.

But he was too late. Harley had seized the small bottle of poison. He swallowed the contents in a single gulp.

"I'm not going back to that fucking asylum," he whispered.

Jack stopped several steps away. Luther straightened, the recovered pistol in his hand. Together they watched Harley convulse and collapse to the floor.

"Never going back," Harley gasped.

In the next moment it was over. He lay, unmoving, on the floor.

Luther opened one side of his jacket and inserted his pistol into the shoulder holster. He looked at Jack, brows slightly elevated. "Now what?"

Jack studied the dead man for a moment, mentally slotting more puzzle pieces into place.

"This isn't over yet," he said.

Luther eyed him. "What happens next?"

"There is a high probability that Rollins Dover will return to Burning Cove as soon as he gets the news of Flood's death."

"Because he will realize there's no one left to drive his mother's limo back to San Francisco?"

"No. There are other ways the car could be managed. Dover will return because he'll realize that Maud Hollister is about to become a serious problem."

"Think he'll try to buy Hollister's silence?"

Jack listened to the chimes clashing gently somewhere in the ether.

"No," he said. "Dover will try to kill her."

Chapter 42

"S o much for staying out of the line of fire," Prudence said. She glared at Jack. *"What could possibly go wrong,* you said. *Everything is under control,* you said. *Luther Pell will be there to cover me,* you said."

She was standing in the center of room 223 in the main wing of the Burning Cove Hotel. It was the room they had been moved to after one of Luther Pell's security guards had driven her back to the hotel and she had discovered what had happened in the villa.

She had flatly refused to spend the rest of the night there. Yes, the body had been removed. No, there was no blood. Yes, the drinks cart and the poison had been taken away, and aside from the bullet hole in the wall, there were no obvious signs of violence. The Burning Cove Hotel knew how to take care of such things in a discreet fashion. It didn't matter. She could sense the bad energy in the atmosphere, and that was enough to make her demand a new room. No one had argued with her.

It was nearly dawn. She was still dressed in the black evening gown she had worn to the Paradise. The veiled hat and black gloves were sitting on the table near the window. Jack was sprawled in a chair, watching her pace the room and wave her arms a lot.

"To be clear, I did not actually say *What could possibly go wrong?*" he said. "I may have said the other stuff, but I did not say that. There is always a possibility of error. I try to allow—"

"Oh, shut up." She stalked across the room and swung around. Her gaze fell on the crystal paperweight. It was on the table next to her gloves. There were no chips or cracks in it. "I knew that paperweight would come in handy someday."

Jack glanced at the crystal sphere. "You were right."

She sighed. There was no point berating him for the risks he had taken that evening. He and Luther had both survived, and a would-be killer had been stopped. The heat in his eyes told her he was still riding the exhilarating energy that came with the triumph.

"I can see I'm wasting my time," she said. "Okay, the stern lecture is over. Time to move on. Congratulations. Your analysis and predictions of Harley Flood's actions were correct. An excellent example of the usefulness of the Wingate Crime Tree. Now what?"

Jack checked his watch. "Now we wait."

"For what? We know the identity of the last one

standing. Rollins Dover. He must have been the one who kidnapped me and murdered his brother. The only question is, how do we prove it?"

"It may not be necessary to prove anything," Jack said.

"I don't understand."

Jack got to his feet and walked across the room to take her into his arms. "It's not over, Prudence."

She shuddered. "Are you certain?"

"That family is slowly but surely being destroyed from within. It's like watching an avalanche. Some forces, once set in motion, can't be stopped."

Chapter 43

Maud Hollister had made her plans for the future. She longed to move forward with them, but she knew she had one more thing to do before she took the next step.

She was sitting in the darkened living room of the house Clara had rented only days earlier, thinking about the past and about how some people were doomed to live lives that had been cursed, when she heard the car in the driveway.

She went to the window, twitched the curtains aside, and watched Rollins climb out from behind the wheel of the Jaguar. She had known he would show up after the phone call she had made late last night. She had told him that she intended to go to the press with the whole sordid story, and that she would be able to back up that story with photographs of a certain birthmark, Clara's check register, and evidence of madness in the bloodline. Rollins had begged her to keep silent. He had promised her a fortune. She had told him he had twenty-four hours to come up with the money, and then she had hung up on him.

He had come to Burning Cove, just as she had known he would. She had practically raised him. She knew him far better than he knew himself. She saw the monster in him, the same monster that had been in Gilbert and Harley. The monster that had been their father.

Chapter 44

I brought the money, Hollister." Rollins walked into the living room and set the suitcase on the floor. It was almost over. He needed a few answers and then he could finish the business. "It's all there." He nodded at the suitcase. "By the way, my mother's will was read yesterday. You are not in it. Neither was Harley Flood. But I suppose that doesn't come as a surprise, does it? Clara was not a generous person."

To his disappointment, Maud did not erupt into tears or shrieks of rage. But then, he reflected, she had known Clara very well.

Maud walked to the window and moved the curtains aside just enough to enable her to see the jewel-bright ocean. "No, Clara was not a kind or generous woman," she said.

"I suppose we shouldn't be too hard on her. I'm

well aware that Clara paid for Harley's boarding school and then, later, his years in that very expensive psychiatric hospital. My mother was, above all else, an excellent businesswoman. She kept very good records. I know all about those checks she wrote on her personal bank account, and I am aware of the blackmail she has been paying in recent weeks."

"Do you?"

Not the dramatic reaction he had anticipated, Rollins thought. Maud looked weary, but other than that, he detected no sign of emotion. Disappointed, he went to the drinks cart and took the stopper off the flask of whiskey.

"I do have a couple of questions for you," he said. "I think I deserve some answers, considering the amount of money in that suitcase."

"What questions?" Maud asked, not turning around.

"Did Clara know that Harley Flood was Copeland's third son? The one she thought was safely locked up in the asylum?"

"How did you find out?" Maud asked.

"It doesn't matter."

"No, I suppose it doesn't," Maud said. "Clara did not know the truth, not until the end. I told her that night when I went to see her at the hospital. At the time I thought you were intending to have her committed, you see. I wanted her to know who had induced her visions and hallucinations. I wanted her to suffer."

"We all wanted her to suffer." Rollins swirled the whiskey in his glass. "Well, maybe not Gilbert. He was the chosen one. The thing is, he wasn't interested in Dover Industries. Clara never accepted that simple truth. When it came to Gilbert, she really was delusional."

"Yes." Maud turned to face him. "Do you have any other questions?"

"Just a few more." Rollins swallowed half the whiskey he had just poured and lowered the glass. "How, exactly, did my father manage to drop dead so conveniently all those years ago? Was that your doing, by any chance? I've always wondered. Only you and Mother were home that night. Gilbert and I were at the movies. The rest of the staff had the night off. That was a rarity in the Dover household."

Maud watched him intently. She no longer looked weary. There was a feverish light in her eyes. "Yes. I made his favorite soup and put the poison into it. Clara and I watched him die. It was very gratifying. And now I'm going to watch you die, just as he did."

Panic ripped through him. There was something wrong in his chest. His heart was beating much too fast. He was getting light-headed. It was suddenly hard to breathe.

"What?" he said, bewildered. He looked at the whiskey glass, horrified.

"I put the poison into the whiskey because you always drink whiskey. I know you very well, Rollins Dover."

His knees gave way. Without warning he was on the floor, staring up at the ceiling. Maud came to stand, looking down at him.

"I stood over your father the night he collapsed at

the dinner table," she said. "I made certain he knew that I was the one who had killed him. You should have seen his face. The fear. The pain. The helpless rage. The same expressions I see on your face now. Like father, like son."

Through the gray fog that was swiftly clouding his vision, he watched her go to the suitcase. She unlatched it and looked inside, smiling a little.

"Of course you didn't bring the money," she said. "No surprise. The Dovers are all liars." She reached inside and took out the gun. "Never mind. This will do nicely."

Chapter 45

S he poisoned Rollins Dover, probably watched him die, and then she used the gun he had brought with him to kill herself," Luther said.

"Yes." Jack studied the two bodies on the floor. "In the end she succeeded in destroying the Dover family and the empire that Clara had built. Dover Industries won't be able to survive this."

They were standing in the hallway of the house Clara Dover had rented with the intention of witnessing her revenge against Prudence. The crime scene did not require any psychic interpretation. It was obvious that Rollins Dover had driven all the way from San Francisco with the intention of shooting Maud Hollister. She had tricked him into drinking poisoned whiskey, and then she had used his gun to take her own life.

Luther went to the phone and picked up the receiver. "I'll call the police. It's their problem now. I don't envy whoever gets the job of notifying Dover's widow. I understand the couple has only been married a few months."

Chapter 46

Another sunny Southern California day, another gorgeous wedding production at the Burning Cove Hotel.

The reception was held in the courtyard. The cake was a multitiered confection of elegantly sculpted icing. The guests were formally attired. The bride wore white, a lot of it. The gleaming white satin, cut on the bias, flowed over her curves. A long white lace veil cascaded to the ground.

Prudence caught glimpses of the elaborately staged affair when she walked back to the room after enjoying a pot of Darjeeling in the hotel's glass-walled tearoom. It was midafternoon and she was on her own. She had been thrilled when Jack had accepted Luther's invitation for a round of golf. She knew the two would probably spend the time talking about the conclusion of the investigation, but that didn't matter. The important thing was that Jack was out on the golf course with a friend, doing something that friends did together. It was only a round of golf, but she took it as a sign that he was returning to real life.

A celebratory shout went up from the wedding guests. It was followed by a round of applause. Prudence glanced at the scene in the courtyard and saw that the newlyweds had just cut the first slice of the cake. The pair looked and sounded happy. Weddings were all about hope. All about the future.

She was startled by the sense of wistfulness that whispered through her. She did not dream of a white gown and veil. She could do very nicely without the cake. She had no need of a gold ring on her left hand. But she was in love, and she was ready for the next step in the relationship with Jack—commitment.

One of these days, she thought. Jack just needed a little time. He was still in the process of reentering the world. It was never going to be easy for him—the scars would not magically disappear—but he could deal with the physical damage. He had always been able to handle that. It was his fear that he might be going mad that had turned him into a recluse. But he was moving beyond that terror, and she was delighted and relieved.

She had a newfound fear of her own, however. She wanted him to love her, but not because he was grateful to her.

She turned away from the wedding scene and continued on to the room she and Jack were sharing—for how much longer? With the case closed, they seemed to have slipped into a strange sort of limbo. Sooner or later decisions would have to be made. Probably sooner. Neither of them could afford to live at the Burning Cove Hotel indefinitely.

A round of applause went up from the bridal party in the courtyard.

The bride wore white.

The closest she was likely to come to wearing a wedding gown was the time she had awakened in a very expensive wedding gown stained with the blood of the very dead Gilbert Dover.

A very expensive wedding gown.

She caught her breath. *Don't be ridiculous.*

But she had to be sure.

She changed course and hurried toward the lobby. When she got to the front desk, she smiled at the clerk.

"Can you tell me how to get to the local library?" she said.

"It's downtown in the civic plaza," the clerk said. "Too far to walk. Mr. Wingate took his car out earlier. Don't worry, the valet can get you a cab."

"Thank you."

She hitched the strap of her handbag over her shoulder and went quickly toward the hotel entrance.

Maybe she was wrong.

But her intuition was whispering to her. *The last one standing.*

Chapter 47

S he was not wrong.

Prudence stared at the photo in the San Fran-cisco newspaper for a long time, her stomach tight with anxiety. Incipient panic did a terrible dance across her nerves.

Maybe she was overreacting. Jumping to conclu-sions. Letting her imagination run wild. On the sur-face, it made no sense. But if you looked below the surface, the logic held.

She touched the crystal pendant. The gentle energy locked in the stone had a calming effect.

She could not wait to tell Jack her theory of the crime. If she was wrong, he would be able to tell her why. If she was right, there wasn't much either of them could do about it. The killer had been very clever and would probably continue to abide in the shadows.

Her intuition was shrieking at her. She checked the wall clock. How long did it take to play a round of golf? What if the two men decided to stop off in the clubhouse for a drink after the game?

She slung the strap of her handbag over her shoulder, carefully refolded the copy of the San Francisco paper, and took it back to the librarian's desk. The small sign declared that the name of the woman behind the desk was Miss Frazier.

"Did you find the information you needed?" Miss Frazier asked.

"Yes, thank you," Prudence said. "I appreciate the help."

"You're Madame Ariadne, aren't you? I saw the news about that terrible fire at Mr. Wingate's house. Thank goodness you both made it out alive. It must have been a dreadful experience."

"Yes," Prudence said. "It was."

She started to turn toward the door. There was a phone booth outside on the corner. She would call the golf club and leave a message for Jack.

"I heard about the incident in Mr. Wingate's villa at the Burning Cove Hotel," Miss Frazier continued. "According to the papers, someone broke into his room and attempted to murder him with poison."

"I must be off, Miss Frazier. Thank you for your help."

"You're welcome. You know, Mr. Wingate moved to town a few months ago. He became a regular patron here at the library, but aside from his visits, he kept to himself. His life has certainly become a lot more active since he hired a personal psychic."

"I've been encouraging him to get out more," Prudence said.

She rushed to the door and escaped onto the front steps. Safely outside, she paused for a moment to collect herself and then went briskly toward the phone booth at the end of the block.

Chapter 48

"Yes, please tell Mr. Wingate that it's urgent," Prudence said. "I'm on my way back to the Burning Cove Hotel. He can reach me there."

She dropped the phone into the cradle, opened the door of the booth, and stepped out onto the palm-shaded sidewalk. She looked at the busy street and realized it might take a while to find a cruising cab.

She did not notice the woman in the black suit and wide-brimmed veiled hat coming up quickly behind her until Ella Dover moved alongside. She had an expensive fur coat draped over her arm. The garment concealed one hand.

"Keep walking," Ella said. "The parking lot. I have a pistol with a silencer under my coat. I really can't miss at this range."

"You own a silencer? I thought only the mob used them."

"It belonged to my father. He bought it for target practice so as not to annoy the neighbors. Then he used it on himself. He probably didn't want to awaken the household."

"Are you going to shoot me down in broad daylight in a parking lot?" Prudence said. "Doesn't that strike you as somewhat risky?"

"You'll notice there isn't anyone else around at the moment. I can kill you and leave your body between a couple of parked cars. By the time someone finds you, I will have disappeared. But I don't think it will come to that."

"Why not?"

"Because I'm not here to kill you, Miss Ryland. I want to talk to you." Ella stopped near a nondescript Ford. "Get in on the passenger side and then slide behind the wheel. You're driving. I will be right beside you with the gun pointed at you."

No, you're here to murder me, Prudence thought.

"And if I don't go along with this plan?" she said.

"Then I really will have to take the chance of shooting you here in the parking lot. But there's no need for that sort of drama. Get into the car."

Prudence opened the passenger side door and scooted across the bench seat to slip behind the wheel. Ella got in beside her and closed the door. She tossed the coat aside, revealing the pistol with its bulky-looking attachment.

"Drive," she said.

"Where am I going?" Prudence asked.

"I gave that a lot of thought before I decided to talk to you today. We need a location where we won't be disturbed. The ruins of Mr. Wingate's house will do nicely."

Prudence got the engine going, put the Ford in gear, and drove out of the parking lot.

Chapter 49

"Room two-twenty-three, please," Jack said. "Yes, I'll hold."

He tightened his grip on the clubhouse phone and checked the time again. According to the golf club manager, Prudence had left the message twenty-five minutes earlier. That was not a long period of time, but the invisible chimes that had convinced him to end the game on the eighth hole were clashing wildly now. When he thought about the time it had taken to walk back to the clubhouse, he wanted to smash the nearest available object. Such an act would, of course, be utterly pointless. He had to focus.

Shit.

"I'm sorry, Mr. Wingate, there's no answer," the hotel operator said. "Can I take a message?"

Twenty-five minutes. Maybe Prudence hadn't had

time to get back to the hotel. She might have decided to do some shopping before she returned to the room, or maybe she'd had trouble catching a cab. But given the urgency of her message and the wildly clashing chimes, neither of those possibilities felt right.

"Transfer me to the front desk, please," he said.

"One moment."

Another voice came on the line. "Front desk, how may I assist you, Mr. Wingate?"

"I'm looking for Miss Ryland. She should have returned to the hotel by now, but she's not in the room. Please page her."

"That won't be necessary, sir," the clerk said. "I can assure you that Miss Ryland isn't on the premises. Both keys for room two-twenty-three are still in the box here at the front desk. She hasn't returned from the library."

"Are you sure that's where she went?"

"Yes, sir. She asked for directions. The doorman called a cab for her." The clerk chuckled. "She's a pretty popular lady today. You're the second person to ask about her whereabouts this afternoon."

Jack told himself to breathe. He had to stay cold and in control. For Prudence's sake. "Who else wanted to know where she was?"

"A Mrs. Smithton stopped by for a visit. Said they were old friends. I told her Miss Ryland was at the library. Why? Is there a problem?"

"What did Mrs. Smithton look like?"

"I didn't get a good look at her, because she was dressed for a funeral. Wore a hat with a black veil. But from what I could tell, she was a very attractive woman with blond hair. Does that help?"

"The widow is the last one standing," Jack said quietly.

"What was that, sir?"

"Nothing. Thanks."

Jack hung up the phone and turned to Luther, who was lounging against the polished bar, waiting. "Let's go."

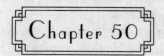

Chapter 50

I t was you all along," Prudence said. She brought the
Ford to a halt in the driveway of Jack's burned-out
house. "You came up with a plan to avenge yourself
on the Dovers, and you set it in motion by marrying
Rollins."

Ella raised the veil of her hat with one gloved hand
and crumpled the netting onto the brim. The pistol
was very steady in her other hand. "The entire Dover line has been extinguished. I now control the
company."

"I've got to hand it to you. Clara never realized that
you were the enemy within the walls of the Dover
household. She never saw you as anything other than
the wife of her second son."

"Before she died, I made certain she knew exactly
who was responsible for destroying her empire."

"You were the one who killed her in the hospital."

"I took my time with that pillow," Ella said. "Dover Industries and her own bloodline were the only things Clara cared about. I wanted her to understand that everything she had built and the future she had planned were all going to disappear."

"If making Clara suffer was your goal, why not follow through with Rollins's plan to have her committed? She would have hated that."

"It was tempting," Ella said. "But I knew Clara well enough to know she would probably escape. Threats. Money. Power. Whatever it took, she would have found a way to use it. That woman was brilliant when it came to manipulating people. Between you and me, I think she actually was psychic when it came to strategy and planning."

"So you are the last one standing, but it looks to me like you may be standing over the smoking ruins of whatever is left of the empire you conquered. Dover Industries may not survive the scandal and the drama that wrecked the family."

"You don't understand. My goal wasn't to inherit Dover Industries. I wanted to see it obliterated, just like the family."

Prudence looked at her. "I guess the only question I have is, why?"

"The Dovers and all of San Francisco society knew me as Ella Norcroft before I married Rollins. Norcroft was my mother's maiden name. But I was born Ella Comstock."

"I don't understand. Should that name mean something to me?"

"No. And the reason it doesn't mean anything is because Clara Dover destroyed my father's business on the way to building her empire. Comstock Manufacturing was one of the many companies she crushed. She barely noticed the damage she caused."

"I think I get the picture."

"When she destroyed Comstock Manufacturing, Clara Dover destroyed my family. My father put a gun to his head. My mother went into a decline from which she never recovered. She started taking pills. One day she overdosed. I found the body. I went to live with an aunt on the East Coast, a bitter woman who resented me from the start because I was so much prettier than her own daughters. She treated me as if I were a servant. She could not wait to kick me out of the house."

"That explains a great deal," Prudence said gently. "I must remember to tell Jack he was right."

Ella looked wary for the first time. "About what?"

"He said at the beginning that this was all about revenge. The problem was that it was literally awash in revenge. So much of it. You and Rollins worked together to murder Gilbert, didn't you? You used your wedding dress to set the scene in the honeymoon suite at the hotel. I recognized it in the newspaper photos at the library."

"Is that what you were doing at the library today? Looking for photos of my wedding?"

"Back at the start I wondered why the killer used such an expensive handmade gown for a murder. We assumed it indicated the depths of a violent obsession, but that wasn't it at all. It was a matter of convenience."

"Not just convenience," Ella said. "I knew buying another wedding gown, even an inexpensive one, would attract attention. I was Mrs. Rollins Dover, after all. There would be talk. Gossip. I could not have that."

"Why did you feel you needed a wedding gown to stage Gilbert's murder?"

"Believe it or not, it wasn't my idea. That scene in the honeymoon suite was Rollins's doing. Once I convinced him it was time to get rid of his brother, he became fixated on a plan to use the death to humiliate Clara. I have to admit, I did find that aspect of it appealing."

"Because you hated Clara, too."

"Oh, yes. We both knew that when the press got hold of the photos of the murder scene, the gossip about Gilbert's sexual eccentricities would be all over San Francisco. Clara would be mortified. Rollins insisted on using you as the Killer Bride. He thought that would not only humiliate Clara but would ensure that her rage was focused on you. Rollins was always afraid of Clara, you see. He did not want her to suspect him."

"How did you find me in Adelina Beach?"

"After we developed the plan, we hired a private investigator. You had moved and left no forwarding address, but you did not change your name. It took a while, but the detective finally located your old housekeeper. She had some correspondence from you that was postmarked Adelina Beach."

"Rollins sent Tapson to murder me back in October, didn't he?"

"Yes. Tapson failed and landed in the hospital. Rollins panicked and got rid of him."

"With a pillow? The same way you killed Clara?"

Ella smiled. "Where do you think I got the idea?"

"When did you find out that Harley Flood had been fathered by Copeland Dover?"

"Rollins and I both realized from the start that he was a fraud," Ella said. "All that nonsense about Clara's delicate nerves due to her psychic talents was almost laughable."

"Because Clara Dover had nerves of steel."

"Right up until she began to receive treatments from Dr. Harley Flood. At first, Rollins and I assumed he was just in it for the money. To give him his due, he was a very good con artist. But I began to realize what was going on when Maud Hollister insisted Flood was an excellent doctor for Clara. There was something about the way she looked at Flood that made me realize the two of them had a personal connection."

"How did you discover the truth?"

"Quite easily," Ella said, her voice suddenly featherlight and inviting and laced with a dark music. "I asked Maud a few questions in private."

Energy shivered in the front seat of the Ford. Prudence felt her pendant grow warm as she resisted the pull of the currents.

"I'm surprised Maud admitted that Harley was her son by Copeland Dover," she said. "Maud had her own plans. Why would she confide in you?"

"It's true that Maud had been keeping Dover family secrets for so long it had become a habit. But she and I had a very interesting conversation." Ella smiled a little, and the energy in her eyes got a little more intense. "Afterward she did not remember anything she said to me."

Prudence cocked her head, listening to the compelling music of Ella's voice, and then she, too, smiled. "Oh, I see. You've got some psychic talent of your own. You're a true hypnotist."

Ella blinked, startled. But she recovered quickly. "You're the only person who has ever understood that. I suppose it takes a psychic to recognize another psychic. At the start I was certain you were a fraud, like most people who claim to possess paranormal talents. But after you escaped the honeymoon suite at the Pentland Plaza without getting caught, I began to wonder if you might be the real deal. After all, you had also survived Tapson's attempt to murder you. What were the odds that you had simply gotten lucky twice?"

"I don't know. Math is not my strong suit. You could ask Jack Wingate. He's an expert when it comes to calculating probabilities."

Ella ignored that. "Did you somehow put Tapson into that coma?"

Prudence smiled. "I'm just a dream reader, one who faked it most of the time."

Ella looked annoyed. "What does that mean?"

"You plan to murder me. Why should I explain myself to you?"

"Tell me about your talent." The dark music surged through Ella's voice once more, compelling, inviting, almost irresistible.

Almost.

"Forget it, Ella. You can't hypnotize me. I'm immune. Probably because of my talent."

"You have no idea what I can do with my ability," Ella warned.

"Do you really believe that you can use a hypnotic suggestion to make me jump off a cliff? That's what you're planning, isn't it? Forget it. You can't make my death look like an accident. There is no way Jack Wingate will believe it, and he won't stop looking for the killer, because he's Jack Wingate. He likes answers."

"I've had enough of this," Ella snapped, the musical currents vanishing from her voice as if by magic. "Get out of the car."

"Good idea, because if you shoot me here, there will be a lot of blood and a great deal of evidence on the front seat. Then there's the problem of the body. You'll have to figure out how to get rid of it. Your clothes will be spattered with blood, too. Sadly, I'm afraid Jack Wingate will take one look at the scene and declare you to be an unhinged, poorly organized killer. How humiliating."

"Get out of the car," Ella hissed.

The pistol was starting to tremble in her hand. Her eyes were heating with a desperate energy. In another few seconds she would pull the trigger and worry about the blood-spattered front seat later.

"All right," Prudence said. "I'll get out of the car."

She gripped the handle and opened the door.

Ella sucked in a steadying breath. The pistol no longer trembled.

"You really are a fraud, aren't you?" she said.

"That has been suggested," Prudence said.

She slipped out from behind the wheel, stepped down onto the ground, and started to back away.

"Don't move," Ella said, negotiating the process of getting out of the front seat while keeping the pistol aimed squarely at her target.

Prudence touched the crystal necklace and cautiously opened her senses to the dark storm of Ella's dream energy. The fierce currents seethed and crashed, threatening to inundate her. Strangely enough, it wasn't the pistol she feared, as dangerous as it was at such close quarters. It was the possibility that her mind might be overwhelmed, drowned, by Ella's powerful talent.

This was what she had accidentally done to Julian on their wedding night, she realized. Now she understood the shock and fear in his eyes. She had glimpsed much worse in Tapson's eyes before he collapsed on the floor of the reading room.

This is what it feels like to have a powerful psychic attack you, Prudence Ryland. But she knew how to fight back, because she was powerful, too.

She braced herself and began to focus her own energy, seeking to slip through the disturbing flashes of lightning, the darkness of nightmares, and the howling of the primal winds that swirled in Ella's dream energy. She knew from experience that she could not fight such energy head-on. The key was to ride the waves to the center without being noticed.

Ella took a step away from the car. Her shoe skidded a little on the rough graveled drive. She steadied herself and motioned with the pistol.

"Start walking," she said. The fierce currents of energy sang a Siren's song in her voice. "The cliff."

"Now, why would I walk to my own death?" Prudence asked softly. "You're really not any good at this, are you?"

"There's nothing to stop me from shooting you right here." Ella tightened her grip on the gun.

"Have you ever actually fired a pistol?"

"I think I can manage. Turn around."

Prudence hesitated and then slowly obeyed. The barrel of the gun pressed against the side of her head. Ella's ungloved fingers touched the back of her neck. Prudence felt a terrifying energy burn through her senses. She knew then that Ella had learned that physical contact made it easier to gain and hold a focus.

"Walk to the edge of the cliffs," Ella said in a powerful voice that would have done credit to a coloratura soprano.

The compulsion was almost overwhelming. Prudence felt like a leaf swept up in a tornado. But the physical connection between herself and Ella worked both ways. She fought her way through the howling winds of Ella's dream energy. The process was exhausting. It took every ounce of strength she possessed to make progress without alerting Ella.

Suddenly she was there, hovering over the dark pit that fueled the other woman's nightmares.

She gathered her nerve and her talent, and sent a lightning-fast burst of energy into the dark pit.

Ella stiffened. Her mouth opened on a silent scream. She convulsed.

And collapsed. The pistol landed on the gravel beside her.

Prudence heard the engine of a powerful car roaring down the drive. She did not look away from Ella's unmoving form. The world seemed to have frozen around her.

Jack leaped out of the Packard and ran toward her.

"Prudence," he said. "It's all right. It's over."

She turned and went into his arms. He held her close and tight.

Luther went forward and crouched beside the fallen woman. He touched Ella's throat and looked at Prudence as if he knew exactly what she was thinking.

"She's alive," he said. "Unconscious, but alive."

"Good," Prudence whispered. "That's good. Thank you."

She pressed her face into Jack's shoulder. She was vaguely aware of him scooping her up and carrying her toward the Packard, and then she dropped into a deep sleep.

Chapter 51

She surfaced on the tide of a dark sea and instinctively tried to swim to an unseen shore. She had to keep moving. If she stopped to tread water, she would be sucked down into the depths. But she could not move. She was frozen, trapped, in the waves.

"Prudence, wake up. You're dreaming again. You are all right."

Jack's steady, reassuring voice brought her out of the last remnants of the nightmare.

She opened her eyes to a heavily shadowed room. Jack was standing beside the bed, a cup of tea in one hand. The thin line of daylight at the edges of the closed curtains told her that it was not yet night. She bolted upright, a fresh flash of panic crackling across her senses.

"How long was I out?" she gasped.

"You were never unconscious, if that's what you're worried about." He put the tea down on the nightstand. "You were asleep. There's a significant difference."

"You're sure?"

"I had the hotel call a doctor to examine you. She said you were fine, just exhausted. You actually woke up a little while she was here. You told her to go away because you wanted to sleep."

A fragment of memory returned—a comfortably rounded woman in a severe business suit and carrying a satchel bending over her, speaking to her in a firm voice. *Prudence Ryland, can you hear me?*

Prudence relaxed a little. "Yes, I remember now." She reached for the cup and took an invigorating sip. "This tastes very, very good."

"I'm going to miss room service after we check out."

"So will I." She really did not want to think about leaving the hotel, but not because she would miss room service. Checking out would signal the closing of the investigation. She would go back to the lonely apartment in Adelina Beach, and Jack would find a place to rent here in Burning Cove while he finished *The Wingate Crime Tree* and decided whether or not to rebuild. She pushed thoughts of the future aside. "What happened to Ella Dover?"

"She's in the hospital, alive and unhurt as far as the doctors can determine, but she appears to have suffered a nervous breakdown." Jack's tone was neutral. So was his expression. Just a man reporting the facts.

"I'm told she's delusional. Insists you destroyed her paranormal senses. Seems to think you're some sort of psychic vampire."

"A psychic vampire." Prudence closed her eyes.

"Like I said, she's delusional."

Prudence opened her eyes and stared at him. "What if she's right?"

Jack got a thoughtful expression and sat down on the side of the bed. "If she's right, my life is going to get even more interesting than it is now, and that's saying something."

"Damn it, Jack, I'm serious."

"So am I. I think you were right. We do have the basis for the perfect relationship. A psychic vampire who reads dreams and a psychic consultant who reads crime scenes. What could possibly go wrong?"

"You told me you never ask that question because something can always go wrong."

"Not when it comes to you and me. But getting back to the subject of Ella Dover, it turns out she is the last one standing on top of whatever is left of the Dover family empire. Whether she will be able to run it from jail or an asylum remains to be seen."

Prudence shivered. "You were right when you said that my case would prove to be a story of revenge."

"Those cases never end well. There's a lot of truth in the ancient warnings about the risks of setting out on a path of vengeance. Like they say, you might as well dig two graves at the start, because you'll need one for yourself."

Prudence nodded somberly. "Too much negative energy can only lead to disaster."

Jack looked amused. "Generally speaking, I don't approve of resorting to paranormal explanations for such things, but in this case, you may be right."

"How did you figure out that Ella had kidnapped me and forced me to drive to House of Shadows?"

"Old-fashioned investigation work. No psychic stuff involved. The front desk here at the hotel came through, as usual. I knew from the clerk's description of the woman who had stopped to call on you that Ella was looking for you. The clerk said you were at the library. By the time Luther and I got there, you had disappeared, but the librarian on duty had seen you and a woman in black walking toward the parking lot. A short time later, she saw you both drive past the front entrance of the library. You were at the wheel and heading south. The Burning Cove Hotel is north of downtown. House of Shadows, or what's left of it, is south. The conclusion was easy."

"Easy?"

"Well, I also knew that killers prefer to use familiar ground whenever possible. Ella wanted an isolated location. She didn't know the local terrain very well, but she knew my property met her requirements because she had been there on a previous occasion."

Prudence smiled. "Leave it to a librarian to point you in the right direction."

"Not that it mattered. When Luther and I arrived, you had the situation under control. Which reminds me, we have an invitation to join Luther and Raina Kirk for dinner at the Paradise this evening."

Prudence brightened. "That sounds like fun. Can I assume Mr. Pell and Miss Kirk are a couple?"

Jack got a knowing look. "Yes, you can definitely assume that." He glanced at his watch. "But we've got plenty of time. Feel like taking a short drive?"

"All right." She pushed aside the covers and swung her legs over the side of the bed. "Where are we going?"

"I want to show you a certain property."

"Did you find a place to rent while you rebuild?"

"Maybe."

The sign in the window of the art gallery indicated that it was permanently closed and that the premises were for lease. It was situated in a palm-shaded plaza near the heart of the town's fashionable shopping district. There were several other galleries and a sprinkling of sidewalk cafés and boutiques in the same plaza.

Prudence fell in love at first sight. "What a perfect spot for a bookshop. This is exactly the sort of location I'll be looking for when I get ready to open One Step Beyond."

Jack looked ridiculously pleased. "I was hoping you would say that. Raina Kirk's office is right around the corner. She says the interior of this space is in excellent condition and that it would take very little to convert it into a bookshop."

"Whoa." Prudence held up both hands, palms out. "It's a beautiful shop and an ideal location, but I couldn't possibly afford the rent in this part of town. And when did you discuss my bookshop plans with Raina Kirk?"

"I talked to Raina while you were sleeping this afternoon. We were clearing up a few last details of the case and I mentioned that you wanted to open a bookshop focused on metaphysics and the paranormal. She said she knew of a place that might work and gave me the address."

"Oh." Prudence flushed. "Well, it certainly is lovely, but as I said, I'm sure I couldn't afford it."

"Raina says she thinks the owner will bargain if you're willing to sign a long-term lease. Also, there's a nice little apartment above the shop. It's included in the rent."

"Is that so?"

Jack cleared his throat. "I could move in with you and share the rent."

"What?"

"I'm going to need a place to live while I rebuild on that very nice chunk of California waterfront property where House of Shadows used to stand."

She stared at him. "Jack, is this your peculiar way of suggesting we destroy what's left of our reputations by living in sin over a bookshop in the heart of downtown Burning Cove?"

"Well, no."

"Good. I don't want you to take this personally, but frankly, I don't think you're the type."

"To live in sin?"

"Right. It takes a certain sort of man to do that, and you are not one of those men."

"You think I'm too serious and too boring and too unsociable to figure out how to live in sin?"

"Nope. But I think it would break your heart. You

want commitment and a vision of a shared future. You want to love and know you are loved. You want a family. Connection."

He looked at her, his eyes steady and certain. "You're right. But I will take what I can get from you, Prudence. I love you. I will love you for the rest of my life."

Joy splashed through her, igniting all of her senses. She wound her arms around his neck and smiled. "Turns out I want commitment and a shared future, too. I want to love and know I am loved. I want a family and connection, and I want those things with you. I love you, Jack Wingate."

He held her close and tight, and when his mouth came down on hers, she opened all of her senses so that she could savor the quiet, bone-deep thrill of the energy resonating between them.

"Feels good, doesn't it?" Jack said against her mouth.

"What?" She gasped and stepped back so quickly she clipped his jaw with the side of her head.

"Okay, that was a close call," he said. Tentatively he touched his jaw. "I don't think you broke anything, but by tomorrow I may look like I've been in a fistfight."

"You felt it, too?" she asked, dazzled by a sense of wonder.

"Oh, yeah." He touched his jaw again and winced. "I felt it."

"Forget your jaw. This is important. Tell me the truth. Do you feel a special sensation when we're close like this?"

"Definitely." He clamped his hands around her shoulders and started to pull her close again.

"I'm serious."

"So am I. If you want to call what we have together a psychic connection, that's fine by me. What I do know is that I felt it the instant I met you in Luther Pell's office. I also knew that I would feel it for the rest of my life."

"Really? That first day you were sure?"

"One hundred percent certain."

"Not ninety-eight percent or ninety-nine?"

"There are a few things in life that you can be sure of, Pru. What I feel for you is one of those things."

He drew her close, and this time she did not resist.

"You really do have some paranormal talent, you know," she said.

He smiled and his eyes burned. "So what? I no longer give a damn."

Delighted and hugely relieved, she wrapped her arms around his neck again. "That's perfect, then."

"It is, isn't it?" he said.

He started to kiss her, but he hesitated, his mouth an inch above hers. "Do you hear chimes?"

"No," she said. "But it's okay if you do."

He laughed, and then his mouth closed over hers and she threw herself into the embrace. She did not hear chimes, but she could feel the energy of love and joy that whispered in the atmosphere. That was more than enough.

Chapter 52

I t occurs to me that if you ever decide to retire from the nightclub business, you should give serious consideration to opening a matchmaking agency," Raina said.

Luther looked up from some notes he was making in his case journal. "What?"

"I just said I see a future in matchmaking for you," she said.

They were alone in Luther's private booth on the mezzanine of the Paradise Club. Prudence and Jack had joined them for drinks and dinner and a relaxed debriefing. It took a while to come down from the rush of a closed case. It was best to do that unwinding with friends. *And lovers.* She smiled at Luther. He returned the smile, leaned close for a moment, and kissed her.

When he straightened, his usually enigmatic eyes heated with a familiar warmth. She recognized it because everything inside her responded to it. They were bound together by so many things now—commitment, secrets, passion, and trust. It all added up to love.

Having met Prudence in person and watched her together with Jack, she was certain the pair shared a bond built on a very similar foundation.

The two had gone downstairs to dance a few minutes ago when the orchestra had begun to play. The floor was crowded, the shadows were deep, and the rain of lights from the mirror ball overhead dazzled the eye. Nevertheless, it was easy to spot Prudence and Jack. Energy seemed to whisper around them as they moved together, lost in the music and each other.

Luther followed her gaze to the dance floor. "I knew those two would get together."

"Did you?"

"Something about the way they looked at each other that first day," Luther said.

"As I recall, you were afraid they might try to strangle each other."

"Exactly. You know, when you think about it, this isn't the first couple I've managed to put together in the course of an investigation. When you look back at recent cases, I've got a remarkably good track record in the matchmaking department."

"Probably a psychic talent," Raina said.

"I'm pretty sure I never possessed that particular talent until I met you."

"Is that so?"

"I do believe you have opened up a whole new psychic pathway for me."

Raina smiled. "What a coincidence. I've been thinking you've done something very similar for me."

"Is that right?"

"That's what happens when you fall in love, I guess. Something about the process makes it possible to see the world in a different light."

He wrapped an arm around her and drew her close. "Yes, it does. And once you have seen it in that new light, you can never go back."

"Uh-oh."

Raina pulled away from Luther's warm grasp and leaned over the railing to get a better look at the dance floor.

"What's wrong?" Luther asked.

"Prudence just came to a sudden halt on the floor and she's waving her arms. I think they are arguing. In the middle of the dance floor."

Curious, Luther leaned over her shoulder and looked down. "Nothing to worry about. That's their idea of foreplay."

"Are you sure?"

"Positive."

"I've got it," Prudence announced in a ringing voice.

Jack was aware that several heads had turned, but for once no one was staring at his scars. They were all watching Prudence, who looked thrilled with herself. *Unpredictable as usual,* he thought. This was a moment that called for action. He knew how to lead.

He tightened his grip on her and drew her firmly back into the pattern of the dance.

"What have you got?" he asked, keeping his voice low.

"The title for your book." She smiled with delight. *"The Art and Science of Criminal Profiling: A Modern Approach to Investigation."*

"My method creates a tree, not a profile or a drawing of the suspect."

"I told you, the word *tree* feels old-fashioned. Boring. The word *profile* sounds much more modern."

"No, it sounds like a cardboard cutout. And there's no art involved. My method relies on observation and logic."

"Your method requires the eye of an artist, someone who can see the whole picture even though only some of it is visible."

"My market is law enforcement," he said. "That crowd won't like the word *art* and it won't know what *profile* means."

"Your book will help shape the future of law enforcement. It needs a thoroughly modern title."

"Forget it."

"Think about it," Prudence urged.

"Okay, I'll think about it. But the word *art* is definitely out."

"Don't make any hasty decisions."

"I am not going to make any decisions, hasty or otherwise, right now. In case you haven't noticed, we are dancing."

"Oh. Right."

"And later we will make love and then we will

sleep, and in the morning we will discuss our wedding."

"Okay," she said. "That sounds like a plan. But just so you know, it's going to be a very small wedding."

"Fine by me."

"A few close friends."

"Not a problem," he said.

"And I definitely will not be wearing a fancy white wedding gown."

"Call me psychic, but I could have predicted that."

Ready to find
your next great read?

Let us help.

Visit prh.com/nextread

Penguin
Random
House